COME RAIN, COME SHINE

Recent Titles by Anne Doughty from Severn House

ON A CLEAR DAY
BEYOND THE GREEN HILLS
THE WOMAN FROM KERRY
THE HAMILTONS OF BALLYDOWN
THE HAWTHORNS BLOOM IN MAY
A GIRL CALLED ROSIE
FOR MANY A LONG DAY
SHADOW ON THE LAND

COME RAIN, COME SHINE

A novel in the Hamiltons sequence
1960 – 1966

Anne Doughty

severn
House

This first world edition published 2012
in Great Britain and in the USA by
SEVERN HOUSE PUBLISHERS LTD of
9–15 High Street, Sutton, Surrey, England, SM1 1DF.
Trade paperback edition first published
in Great Britain and the USA 2012 by
SEVERN HOUSE PUBLISHERS LTD

British Library Cataloguing in Publication Data

Doughty, Anne, 1939-
  Come rain, come shine.
  1. Armagh (Northern Ireland : County)–Social conditions–
  20th century–Fiction.
  I. Title
  823.9'2-dc23

ISBN-13: 978-0-7278-8176-2 (cased)
ISBN-13: 978-1-84751-433-2 (trade paper)

All Severn House titles are printed on acid-free paper.

Severn House Publishers support The Forest Stewardship Council [FSC],
the leading international forest certification organisation. All our titles that
are printed on Greenpeace-approved FSC-certified paper carry the FSC logo.

MIX
Paper from
responsible sources
FSC
www.fsc.org   FSC® C018575

Typeset by Palimpsest Book Production Ltd.,
Falkirk, Stirlingshire, Scotland.
Printed and bound in Great Britain by
MPG Books Ltd., Bodmin, Cornwall.

For
Edwin Buckhalter
and all my friends at Severn House
without whom the Hamiltons and many like them
would have lived and died unknown and unacknowledged

Acknowledgements

Come Rain, Come Shine is a novel about hopes and dreams and what happens when circumstances change and cut right across the plans people make. Friends and family, as well as writers and historians, have enabled me to be accurate about the detail of 1960 to 1966, but without one person in particular this novel would not be in print.

As I worked on Clare and Andrew's story, I began to realize what happened to them in the 1960s was already beginning to happen to so many as a consequence of the financial crash of 2008. The hopes of young and old in many places and at all levels in society were put at risk and threatened with failure.

Publishing was no exception, so that, by the time I completed *Come Rain, Come Shine* the possibility of it ever seeing the light of day had receded dramatically. Libraries were closing, both in the UK and in America, and funds for buying books seriously reduced. The climate had changed for me just as it had for Clare and Andrew.

In the event, I have been very fortunate. Edwin Buckhalter, Chairman of Severn House, did accept *Come Rain, Come Shine* even in this hostile climate. As a result of his generous act, I have been able to complete a century of Irish history as seen through the eyes of one ordinary family. So it is to Edwin and all my friends at Severn House that I gratefully dedicate this book. Without them, the Hamiltons would have lived and died unknown and unacknowledged.

Anne Doughty
January 2012

One

September 1960

The moment the Belfast flight was announced, Clare Hamilton put down her coffee cup and picked up the large, beribboned box parked neatly under the table. She walked quickly across the departure lounge, a small, slim figure in an elegant moss green suit and was among the very first passengers to enter the quiet, echoing corridor that led down to the roar and whine of engines, the oscillating turbulence of aircraft movements and the dazzling glare of acres of pale tarmac.

The waiting Vanguard shimmered in the strong evening sun as she paused to hand over her ticket. How long it might be before she flew again she could not guess, but if this was to be her last flight for some time, she hoped it would be like the one she'd made back in April. On just such a sunlit evening she'd flown into Aldergrove over the green landscape she so loved to the totally unexpected sequence of events which had changed her life.

'May I put that in the hand luggage store for you, madam?' the young steward asked politely, with a small bow towards her silver and white striped box.

He put out his hand for the box, large and rectangular, but clearly light in weight.

'I'll put it down by my side where it won't get in the way,' she said, smiling at him. 'It's my wedding dress,' she added, as he seemed about to protest.

'Who's the lucky man?' he asked, his careful pronunciation replaced by a familiar Ulster accent.

She laughed, suddenly delighted by the sound of home and the broad grin that creased his face as he waved her past.

She made her way to the window seat she'd booked weeks ago from her office in the Place de l'Opéra, settled herself and tried to relax, but the excitement that had pursued her all day was not to be dispersed so easily. She was going home, home to Andrew and to her beloved little green hills. In three days they would be married, ahead of them a life together quite different from any they had once imagined.

She looked down through the dusty window at the familiar activities of the airport, the small vehicles scurrying to and fro bringing luggage and catering supplies, the large fuel tankers now uncoupling their hoses and returning to their depot. Luggage manifests were being exchanged. A Royal Mail van appeared at speed, its back doors sprang open, sacks of mail flew out on to waiting trolleys that quickly disappeared from view. She listened for the familiar sound of the hold doors being banged shut.

Whenever she watched the familiar scene, whether in London or Toulouse, Zurich or Athens, she always thought of the summer of 1957, shortly before graduation, when she'd arrived in London, wearing her best summer dress and carrying a single suitcase. She had tramped the dimly lit platform at Euston Station, struggled with the escalator to the Tube, spent a night in a student hostel, got herself to Victoria for the train to Paris and wept. Whenever no one was looking, and even sometimes when they were, tears had streamed down her face. She was quite alone, without home, or job, or future. She had taken the Liverpool boat, because she had broken off her engagement with Andrew. She had loved him for so long and been so happy, but their bright hopes had been shattered and she could see no way forward for them.

The engines roared and the aircraft rose into the clear sky. The wing dipped over the Hounslow reservoirs as they turned west and she studied the streams of traffic flowing in all directions, the veins and arteries feeding the great city at their heart. She tried to take in every detail of the moving pattern for she might never come this way again. Moments later, the course correction complete, she caught sight of the Chilterns, wisps of cloud blurring their outline.

She moved uneasily in her seat, adjusted the box propped between the window and her left foot. Everyone had said she'd got it wrong, that she and Andrew were made for each other, but after his cousin was killed in a road accident, he'd abandoned their plan to go to Canada and had taken over the running of the Richardson family estates. She'd seen him shoulder the responsibility for his grandmother, his aunt and uncle, his cousin Ginny. In fact, it seemed he'd accepted his obligations to everyone except herself, so that all they'd planned together appeared just a beautiful dream.

It was not the first time in her life the world had come crashing down around her. Long years earlier, on a hot June afternoon in 1946, she and her young brother William had been taken to the Fever Hospital outside Armagh by the Headmaster of their school. Days later, her mother and father, Ellie and Sam Hamilton, had both died in the typhoid epidemic of that year leaving them parentless and homeless.

She had found a new home with her grandfather, Robert Scott, and then, only weeks after a scholarship had taken her to university in Belfast, he'd walked down the lane to stand by the anvil in the forge where he'd worked all his life and died instantly of a heart attack.

Once again, she had found herself homeless. The landlord had given her two weeks' notice to dispose of the contents. There'd been help with that sad task from Jack Hamilton, the youngest of her uncles, but dealing with the memories of a house lived in by Scott blacksmiths for over a century was a different matter. Harder still was the loss of what had been her second home, the one she'd lived in for half her eighteen years.

Suddenly the distant pattern of the English Midlands far below disappeared completely. The grey mizzle that swirled around the aircraft and streaked her window with tiny raindrops as they continued climbing into cloud enveloped her in the chill remembrance of that bleak time. After Granda Scott died the only comfort she knew came from Andrew's letters and their occasional short phone calls in the dim hall of the house in Elmwood Avenue where she'd inherited her cousin Ronnie's old student room after he packed up and headed for Canada.

She went on staring through the window, perfectly aware she was rigid with tension. She had never been afraid of flying, had enjoyed all but the most turbulent of flights, but what she could never bear was this grey blanket that removed all light and joy from a world where previously there had been sunshine and colour.

She took a deep breath, extracted her book from her handbag, tried to focus on the words on the page. Then, as suddenly as it had disappeared, the sunlight returned. It poured down from a blue sky, glancing off the moist, glistening wing, the view below now of dazzling white cloud caps. She shut the book gratefully. Yes, she had known the light would return, that above the murk the sun always shone. But no matter how many times it happened, she still feared the grey mist. It was not the mist in itself. It was the fear that, like some of the worst times in her life, the bleakness would go on for so long she would finally lose heart and give up.

The cloudscape below always made her think of the Rocky Mountains, though any postcards she'd ever seen of them made it perfectly clear they didn't look like this at all. Probably her Rocky Mountains were pictures in her imagination, something she had called up when she and Andrew were planning to go to Canada.

The plan itself emerged quite unexpectedly one day when they'd had an outing with lunch as a special treat. Andrew had looked so miserable most of the time she'd forced him to tell her what was wrong. He'd finally admitted that being back in Belfast and near her didn't make up for the misery of his job with the firm of solicitors his uncle had arranged for him.

He'd been so negative to begin with, had said there was no other way of earning a living, given all he had was a Law Degree from Cambridge. Gazing down at the towering mountains of cloud, silhouetted against the brilliant blue sky, she remembered how she'd refused to go along with his negative view of himself and asked him what he'd do if he were rich and if money were no object. His answer had delighted her, for it was the same answer he'd given years earlier when the two of them were playing Monopoly with his cousins Ginny and Edward at Caledon that very first summer they'd been able to spend time together.

'I'd buy cows,' he said firmly. 'But not here,' he added, looking just as dejected as when they'd begun to talk.

She'd stopped smiling instantly, but she went on asking questions and by the time they'd left their sitting place, they'd made their decision. Canada it would be. The Palliser Triangle to be precise, because Andrew had a relative who had gone out there in the 1920s and now had a very large ranch with a substantial herd.

The plan to go to Canada had sustained her through the last year of her Honours course at Queens and Andrew's year in Linen Hall Street, a junior solicitor at the beck and call of elderly partners. They were very experienced and quite meticulous over points of law, but they had a set of values and attitudes towards the people they encountered that he found almost impossible to stomach.

Then, on that wonderful day when Clare finished her last exam and they'd planned a picnic supper in the Castlereagh Hills to celebrate, it all began to go wrong. Ginny and Edward had had a head-on collision on a narrow country road with a vehicle that shouldn't have been there. Edward never regained consciousness, Ginny was left with scars on her face and arms and Andrew found himself head of the family and responsible for both the house in Caledon and his grandmother's home at Drumsollen. The vision of wide acres of prairie and glistening mountains crumbled at a touch, like a warm and comforting dream dissolving as one wakes to the chill of a winter morning.

Perhaps she *had* been wrong to break off their engagement. If she'd stayed with Andrew, not the most practical of men, she could have helped him cope with the tangle of financial affairs, mortgages and death duties that enmeshed him. She could have supported Ginny, who'd taken her half-brother's death so very badly and whose scars would need more than plastic surgery if they were not to affect her for the rest of her life.

She felt the bite of tension in her shoulders as the images flowed back. From a point in the future, it's always easy to see how things could have been different. Here and now, after more than two years in a demanding job, with a new life, new friends, renewed hope for the future and a wedding dress waiting to be worn, it was just possible to see that there *might* have been an alternative. But the person she was now was not the person she was then. The girl who set off on the Liverpool boat could not have shared Andrew with all the many and conflicting demands he had accepted without question.

She looked at her watch. The time had gone so quickly. Any minute now the familiar tape-recording would tell them to fasten their seat-belts. As they began to lose height, she took a last look at her Rocky Mountains and continued to argue with herself, as if it were a matter of great urgency that she decided what she really thought. Without their parting, there would have been no job in Paris, no new friends like Louise and Jean-Pierre. Especially, there would have been no Robert Lafarge, the eminent French banker who had given her a job and had now become a dear friend, one who treated her like the daughter he'd lost when his wife and children disappeared in the Fall of France.

Parting with Andrew had been heartbreaking, but she'd done her best to begin all over again. When they'd met up again by accident last April and spent a weekend together, they'd admitted they'd found out things about themselves they might never have learnt in any other way.

She prepared herself as they descended rapidly. What did it matter if she arrived home in a rainstorm? She smiled to herself as she remembered her leaving party, the laughter and the gaiety in her favourite restaurant. Her colleagues had teased her, wished her luck, drunk her health with rather a lot of very good champagne and promised to visit her in Ireland, even if it *did* rain all the time.

Moments later, they came out below the base of the cloud. To her absolute amazement, she saw the familiar outline of the Isle of Man lying in the midst of a deep blue Irish Sea. Beyond, to the west, as far as the eye could see, there wasn't a cloud in sight, the green and lovely land she called 'home' stretched into the far distance, radiant in the low evening sunshine. The Mourne Mountains threw long shadows towards the gentle hills of County Down as the aircraft moved northwards. As the wing dipped over the brick-covered acres of Belfast, she caught the first sight of the Antrim Hills. Dark, hard-edged basalt, as uncompromising as the six-storey mills that sprouted at their feet. Beyond lay the gleaming expanse of Lough Neagh, set amid green fields dotted with small, white farmhouses, placed like models on a playroom floor, a handful of trees alongside each one to shelter it from the prevailing wind.

She wished she could pause, however briefly, so that this moment would be fixed forever in her mind. She needed time to gaze at the far horizon, to separate out the Sperrins and the mountains of Donegal from the distant banks of cloud, beyond which the sun would descend into the Atlantic. But only seconds later they were low over the calm water of the lough. They bumped slightly on the new concrete runway at Aldergrove, disturbing, if only for a moment, the hares who were feeding on the rich grass alongside.

The engines roared in reverse, the whole cabin vibrating, then as the noise and vibration died away the plane taxied so slowly towards the new terminal building that she was able to look down into the yards of the nearest farms. The newly-milked cows moved back from byre to meadow, as indifferent to the noise of their new neighbours as the hares who grazed on the margins of the runways.

'Andrew, I'm here,' she said, catching the sleeve of the tall, fair-haired young man who was leaning over the balcony and peering down anxiously into the baggage hall.

'Clare,' he gasped, relief spreading across his face as he spun round and clasped her in his arms. 'I thought you hadn't made it. I was down at the gate to meet you.'

'I thought you would be, but I couldn't see you,' she explained, shaking her head. 'The plane was full of large men. All I could see was business suits.'

He laughed and clutched her more firmly. 'I don't think I'll be able to let you out of my sight for a very long time,' he confessed. 'I've been going mad for the last hour.'

He stopped and looked sheepish as he released her.

'I know I'm silly, but I can't bear the thought of losing you again,' he began. 'Now tell me, did you have a good flight?' he went on, making an effort to collect himself.

'Not entirely,' she replied honestly, as she smiled up at him. 'In the end, it was quite wonderful, but I had a bad time too. There was thick cloud and I kept thinking about what happened to us two years ago. And then, when I did get here I couldn't find *you* either.'

'*Pots and kettles*,' he said, his blue eyes shining, as he kissed her again. He dropped his arm round her shoulders and held her close as they made their way downstairs to the empty carousel.

She laughed, delighted by the familiar phrase. It was one she'd learnt from her grandfather. She could hear him now, see the wry look on his face; '*Shure them two are always right, one's as bad as the other, and when they give off about each other, it's the pot callin' the kettle black.*'

All the pots and kettles at the forge house were black from the smoke from the stove. They'd have been even worse when they were hung on a chain over an open fire, as once they were in the days before there was a stove at all. Like everything else she had shared with Andrew from her life with her grandfather, he'd remembered it.

'*Six of one and half a dozen of the other*,' she replied, offering him back the phrase *his* mother would have used.

For so many years, they'd exchanged words and phrases as they'd explored their very different life experiences. While Clare had never moved beyond 'her teacup', a small area round Armagh itself and her grandparents' homes, Andrew had spent most of his time in England. He had been born at Drumsollen, the big house just over a mile from the forge, where his grandparents had lived, but after his parents had been killed in the London blitz, the very day they had taken him over to start prep school, Andrew was seldom invited back. Only when his grandfather, Senator Richardson, insisted on his coming, did his grandmother agree to a short visit.

'Here, let me carry that,' he said, reaching out his free hand for her cardboard box.

'No, I'm fine. It's not heavy.'

'What is it?'

'My wedding dress.'

He laughed and shook his head. 'My dear Clare,' he began with exaggerated patience, 'it is only *seeing you in it before the wedding* that brings bad luck, not me carrying it.'

She laughed aloud, relief and joy finally catching up with her as he began to tease her.

'Well, I'm taking no chances anyhow,' she came back at him, as the first of the luggage appeared in front of them.

She had arrived and all was well. It wouldn't even matter now if her luggage had gone to Manchester or Edinburgh. She had her dress. The rest could be managed.

'So where are we spending the night?' she asked, as they drove out of the airport.

'Officially, you are staying with Jessie's mother at Ballyards,' he said, glancing across at her.

'And unofficially?' she replied, raising an eyebrow.

'Jessie told her you were arriving tomorrow. Slip of the tongue, of course, but we can't just have you arriving when she's not expecting you.'

'Of course not,' she agreed vigorously. 'I'll just have to come home to Drumsollen with you.'

'I was hoping you'd say that,' he said, as they turned on to the main road and headed for Armagh.

The sun had dipped further now, and with the light evening

breeze that had sprung up, its golden light rippled through the trees that overhung the road. The first autumn leaves caught its glow and small heaps lying by the roadside swirled upwards in the wind of their passing.

'Let me, Andrew,' she said, as they drew up at the newly-painted gates of Drumsollen.

She paused as she waited for him to drive through, looking across the empty road, grateful for the fresh air after a day of sitting in cars and planes. This was where it had all begun, so many years ago. She and Jessie had left their bicycles parked against the wall by the gates while they went down to their secret sitting-place by the little stream on the opposite side of the road. They'd come back up to find Andrew bending over her bicycle. Jessie thought he was letting her tyres down, but Clare had taken one look at him and known that could not possibly be. In fact, he'd been blowing them up again after some boys from the nearby Mill Row had indeed let them down. She closed the gates firmly and got back into the car.

'I can hardly believe it, Andrew. Drumsollen is ours.'

'God bless our mortgaged home,' he said, grinning, as they rounded the final bend in the drive. Ahead of them stood the faded façade of the handsome house where generations of Richardsons had lived, its windows shuttered, its front door gleaming with fresh paint.

'Andrew! My goodness, what *have* you done?' she demanded as he stopped by a large, newly-planted space in front of the house.

'Parterre, I think is the word,' he said, looking pleased with himself. 'But we could only manage half. John Wiley found the plan inside one of the old gardening books Grandfather left him, so we poked around to see if we could find the outline. We knew where it ought to be, because June remembered it from before the war. It showed up quite clearly when we started mowing the grass. What d'you think?'

'I think it's quite lovely,' she said, running her eye over the dark earth with its rows of bushes. 'Did *you* choose the roses?'

'No, not my department,' he replied, shaking his head. 'Given I hadn't got my favourite gardener at hand, I thought Grandfather's choice would be more reliable. There was a list with the plan. We got the bushes half-price at the end of August, so I'm afraid there's not much bloom.'

'There's more than enough for what I need,' she said happily, as they parked by the front door and got out together. 'Have we time to go up to the summerhouse before the light goes, or are you starving?'

'There's plenty of time if you want to,' he said easily, drawing her into his arms again. 'June left me a casserole to heat up. I think by the size of it she guessed you were coming, but she didn't say a word,' he added, as he took her hand.

They crossed the gravel to the steps that led up the low green hill which hid Drumsollen from the main road and climbed in silence. This was where they had come in April after their unexpected meeting. This was where they had agreed their future was to be together after all.

'Little bit of honeysuckle still blooming,' she said, as they came to the highest point and stood in front of the old summerhouse, which Andrew had restored over a year ago, his first effort to redeem the loss of the home he thought he must sell. They stood together looking out to the far horizon. The sun appeared to be sitting on the furthest of the many ridges of land between here and the distant Atlantic.

'Clare, do you remember once saying to me that you loved this place, that you wanted to be here, but you'd be sad if you never saw anything beyond these little green hills?' he asked quietly.

'No, I don't remember saying it, but I'm sure I did,' she said slowly. 'It's true, of course. And you always did pay attention to the really important things I said.'

'Makes up for my other unfortunate characteristics,' he added promptly.

She turned towards him and glared at him until he laughed.

'Sorry. I'm not allowed to refer to my less admirable qualities.'

'Oh yes, you can refer to them if you want, but you are not allowed to behave as if they were real.'

'But they *feel* real,' he protested. 'I'm no use with money. I can't stand sectarianism, or arrogance, or injustice. What use is that in the world we've got to live in?'

'Andrew dear, it only needs one of us to be able to do sums. I've had a holiday from the things you've been living with. I'm not ignorant of them, just out of touch. Does it matter?'

'No, nothing matters except that we are together. I'm sorry. I shouldn't have said what I said to spoil your homecoming. Here of all places, where we were so happy last April.'

Clare looked at him and saw the distress and anxiety in his face. She thought of the little boy who'd been told on his very first day at prep school that he had lost his parents. 'Andrew, my darling. We *both* have weaknesses. Look at the way we *both* got anxious when I was flying. With any luck our weaknesses won't attack *both of us* at the same time,' she began gently, taking his hands in hers. 'Let's just say that between us we'll make one good one.'

He nodded vigorously and looked away.

She knew he was near to tears but said nothing. He'd been taught for most of his life to hide his feelings; it would take many a long day for him to be easy even with her.

They stood for some time holding each other and kissing gently. As the sun finally went down, they stirred in the now chill breeze and noticed that the sky behind them had filled with cloud. A few spots of rain fell and sat on the shoulders of Andrew's suit until she brushed them off.

Clare laughed. 'We're going to get wet,' she said cheerfully, as they turned back down the steps to the empty house below.

'No,' he replied, 'it's been doing this all day. We'll be fine. And what does it matter anyway,' he added, beaming, as he put his arm round her. 'We'll be all right, come rain, come shine.'

Two

The little grey parish church built by the Molyneux family in the early 1770s for the workers on their estate at Castledillon, and their many tenants in the surrounding farmlands, sits at the highest point of the townland of Salters Grange. Not a particularly high point in effect, for the hills of this part of County Armagh are drumlins, low rounded mounds, their smooth green slopes contoured by moving tongues of ice that reshaped the land long ago, leaving a pattern of well-drained hillsides and damp valley bottoms with streams liable to flooding at any season after the sudden showers carried by the prevailing, moisture-laden west wind from the Atlantic, a mere hundred miles away.

Despite its modest elevation, the church tower and the thin grey spire above has an outlook that includes most of the six counties of Ulster. From the vantage point of the tower's battlements, you could scan the surrounding lowlands, take in the shimmering, silver waters of Lough Neagh and, on a clear day, penetrate the misty blue layers of the rugged hills of Tyrone to glimpse the far distant mountains of Donegal.

From the heavy iron gates that give entrance to the churchyard, the view is more limited, a prospect of fields and orchards, sturdy farmhouses with corrugated iron hay sheds and narrow lanes leading downhill to the Rectory, the forge or the crossroads. Through gaps in the hedgerow, a glint of sun on a passing windscreen marks the line of the main road linking the nearby villages with their market town, Armagh, dominated by the tall spires of the Catholic cathedral and the massive tower of the Protestant one, regarding each other from their respective hills.

On this bright September afternoon, the sun reflecting off the grey stone of the tower, the gates stand open, a small, battered car parked close by, as two women make their way up to the church door, their arms full of flowers and foliage.

'You divide them up, Ma, and I'll get out the vases,' said the girl, as she lowered her burden gently on to the pedestal of the font. 'Aren't they lovely? Where did Clare get them?'

'Sure, they're from Drumsollen,' June Wiley replied, watching her eldest daughter finger the bright blooms. 'Hasn't Andrew and your Da replanted one of the big beds at the front?' she went on, as she began to strip green leaves briskly from the lower stems. 'They've half of it back the way it was in the old days when the Richardsons had three or four gardeners,' she added, with a little laugh. 'You'll see great improvements at Drumsollen. Mind you, that's only the start. They've great plans, the pair of them. They'll maybe take away some of your trade from the Charlemont.'

'That'll not worry me after next week,' Helen replied cheerfully. 'I'll have my work cut out keeping up with all these Belfast students cleverer than I am.'

'Now don't be sayin' that,' June replied sharply, as Helen lined up a collection of tall vases. 'Sure didn't Clare go up to Queens just like you're doin' and look where she's got to. Just because you come up from the country, ye needn't think those ones from Belfast are any better than you are. Didn't *you* get a County Scholarship? How many gets that?'

'Clare was the first one from round here, wasn't she?'

'She was indeed, an' I'll never forget the day she got the news. Her grandfather was that pleased he could hardly tell me when I called at the forge to ask. I thought he was going to cry.'

'Wish he was here for tomorrow, Ma. He'd be so proud,' Helen replied, looking away, suddenly finding her own eyes full of tears, so sharp the memory of the old man in his soot-streaked clothes.

'Aye, he would. But the other granda's coming from over Richhill way with her Uncle Jack. So I hear. But she hasn't mentioned her brother who lives with them. She talks about the uncle often enough, but the brother I've never met. They say he's kind of funny. Very abrupt. Unsettled. Apparently the only one can manage him is Granda Hamilton. The granny pays no attention to him at all.'

'Is she not coming to the wedding?'

'Oh no. Not the same lady,' the older woman replied, her tone darkening. 'Apparently she won't go to weddings *or* funerals. Says they're a lot of fuss about nothing. But I hear she's bad with her legs, so maybe it's an excuse,' she added, a frown creasing her pleasant face as she laid roses side by side and studied the length of their stems.

They worked quietly together as the afternoon sun dropped lower and the light faded in the north aisle. June Wiley had always loved flowers and had learnt long ago how to make the best of whatever the gardener's boy had brought into the big kitchen at Drumsollen. She'd started work there as a kitchen maid, progressed to the parlour and had been instructed in the art of flower arranging by Mrs Richardson herself, a formidable lady known to all the staff as The Missus. It was later that young Mrs Richardson had chosen June as nurse for her son. She was a very different woman from her mother-in-law, warm-hearted and kindly, devoted to her little boy. June herself had gone in fear of The Missus for most of her working life, but she ended up by caring for her right up until her death in the house only eighteen months earlier.

'Have you seen her dress, Ma?' Helen asked, as she knelt down and swept up small fragments of foliage and discarded thorns from the step of the font.

'No, not yet. She said she'd bring it when she came to help me with the food this morning, but she had to leave it behind at Rowentrees. She said she hung it up for the creases to drop out for she didn't want to risk the iron. I think it has wee beads sewn into it here and there.'

'I wonder what she's thinking about today,' Helen said, half to herself. 'She used to work at Drumsollen with you, didn't she, washing dishes and making beds like me at the Charlemont, and now she's the lady of the house.'

June gave her daughter a thoughtful look. A clever girl she was by all accounts, but she'd always made up stories in her head. That was not something June had much time for, her own life having been hard. She had tried to bring up her three girls so they wouldn't get ideas that would let them down.

'Oh, something sensible, I wouldn't wonder,' she replied crisply. 'Oh, she loves him all right, she always has from ever they met, but she'll not think of him and her till she's seen to what has to be done. Them visitors ye have at the Charlemont, Mr Lafarge and the French lady and her daughter. She'll make sure they're all right before she thinks about her and Andrew. Can't remember their name.'

'The girl is Michelle.'

June shook her head. 'No, I meant the mother, Madame Saint-something. Clare said she was awful good to her when she first went over to France, bought her a suit for her first interview and taught her how to dress like the French do.'

She stopped suddenly, straightened up and laughed, so unexpectedly that Helen nearly dropped her dustpan.

'What's the joke?' she demanded.

'You should've seen her this mornin',' her mother said, shaking her head. 'A pair of jeans I wouldn't let any of you girls be seen dead in and an old shirt. It must have been Andrew's before it shrank in the wash. I wonder what the French lady would have thought of that.'

'It's Madame St Clair, Ma, and she's very nice. Speaks beautiful English. And Mr Lafarge is very polite. But I though he was American. He has an American accent.'

'Oh aye. That's another story too,' June replied, lifting the first of the arrangements into place. 'Clare says he learnt English from the Americans at the end of the war and he has some awful accent. Not the right thing at all in his job. I suppose the French are just as fussy about that sort of thing as they are here. Sure old Mrs Richardson, God rest her, was furious when young Andrew came back from a visit to Brittany with some country accent he'd picked up. Clare told me once that when he wants to make her laugh he asks her would she like 'fish and chips'.'

'*Poisson et pommes frites.*'

'Aye, maybe that's the right way of it, but that's not how Andrew says it. The Missus always used to talk French to him when he came visitin' and when he landed back with this accent she was fit to be tied. A Richardson talkin' like a servant.'

'But it was only in French, Ma. What did that matter? It was how he spoke English that would matter here, wouldn't it?'

'Well, I suppose you're right, but these gentry families are full of things you wouldn't believe. They're always lookin' to see whose watchin' them. An' the less money they have, the more they look,' she added, nodding wisely. 'Now the Senator was always the same to everyone, high or low, but The Missus, she was a different story. She was always on her high horse about somethin' and yet she once told our Clare that Andrew wasn't good enough for her, that she could do better for herself. An' Clare a wee orphan with her granda a blacksmith.'

'Even though Andrew was a Richardson and might some day have a title?' Helen asked, her dark eyes wide and full of curiosity.

'Yes. She hadn't a good word for Andrew an' I'll never understand it, for you'd travel a long way to meet a nicer young man. She always said he had no go in him. He was clever enough, but he never made the best of himself, even with the posh boarding school in England and the uncle behind him sending him to Cambridge to do Law.'

'Was Law what he wanted to do?'

June removed a dead leaf from the spread of colour which would grace the font itself and looked at her daughter thoughtfully.

'Maybe it wasn't,' she said flatly. 'I've often wondered about it, but I never had the heart to ask him,' she went on. 'When you got your scholarship to go up to Queens, it didn't matter whether you did Geography, or History, or English. I know your teachers advised you, but it was *you* decided what you wanted to do. But then we're only working people. If you're a Richardson, it's a different kettle of fish. The family will tell you what to do if you don't already know what's expected in the first place. As far as I can see there's no two ways about it, you just have to do it.'

'Well, there's none of the family left, now The Missus is gone. There's just Andrew and Clare. They can do what they like, can't they?' Helen responded cheerfully, her face lighting up with a great beaming smile.

'Aye well, I suppose you're right. But you needn't think, Helen, that falling in love and getting married is all roses. You can't know what's up ahead and it may not turn out the way you hope.'

Helen nodded and said nothing. Her mother was always warning her against disappointment. There was no use arguing. She just didn't seem to see how wonderful it was for Clare and Andrew to have found each other and to make such a marvellous plan for turning Drumsollen into a guest house. They were going to save up and buy back the land that had once made up the estate, then Andrew would give up his job and farm just as he had always wanted. Helen smiled to herself. It was exactly the sort of plan she'd make herself if she found someone she really loved.

'Time we were gettin' a move on, Helen,' June said abruptly, as she turned round and saw her daughter gazing thoughtfully at a handful of rose leaves in the palm of her hand. 'Yer Da'll be home soon and no sign of his tea and we've both got to go back up to the house tonight to give them a hand.'

'Right, Ma, what do you want me to carry?' asked Helen quickly, as she dropped the petals in her pocket. *One day*, she thought, *I'll marry someone lovely and I'll have a shower of rose petals as I come out of the church just like they have in films.*

'D'ye not think that neckline is a bit much for Salters Grange?'

Clare, who was dressed only in a low cut strapless bra and a slim petticoat, turned round from the dressing-table and laughed, as her friend Jessie pushed open the door of the bedroom, dropped down on the bed, and kicked off her elegant new shoes.

'I hope ye slept well in my bed,' Jessie continued. 'I left ye my teddy-bear to tide you over till tonight,' she went on, looking around the room that still had her watercolours and photographs covering all the available wall space.

'Oh, I slept all right,' replied Clare, as she dusted powder over foundation with a large brush. 'By the time June and I had got all the food organized and the tables laid I could have slept on the floor. But your bed was much nicer. Thank you for the loan of it.'

'Or *the lend of it* as we always said at school and got told off for.'

Clare smiled, relieved and delighted that Jessie seemed to have fully recovered her old self after the hard time she'd had with her second child.

'How's Fiona?' she asked, as she turned back to the mirror.

'Oh, driving us mad,' she said calmly. 'I sent Harry to walk her up and down and tire her out a bit before Ma tries to get the dress on. She can talk about nothin' but Auntie Clare and Uncle Andrew. Does it not make you feel old?'

'No. Old is not what I feel today,' she said lightly. 'Blessed, I think is the word, as long as you don't think I've gone pious,' she added quickly. 'It's not just Andrew. It's being home and having family. It's you and Harry and wee Fiona and your mother and all the people who'll come to the church. Even the ones that come to stand at the gate, because they go to all the weddings, or because they remember Granda Scott.'

'Aye, there'll be a brave few nosey ones around,' Jessie added promptly. 'Ma says she heard your dress was made by yer man Dior himself.'

Clare laughed, stood up and reached out for the hem of the gleaming, silk gown hanging from the picture rail.

'Look Jessie, I only found it this morning.'

Jessie leaned over and looked closely at the inside hem. 'Good luck, *Bonne chance, Buenos* . . . something or other . . . and there are names as well. Ach, isn't that lovely? All the way round. Who did that?' she demanded, her voice hoarse, her eyes sparkling with tears.

'The girls in the work room. I knew them all, because I had to have so many suits and dresses, but when I had the last fitting there was nothing there. I'm sure I'd have noticed.'

'So you'll have luck all round ye and in whatever language takes your fancy . . .

Clare nodded, her own eyes moistening at the thought of all the little seamstresses taking it in turns to embroider their name and their message. She paused as she slipped the dress from its hanger and took a deep breath. The last thing she must do was shed a tear.

Whatever it said on the packaging she had never found a mascara that didn't run if provoked by tears. Tears of joy would be just as much of a disaster as any other kind.

The crowd of women and children gathered round the churchyard gates were not expecting very much. They knew it was to be a small affair with only close family. In fact, there were those who thought there couldn't even be much in the way of close family if June Wiley, the housekeeper, her husband John and their girls were to be among the guests, even if June had once been Andrew Richardson's nurse. They certainly did not expect any 'great style' from anyone except the bride. Even that was a matter of some doubt as rumour had it she'd bought her dress on the way home from Paris and arrived with it at the Rowentrees in a cardboard box.

The first guests to arrive did little to disperse their expectations. Jack Hamilton drove up in a well-polished, but elderly Hillman Minx. He was accompanied by his father, Sam, now in his eighties, who got out of the car with some difficulty, but once on his feet, smiled warmly at the waiting crowd, pushed back his once powerful shoulders and tramped steadily enough up to the church door.

Charlie Running, old friend of Robert Scott, walked briskly up the hill from his cousin's house and said, 'How are ye?' to the gathered spectators, for Charlie knew everyone in the whole townland. Before going inside he tramped round the side of the church to pay his respects to Robert.

Next to arrive were the Wileys. June, John and all three girls, as expected. No style there. Not even a new hat or dress among them. Just their Sunday best. Charles Creaney, Andrew's colleague and best man, parked his almost new A40 under the churchyard wall somewhat out of sight of the twin clusters of onlookers by the gates. Andrew and the two ushers got out and the four of them strode off, two by two, heading for the church door without a glance at the women in aprons or the children fidgeting at their sides.

Moments later, a small handful of husbands and wives, some of them clearly from 'across the water', arrived by taxi. But there was no one among them to excite more than a brief speculation as to who they might be. Only the need to view the bride and to have the relevant news to pass on in the week ahead kept some of the women from going back to their abandoned Saturday morning chores.

Then, to their surprise and amazement, one of Loudan's smaller limousines, polished so you could see yourself in its black bodywork, and bedecked with satin ribbons, drove up and slid gently to a halt. The driver opened the passenger door, touched his cap, offered his hand and a woman stepped out into the morning sunshine, a pleasant smile on her face. In the total silence that followed her arrival, she walked slowly towards the church door.

Salters Grange had its own version of 'great style', but they had never seen anything to equal the poise and presentation of Marie-Claude St Clair. Her couturier would have been charmed.

'I think she's a film star,' said the first woman to find her voice. 'She's like somethin' ye'd see on the front of *Vogue*.'

'I'm sure I've seen her on our new telly.'

'Young Helen Wiley said there was a French woman and her daughter staying at the Charlemont in Armagh. Would that be her?'

'Where's the daughter then?'

It was then that Loudan's largest limousine appeared, driven by none other than Loudan himself. It drew to a halt in front of the gates. From the front passenger seat, a small man in immaculate morning dress stepped out, drew himself to his full height and waited attentively until first one lovely young woman and then another was assisted by the bowler-hatted Loudan to alight from the back seat.

Robert Lafarge bowed to them both and then offered his arm to the older one. So it was that, Cinderella no more, Clare Hamilton entered Grange Church on the arm of an eminent French banker, attended by a smiling young woman, whom she had cared for in her student days as an au pair on the sands at Deauville.

As the quips and comments flew back and forth across the gravel driveway it was clear the wait had not been in vain.

'Did ye ever see the like of it? Was that necklace emeralds?'

'How would I know? But I can tell you somethin'. That dress was such a fit you'd not buy that in some shop. An' her that slim. Shure it must have been made for her, and those wee pearl beads round the skirt with the green and gold threadwork in-between to match the necklace.'

'Was it silk or brocade? It was white all right, but there was green in it somewhere when she moved.'

'Who was the wee man giving her away?'

'They say that's Robert Scott's younger brother, the one that went to America an' niver came back.'

'Well, he doesn't look like a Scott to me, that's for sure. Sure he's only knee high to a daisy. Robert was a fair-sized man in his day . . .'

While the women of Church Hill speculated on the past and future of Clare Hamilton, granddaughter of their former blacksmith, and of Andrew Richardson, sole surviving member of the once wealthy family who had lived in the parish since the seventeenth century and served in the Government since it was first set up 1921, the two individuals themselves stood together on the newly-replaced red carpet of the chancel and exchanged rings.

In the September sunshine filtering through the windows on the south aisle, the two rings gleamed just as they had when Clare found them in the dust and fluff under the wooden couch by the stove in the forge house. As the smaller one, once bound with human hair inside the larger one, was slipped on her finger, Clare feared for her mascara once again. She had found the rings a mere fortnight after her grandfather's death. Then, she had lost both her grandfather and her home and had only a student room to call her own. Now, so much had been given back. Someone to love who loved her as dearly. A home that was theirs, Andrew's family home, the place he had longed to be for most of his life.

With hands joined and heads bowed for the blessing, they both felt the touch of gold. The rings that had lain in the dust for a hundred years or more had emerged untarnished. Engraved on each of them were the initials EGB. It was a message of hope: in Irish, *Erin Go Bragh*; in English, *Ireland Forever*. Or better, the words the minister had used earlier . . . *for as long as you both shall live.*

Three

The first day of January 1961 was dull and overcast in Armagh. Clare stood at the bedroom window and looked out across the lawn and over the curve of Drumsollen's own low hill. Even under a grey sky the grass was a vibrant green and shaggy with growth. So far this winter there had been no severe weather and no snow at all, but spring was still a long time away.

After breakfast, Andrew stepped out into the early morning, left crumbs on the bird table and came back in again looking pleased. The wind was light and from the south-east. Echoing a phrase of her grandfather's, he announced: '*There's no cold.*'

'Thank goodness for that,' Clare laughed, as she carried their breakfast dishes to the draining board. 'It'll be draughty enough by the lake at Castledillon without a cold wind as well,' she declared, as he shrugged his shoulders into his ancient waxed jacket and took his binoculars from a drawer under the work surface.

'You're sure you don't mind me going, Clare? We were supposed to have a holiday today and you're left with all the work,' he added, a hint of anxiety creeping into his voice.

'Oh Andrew, don't be silly,' she responded, giving him a hug, 'We BOTH work so hard. You must take some time to do the things you want to do. You go and help with the count and get a look at the heronries. Another day when YOU are at work, I'll go and see what Charlie's added to his archive and talk local history with him. *Fair shares for all*, as your mother would say.'

They went upstairs and crossed the dim entrance hall where a small collection of ancestors still stared gloomily around them as if they had mislaid something they needed. A light breeze blew in their faces as Andrew opened the double glass doors into the porch, stepped through and swung the heavy outer door back into its daytime position. He put an arm round her shoulders as they walked across the stone terrace and down the broad sandstone steps to the driveway.

'I'll be back by twelve,' he said, kissing her. 'If you do start on Seven you can have my paintbrush ready. Don't do too much while I'm gone.'

'I promise. I'll have your lunch ready. You'll be starving. You always are. It'll only be a toasted sandwich,' she warned, as he opened the car door.

She went back indoors and ran upstairs to their bedroom. The kitchen had been warm from the Aga but the unheated bedroom was cold. Not as cold as her old bedroom at the forge house had been in winter but bad enough to make her grateful for the thick wool sweater she pulled out from a deep drawer below the handsome rosewood wardrobe.

She retrieved the hot water bottles from under the bedclothes, made the bed and took the bottles into the adjoining bathroom to empty them. The plasterwork was still drying out and the acres of white tile and gleaming taps made it feel even colder than the bedroom. She did a quick wipe of the hand basin and turned back gratefully into the room once used by The Missus.

Unlike the cold linoleum of the forge house, this room had always had the comfort and pleasure of a carpet but when they moved in they found it was so full of holes it would have to be replaced before they handed it over to the guests they hoped to welcome in April. Given the new bathroom, they had assumed this would be their best room until they realized the state of the carpet. She was still trying to decide what to do about it when their good friend Harry spotted a carpet when he was buying antique furniture in a house scheduled for demolition. He'd tipped the workmen to carry it to his van, brought it up to them and stayed to help them cut up old one up.

Harry said the 'new' carpet was probably older than the one they'd just carried to the compost heap. It was full of dust and dirty from the tramp of workmen's feet but it showed very little signs of wear. They'd spent the best part of a warm, autumn weekend beating it, vacuuming it and sponging it. By the time they'd managed to lay it they were exhausted, but the carpet with its exotic birds and plants transformed the room. It even matched the faded curtains so well they decided they'd not replace them after all.

The bed made, the room tidied, Clare sat down at her dressing-table and began her make-up. For weeks after their brief honeymoon, she had applied only moisturizer, but as day followed day and she spent most of her time sorting, cleaning, or gloss painting, dressed in the oldest of old clothes, she began to feel something was wrong. The day before the surveyor came to estimate for the new central heating system she made up her mind. Cheap jeans from the cut-price shop in Portadown and well-worn shirts that could go in the machine would be fine for the job in hand, but she needed her go-to-work face to keep up spirits. To her surprise, that simple decision steadied her when she was presented with the enormity of the surveyor's estimate next day.

She smiled to herself as she applied powder with a sable brush just as her dear friend Louise had taught her when they'd first shared an office in Paris. She missed Louise. She missed Paris. She missed that whole other world where she had been mostly happy and certainly successful. But now she and Andrew had each other and a life they could make together. You can't have everything and she knew she had chosen what she really wanted.

She thought again of that sunlit October morning when the surveyor had presented his estimate. It brought back memories of all the meetings she'd sat through with Robert Lafarge, listening to companies putting forward plans, projects and requests for loans. She had smiled at him, given him coffee in the kitchen and negotiated the price. By suggesting the project be spread over the winter period when the company would be short of work, she'd secured a substantial discount. Andrew laughed when she told him. What delighted him was the thought of the unsuspecting surveyor coming face to face with a woman who had once been party to negotiating sums in seven figures.

By Christmas Eve, three of the five large bedrooms on the first floor had been freshened up or completely redecorated. Apart from the high ceilings and cornices, they'd done all the painting themselves. While Andrew was at work, Clare did as much of the brushwork as she could while supervising the installing of the two new bathrooms. When Andrew got home from work, he'd hang his suit over the bedroom chair, pull on his dungarees and take over her brush while she prepared a meal. Afterwards, they'd share the day's news over coffee and then go back together to where he'd left off.

'What do we tackle next?' he asked, as they put up a holly wreath on the front door and looked forward to a few days holiday from paint.

'Your guess is as good as mine,' she said honestly. 'A double brings in double the money and there's only one set of bed linen to launder, but the single rooms will be cheaper and might attract more business. The five singles on the top floor *could* be very important. It all depends on who we manage to attract.'

'Some of each, then?' he suggested. 'Doing a single would take us half the time it's taken for the doubles. And we could do our own ceilings up there. Or rather *I* could do them.'

Clare pulled the bedroom door shut behind her and headed for the top floor, turned along the narrow corridor and stopped at a door with a dim and worn brass number seven. This was the largest of the upper bedrooms with a view over the garden. She stepped into the almost empty room and smiled to herself. It was in a much better state than she'd remembered.

Back in October, she and June had cleaned all the rooms in the house, getting rid of anything that could not be restored or reused. The windows on both floors had stood open for long, sunny days till finally the odour of damp and neglect had been overwhelmed by the faint perfume of lavender polish, the fresh smell of emulsion paint and the strange odour of the new rose-coloured carpet in two of the double bedrooms. Tomorrow, when June came back to work she must ask her who had slept in number seven when she had arrived straight from Grange School to begin her service at Drumsollen.

'Dust sheets,' she said aloud, as she tried to remember where the nearest pile of clean ones might be.

She looked more closely at the window frame. 'And sandpaper,' she added, wearily. You could paint over fine cracks but loose flakes like these came off on the brush. It was more trouble than it was worth trying to take a short cut.

It was just as she was about to go in search of her materials that a movement caught her eye, a glint, or a gleam from a vehicle just coming into view. She looked down in amazement and watched as a large black taxi drew up at the foot of the steps.

Could it possibly be someone who had misread their opening date? She'd been advertising in a whole variety of newspapers and magazines but she'd stressed: *Springtime in the countryside. Special offers for our first guests from April the First. Bookings now accepted.*

She peered down. She could see the driver perfectly well as he opened his door, strode round to the boot and took out a large and heavy suitcase, but she couldn't get a good look at the figure emerging from the front passenger seat.

She ran along the top corridor and hurried downstairs. As she strode across the entrance hall, she caught a glimpse of a familiar figure through the glass panels of the porch door. *It can't be, she's supposed to be in America*, she said to herself, as she pulled them open. But there was no mistaking that red hair. It was Ginny, whom she hadn't seen since they'd met in a hotel in Park Lane just over a year ago.

'Clare, I'm sorry, I haven't any money,' Ginny said bleakly, as she walked round the vehicle, her face pale, her eyes red rimmed.

Clare threw her arms round her and hugged her. She could feel Ginny's shoulders trembling ominously. Something was dreadfully wrong.

'How much is it?' Clare asked as steadily as she could manage, stepping back and smiling rather too brightly at the taxi man.

She was completely taken aback by the sum he named. She wasn't sure she had that amount of money in the house, even with the reserve she still kept in Granda Scott's old Bible.

'Hold on a moment, will you. My handbag is probably upstairs,' she said quickly. 'Perhaps you could bring in my friend's suitcase.'

'Right y'ar,' he replied agreeably, eyeing the well-swept steps and the heavy, white-painted front door.

Clare ran upstairs, emptied her handbag on to the bed. There was a wallet and a purse and some loose silver she'd dropped in when she was in a hurry. Putting it all together, she was still well short of the taxi fare even if she added the pound notes from the Bible and the bread man's money from the kitchen drawer.

'Where on earth has Ginny come from?' she asked herself. Not Armagh certainly. Not since the railway had been closed down. And hardly Portadown to chalk up a bill like that. She stood breathless, a handful of pound notes in her hand and looked around the room as if an answer might lie there somewhere if only she could think of it.

'Oh, thank goodness,' she gasped, as she remembered Andrew's wallet in the top drawer of his bedside table.

It was empty, as usual, but all was not lost. Not yet. She unzipped an inner compartment. There sat the balance of the fare. She ran back downstairs triumphant, delighted by the irony that the reserve she insisted he carry for emergencies was what had saved the situation for *her*.

'Thank you very much, ma'am,' the taxi driver said, as he folded the notes away into his back pocket. 'I think this young lady had a rough crossing last night,' he added kindly, nodding at Ginny, as he took a battered card from his pocket. 'If I can be of service, give us a ring. Distance no object,' he added, raising a hand in salute to them both as he drove off.

*   *   *

'That smells good,' said Andrew as he tramped into the kitchen and struggled out of his jacket. 'I thought you said *a toasted sandwich*,' he went on cheerfully. He ran his eye across the large wooden table. The end nearest the Aga sported a red checked cloth, three place settings and a bottle of wine. 'Has Harry found us another carpet?'

Clare pushed a covered dish into the bottom oven, closed the door, straightened up and shook her head. His eyes flickered away from her face as he caught her sober look.

'Don't tell me the bailiff has arrived before we've even started?' he said, trying to sound light.

Clare knew the tone only too well. He was going to be upset, but there was nothing for it but to tell him the truth.

'Ginny arrived a couple of hours ago, by taxi. She came over on the *Ulster Queen* from Liverpool. Mark's gone off with an American heiress.'

'But they were supposed to be getting married last year,' Andrew protested, as he dropped down into the nearest chair. 'In June, wasn't it? But his father was ill, so they had to postpone it. And then they weren't able to come to our wedding, because of something else. Some big job came up in America and he couldn't say "No" to it. Wasn't that what she told us?'

Clare nodded. 'I though it sounded funny at the time, but I can see it all now. Ginny tried to cover up for him. He lost a lot of money on the Stock Market. She said they couldn't even afford *her* fare to come to the wedding. There *was* something came up in America, so she gave him all she had in the bank for his airfare. But nothing came of it. At least, that's what he said when he came back. Apparently he thought she'd got a lot more money somewhere and he kept on asking her to help him out.'

'But what made him think Ginny had money? The bit she gets from Grandfather Barbour's shares goes down all the time. It's hardly more than pocket money. She had a job, didn't she? Did it pay well?'

'I really don't know. But remember she was living with your aunt in Knightsbridge while she had her plastic surgery. You know what a splendid house that is and how much you had to raise for the Clinic. It must have looked as if there was a lot of money around.'

'So, what happened?'

'She found a letter from this American woman. She thinks he

left it lying around deliberately. They had a terrible row. He was planning to fly out next week. Told her he wasn't cut out for poverty. Sorry and all that. They'd had some good times. But it was over.'

'God Almighty! Where is she now?'

'Asleep on our bed under a couple of rugs. There isn't a bed made up. Anyway, ours is the only room that gets any heat from below. That's why you chose it. Remember?'

Andrew leaned his arms on the table and dropped his head in his hands. For one moment, she thought he might be crying. He'd always been fond of Ginny. At one time, while she was in Paris, she'd thought there was something between them. Harry had said he'd seen them together quite often, but it turned out it was simply Andrew trying to get her back on her feet after Edward was killed.

Ginny had been driving when they were hit by the speeding lorry and his death had left emotional scars as well as the obvious physical ones. She'd needed a psychiatrist as well as a plastic surgeon. Andrew had raised the money by mortgaging their family home at Caledon which he'd inherited, but that had left him in serious financial difficulties because he couldn't pay the death duties owed by the estate.

'So what do we do?' he asked steadily, lifting his head, a hint of a smile on his face. 'There's two of us this time, isn't there?'

She nodded reassuringly, bent down and kissed his cold cheek and put her arm round his shoulders.

'There might be some brandy left from that bottle Harry and Jessie gave you for your birthday,' she said softly, 'I seem to remember Ginny doesn't like whiskey.'

'I'll go up and see,' he said briskly, as he got to his feet and headed for the morning room, now their own small sitting-room.

Clare took a deep breath and felt herself relax. She'd been dreading telling him what had happened because she was so anxious about how he would react. He was always so responsible. Far too responsible. For the moment she would keep to herself the fact that Ginny thought she might be pregnant.

'So you're quite sure, Ginny?

'Yes,' she replied, beaming, as she closed the door behind her and sat down by the sitting-room fire. 'I feel awful and I've got through half that packet of Tampax you gave me yesterday, but I don't feel sick any more. I think I was just sick with worry, Clare. What would I have done without you and Andrew?'

'Unhelpful speculation,' Clare replied easily, as she closed her account book, got up from her desk and came over to sit opposite her in front of the comforting blaze. 'I can't say I'm not relieved, though we'd have managed somehow.'

'I feel I've been such a fool. I've made such a mess of things after all the hard work Andrew put in to help me,' she began, throwing out her hands in a typical Ginny manner.

Clare looked at her pale face and listened, comforted by the fact that she seemed so much herself again only a week after her flight from London. Exhausted she had been and still was, but the gestures, the eye movements, the toss of her head, all said this was the Ginny she had known since that wonderful summer she and Andrew had stayed with his cousins at The Lodge.

Since she'd taken up decorating herself, Clare often found herself thinking of that happy summer when they'd all painted the big sitting-room at Caledon. Ginny's mother had made sketches of all four of them and Edward designed extraordinary games of skill for them to play in their free time. She still found herself thinking of Teddy and the long conversations they had about Irish history, which was his great passion.

He'd told her it was high time Ireland sorted out what actually happened from all the myths that had been invented. Whether you looked at 1690, or 1847, or 1916, there were facts to be had. What he wanted to do was put the record straight, one way or another, so that this group or that could not select their version of events and use them to justify the unjustifiable, nor to prop up corrupt or idle governments, North or South.

'But I can't impose on you and Andrew any longer, you've been more than kind. Besides, it's not fair . . .'

Clare had been listening, but only with part of her mind, knowing what Ginny was likely to say and having her answer ready.

'Ginny dear, you've only been here a week and you've been helping with jobs every day. Now, come on,' she continued. 'You've not moaned, you've been good company. You just had a lot of sleep to catch up on.'

Ginny smiled ruefully. 'I haven't even got the price of a packet of Tampax, never mind the bus fare to go and see Mother and Barney in Rostrevor.'

'Well then, let me make you an offer,' said Clare lightly. 'Like Robert Lafarge, when he offered me my job, I will hope to make it irresistible. Part-time work for three months, starting tomorrow. Artistic director to the Managing Director of Drumsollen House Limited. Full board and lodging, one long weekend per month in Rostrevor, transport provided and five pounds per week. First month's salary paid in advance so you can repay your friend who lent you the money for the train and boat. I'm the Managing Director and the artistic bit means you'll have a lot of painting to do! How about it?'

'Oh Clare, you can't pay me as well as giving me full board and lodging. I should be paying you for that!'

'Well, if it'll make you feel any better, I hope to make a profit on the deal,' Clare said, looking as sober as she could manage.

'But how can you possibly manage that?'

'Well, if you say "Yes" I'll tell you.'

'You're not just being kind?'

'No. Can't afford to be,' Clare responded honestly. 'I'm supposed to be good with money and I can help you with yours, but I can't start being kind enough to help you manage your money rather better if you haven't got any money to manage in the first place, now, can I?'

Ginny laughed and threw out her hands in a gesture of complete defeat. 'All right. Yes. Yes. Yes. Yes. Now tell me how you are going to make a profit on this outrageously generous offer.'

'Well, I've managed to do some "sharp deals" as one of my American clients used to say, but buying sharp means a lot of research to find what we need at special prices. If I had someone here who could carry on with my painting efforts and keep an eye on workmen when we have them in, then I'd be free to hunt for all the stuff we need, like bed linen and towels, china, glass and so on. I'd like to check out these new Cash and Carry places for basics, but I can't leave June on her own all the time, especially when there might be bookings coming in and we've still got to get the place up and running for April.'

'Right. You're on. If you can tackle something you've never done before, then why can't I? Even if I have been an idiot, I can still do all sorts of useful things when I remember what they are,' she added dryly.

'That's got that settled then.'

Clare paused, suddenly uncertain that what she wanted to say next was quite the right thing.

'What is it, Clare? I know that look of yours. You're thinking.'

'Yes, you're right. I am, but about something quite different,' she began slowly. 'I keep looking at your face. You're still very pale, but that's what makes it so wonderful. Even when you are so pale and have no make-up on at all, I can't see *any* of your scars, even though I know exactly where they are.'

Four

The small, pebble-dashed bungalow overlooking the road from Armagh to Loughgall and the local landmark of Riley's Rocks had been part of Clare's life for as long as she could remember. As a child, hand in hand with her mother or father, she'd walked past often on a Sunday afternoon to visit Granda and Granny Scott at the forge. She could still remember how she had gazed up the steep slope and said proudly, '*That's where Kate and Charlie Running live, isn't it?*' She had known the names of all the people who lived in the scattered houses beyond the Mill Row and even the names of those who lived out of sight at the ends of lanes that dipped down under the railway bridge or curved round the low hill on which the Runnings' bungalow was perched.

Later, after she had lost both her parents and had come to live with her grandfather, she'd cycled the road each day on her way to school in Armagh. Sometimes, on days as hot as today, she would stop at the rusting iron pump opposite the bungalow, to drink the cold water that came gushing up from deep underground. It certainly gushed up when Jessie was with her. Jessie did nothing if not wholeheartedly and when she put her hand to the pump, Clare was sure to end up with a wet gymslip or splashed shoes.

Today, on the loveliest of June days, the sky a perfect blue, the heat tempered by a hint of a breeze, Clare parked Andrew's ancient bicycle on the hedge bank beside the gate her grandfather had made for his old friend, took a cake tin from her front basket and prepared to climb the two flights of steps to his front door.

All morning she'd looked forward to visiting Charlie, a pleasant walk of about a mile if one counted in the long driveway of Drumsollen, but by the time she'd dealt with checking out their overnight guests, sorted the paperwork from the morning's deliveries and answered a scatter of telephone enquiries, she knew she was going to be late. While Charlie had such a relaxed attitude to time he often forgot what day it was, nevertheless, she felt sad that events had cut into her time with him.

Charlie did not suffer from the absent-mindedness that was some-times a feature of age, nor did he have the habit of looking the other way from what he would prefer not to see. Charlie saw so much he was perpetually preoccupied, thinking through some item he had read or teasing out some puzzle he'd encountered in his formidable reading programme. Given how often his mind was elsewhere, Clare took it as a great compliment that he never forgot when she was coming. Not only did he have the kettle boiling, but he always cleared away enough of his books, papers, maps and sketches to leave them a seat each in his small front room.

'Well now, tell me all your news, Clare. How is that good man of yours? I hear he's been down in Fermanagh again. Did he prosper, as the saying is?'

Clare laughed. Not only did Charlie know everyone for miles around, but he knew everything going on in the entire area as well. When she'd last seen him a couple of weeks earlier, the complicated land dispute in Fermanagh involving one of Charles and Andrew's biggest clients had not yet arisen.

'Well, Charlie, as you well know, Andrew hasn't much time for litigation or the criminal side, but he's in his element when it's land. As long as he has a good dispute, preferably with boundaries, so he can get his feet on the ground, he's happy. I wish there was more work of that kind,' she ended sadly.

'Too soon for him to give up being a solicitor and take to farming?'

''Fraid so. I can't give him much hope till we've a year behind us, or more likely two. It *has* gone well though, so far, as I'm sure you've heard. But we can't think of buying land till we've repaid all the loans for the structural work,' she admitted honestly. 'The trouble is, the more we do, the more we find to do. We had to have the gutters cleared and the bad bits replaced and one of the men who'd been up on the roof told us the west chimney is in a bad way. How bad it is we don't know yet. We're just keeping our fingers crossed.'

'Aye, I can see that would be a worry. But I did hear you were fully booked in May.'

'Yes indeed,' she laughed, as he filled the teapot from his electric kettle and took the lid off the cake tin. 'Full up in May and bookings coming in all the time. The local papers did us proud with that piece about Armagh in apple blossom time. That was *your* idea. But there's more good news. Besides *visitors*, we've a couple of surveyors booked for the whole of June. I don't know how they got to hear of us but more long stays like that would be just great. Steady income and *less laundry*,' she added, making a face.

'Surveyors now?' he nodded, as he laid out the cups and saucers methodically. 'Would that be a new factory or suchlike?'

'Yes, it's an American company. Textiles. I think it's probably synthetics. Steve and Tom aren't American, they're English, so they're not really much interested in the end product. In fact, to be honest, though they're very friendly, I think they're only interested in doing the job, watching TV in the evening and getting back home to their wives.'

'So you got the TV then?' he demanded, raising his shaggy eyebrows.

'I got two actually,' she confessed, only too aware of Charlie's thesis that television prevented conversation and was undermining the quality of local visiting. 'The sixteen inch is in the old smoking room for the use of guests. I told you we'd have to have that. But I was in luck. Apparently fourteen inch ones are out of date already, so I got one cheap and we have that in our sitting-room. Mind you it's much bulkier than the sixteen inch and it's a tight squeeze with my desk and the typewriter and the office stuff we need in there as well, but we've been so busy we were beginning to think we'd no idea what was going on in the world at all. Not even what's going on here in Northern Ireland.'

'Not a lot, Clare, not a lot. I can tell you you're not missing much, though I have to say the unemployment has dropped a bit and there's a few more houses going up,' he said, between mouthfuls of cake. 'There'll not be much happening unless your man

Brookeborough exerts himself. And that's not very likely. Sure, it's time he was retiring. The man's a few years younger than I am but I can't say the same for his ideas. We need someone with a new perspective and some notion of how to create jobs and a whole different attitude to people forby. Sure, the ship building's going down the plughole and the linen industry isn't far behind. Emigration is way up again and there's desperate poverty, and not just in Belfast and Derry. Even the small farmers are laying off men and bringing in tractors . . .'

She nodded silently and drank her tea, listening hard as she always did when he started to talk like this, running on from one topic to another. She could never guess what he might bring to her attention next. The progress of the Erne hydroelectric scheme, the fate of Georgian terraces in Central Dublin, the development of an industrial park adjacent to Shannon Airport. Charlie was as committed to the whole island of Ireland as he was to their shared interest in their own small corner.

Today, he moved quickly away from matters social and economic and began musing on matters political. The manoeuvrings of political parties and the protests of activists was not something Clare had ever found easy to follow. She relied on Andrew to keep her informed and recently there'd been so little time to talk at all. When they did have the opportunity there were far more personal matters to concern them.

'Ach, I think the IRA has just about had it if the truth be told,' he said suddenly.

Clare was quite amazed at this unexpected comment. Long years ago, when she was still at school, her grandfather had let slip that Charlie was an old IRA man. It had taken her aback completely, for she could not see how even an ex-IRA man could be so good a friend to a stout Orangeman who never missed marching behind Grange band every Twelfth of July, despite his limp.

'One of these days, they'll lay down their arms and that'll be that,' Charlie went on, as he drained his teacup. 'They did their best, but circumstances change. It's economics will change the future of this place, *not* revolution,' he said firmly. 'Though mind you, that doesn't mean there won't be trouble. When people are convinced they're right, however wrong they are, there'll always be those that can manipulate them for their own purposes. But they have to find out for themselves. It's like everything else, no one can tell you you're wrong, you have to see it for yourself.'

'Is that what happened you, Charlie?' Clare asked quietly.

She had spoken before she had thought about it, which wasn't like her at all, but something had prompted her to take her chance and try to resolve this old puzzle.

'Did you know I was a member?' he asked, his large grey eyes widening. 'Your Granda told you?'

She nodded.

Charlie shook his head and looked around his small, overcrowded sitting room. 'I'll never understand that grandfather of yours,' he said abruptly. 'He was as traditional, conservative and Orange as any man I've ever met and yet, when I got into trouble, sure he took an awful chance hiding me, him and Kate, the pair of them.'

'From the police, Charlie?'

'No, not at all,' he said laughing aloud. 'The police wasn't the problem. It was the fact I'd changed my mind. When you join the IRA, you're in for life. If you want out you get out with a bullet in your back or maybe just a couple of shattered kneecaps on a day when the disciplinary squad are in a good mood,' he explained easily.

'So where did you hide?'

'D'ye remember where your granny kept her hens?'

'Yes, of course. The nearest bit of that old house across from the forge. Beside the white lilac.'

'Aye. In my young days, there was still a bit of roof away at the opposite end, the forge end. I suppose it would have been the bedroom when it was still a home. But I spent weeks in there till they thought I'd left the country. I did a powerful lot of reading and writing and Kate brought me food. And that's how she and I fell in love, if that's what you're thinking about now.'

'Yes, I knew that bit,' she admitted shyly. 'He told me she'd been his sweetheart and she did love him, but she loved you too and she said if she didn't marry you, you'd end up on the end of a rope.'

'She was right, Clare. She was right enough,' he said, nodding sadly. 'I was headstrong. I thought I could put the world to rights, but all I did was nearly get myself shot as a traitor. Me? Me, a traitor to the country I love. *Erin go Bragh*! Ireland for ever!' he shouted, as he jumped to his feet.

Clare laughed at his vehemence, remembering all those nights he had come to visit them, putting his head around the door and saluting them with the same Irish rallying cry. Her grandfather either pretended not to hear, or else he made a joke of it.

'Your grandfather was the straightest man I ever knew. There was no badness in him anywhere, but he was unsure of himself. There was something about him, or something had happened to him, maybe when he was a child, and it seemed to stop him from making up his mind about things. But if he knew where he stood, like helping me, then he'd let nothing get in his way of doing what he thought was right, even at risk to himself. I owe him my life, Clare, and I'll never forget him,' he said, as he sat down again, took out his large striped handkerchief and wiped his eyes unashamedly.

Despite the loveliness of the late afternoon, the softness of full leaf not yet darkened by summer growth, the flowers in coloured profusion leaning over garden walls and the dancing flight of swallows hawking over the water meadows, Clare was so bound up in her own thoughts that she found herself cycling up her own driveway without having registered any of it. What preoccupied her was what Charlie had said about her grandfather not being able to make up his mind. He was right, of course. Outside the forge, where he was protected by his long-learnt routines, he was so hesitant. Time and again, she had to make up his mind for him. Just like Andrew, her beloved Andrew, who tried so hard and so often had not the slightest idea what to do for the best.

For all their difference in age and background, in education and context, she'd always sensed these two men shared something in common. It was not that they were unworldly or impractical, but so often, faced with a straightforward, everyday situation, they simply couldn't decide what to do. She confessed to herself, it was a problem she had never had. Mostly because there'd never been many options. She'd always taken what seemed the most sensible course whether she liked it or not. But as Andrew had once pointed out, *there was no one to get in her way*.

Of course, she hadn't always got it right, she reflected, as she pedalled along beside the new rose bed, but that wasn't the problem. What mattered was being able to decide in the first place.

Drumsollen looked lovely in the sunshine, the sun lower now and throwing longer shadows. She freewheeled down the slope and parked the bicycle in the covered area by the steps that led down to the basement and the big kitchen, next to which was the room they now used as their bedroom. All was silent as she walked along the echoing corridor that ran the length of the house. The big kitchen was cool, clean and very empty. Except for two trays on the well-scrubbed table, carefully covered with white cloths, there was no sign of life. She saw the note penned in June's schoolbook copperplate sitting between the trays. It read:

Supper for No. 6 and No. 7 when they come in. Your Uncle Jack rang. Said to ring him back before 6 p.m. Andrew rang said he hoped to be back fiveish. Mr and Mrs Moore picked up Ginny. Said they'd see you Sunday afternoon. Sent their love. John will be back as soon as he drops me home. See you tomorrow. Best. June.

Clare glanced at her watch. Twenty-five past five. Judging by the lack of cars parked outside, it looked as if she was the only one at home. Unsurprising on such a lovely evening, when their guests would stay out as long as possible. Tom and Steve were seldom in before seven.

She smiled to herself as she ran along the corridor, hurried up the carpeted stairs and made for their sitting-room. *Headquarters*, as Ginny had christened it. She'd thought Andrew might not get away till late afternoon, but he was already on his way home which was lovely. Friday was their *evening off*. Though they seldom went anywhere, they were always pleased to have John keeping an eye on things which meant they could garden, or go for a walk, or have a proper dinner with a glass of wine in the bay window of the dining room.

She moved carefully through the narrow gap between their everyday dining-table and her large roll-topped desk, picked up the receiver and dialled Jack's number. Jack had been so good at advertising Drumsollen House, she'd told him when he rang last week that he ought to be getting a fee.

'Frootfield Prisserves, ken I help yew?'

'Oh hallo, Josie. Can I speak to Jack please?'

'Houl on a minit,' Josie replied, abandoning her telephone voice. 'He said ye'd phone.'

Clare suddenly found herself feeling anxious. Unless he had a new guest for her, Jack usually phoned at the weekend. By this time on a Friday, he should have been on his way home.

'Clare, how are you?' he asked, in his usual relaxed manner.

'I'm fine, Jack. Is something wrong?'

'Well, we've had a wee problem,' he said soothingly. 'Da had a bit of a turn last night. He was fine this morning, but the Doctor said he should stay in bed a day or two and rest. But he was asking for you, so I told him I'd give you a ring. That was fine by him. Maybe you'd take a wee run over at the weekend if you can.'

Clare found her hand shaking and beads of moisture were making the receiver slippery. She would never forget it was Uncle Jack who had come up to Belfast to look for her at Queens so he could tell her that Granda Scott was dead.

For a moment, she could think of nothing to say. As she stared helplessly at the black mouthpiece, she heard the sound of an engine and a small, familiar toot-toot. It was Andrew. With a steadiness she certainly did not feel, she said quietly; 'Thanks, Jack, we'll be over shortly.'

Andrew insisted he wasn't in the least tired. He'd be happy to drive her over if she wanted to go to Liskeyborough right now. They paused only long enough to drop his briefcase in Headquarters and lock its door behind them. They waved to John Wiley when they met him on the road but spoke little on the short journey. In the farmyard in front of the long, low house they found several other vehicles parked randomly in the wide space, but no sign of anyone about.

'I think perhaps you should go in on your own, Clare. I'm here if you want me,' Andrew said, as he switched off.

She nodded, not sure what she would find when she stepped into the big kitchen where her grandmother habitually sat by the fire complaining about her legs and commenting sharply on everything that came under her gaze. She didn't even know where her grand-father would be. For all of the years she had visited this house, his bedroom and those of whichever of her uncles were 'at home' had been out in the large, upper storey of the big barn where he had his workshop.

'Ach, hello, Clare. You're a stranger.'

Her youngest aunt, Dolly, now in her early fifties, a dressmaker by trade and a spinster by choice, rose from the fireside and looked her up and down.

'Granny's lying down. She says her heart's broke with people trippin' in and out all day. She's not had a minit's peace.'

'How is Granda?' Clare asked cautiously, knowing Dolly's view of her father would match in all respects the view held by her mother.

'There's not much wrong with him if he'd just content himself and not go poking at things in that workshop of his,' she said sharply. 'The doctor said he was to rest. He's in Jack's room to save us both running back and forth to the barn.'

Clare took a deep breath. She'd never liked Dolly, though she'd done her best over the years, especially when she'd had to share a tiny bedroom with her. Perhaps it wasn't entirely her fault that her manner was so sharp. She'd been spoilt and petted by her mother and allowed no life of her own. On the other hand, as a grown woman, she could have tried harder.

'Has he a visitor at the moment?'

'No, not one,' replied Dolly airily. 'Some of the boys were in earlier and a couple of neighbours came a while ago, but they're all over in the workshop now fiddling with something or other,' she added, with the dismissive sniff that had become habitual, as if nothing in the world was ever likely to please her.

'I'll away and see him then,' Clare said quickly before Dolly could offer any reason why she might not.

She stepped into the short passageway behind the fireplace, her feet echoing on the wooden floor. The bedroom she'd shared with Dolly on her visits from Belfast was small, but Jack's room next door was even smaller. She opened the door quietly in case her grandfather was asleep. But he was not. He was sitting up and a slow smile spread across his face as his bright blue eyes met hers.

'I thought I heerd yer voice,' he said, as she squeezed down the side of the bed nearest to the window to give him a kiss. 'How're ye doin'?'

'More to the point, how are you, Granda?' she came back at him.

He laughed and put out his hand for hers. It was large and warm, broad fingered and deeply lined. She had to admit he looked well enough, his face and almost bald head suntanned and shiny. Were it not for the two bright spots of colour on his cheeks, a bit like badly applied rouge, she might have been reassured, but there was something about him that was different from the last time she'd seen him.

'D'ye see that wee box?' he asked, glancing to the other side of the bed, where a jug of water and a glass sat on a small chest of drawers beside his well-thumbed Bible. 'Bring that roun' to me like a good girl,' he said, speaking in that soft tone she had always found so comforting and reassuring. The box, a few inches square, was made of battered white cardboard.

'This is for you,' he said, taking out a gold fob watch. 'D'ye know what this is?' he asked, handing it to her.

She pressed the raised catch and looked at the elegant numerals on the clock face. It must be his retirement present from Fruitfield. Jack had sent her the newspaper cutting from the *Portadown Times*.

'D'ye see what it says?' he asked softly.

The room was already becoming shadowy, so she turned it to the light and looked closely. '*Sam Hamilton, a good and faithful servant. With gratitude from the Lamb Brothers and all their staff,*' she read slowly, looking up at him.

'There's some says it's a lot o' nonsense, Clare, givin' a man a watch when he retires and has time to himself, but maybe they don't understand that somethin' in your hand helps somethin' in your heart,' he said slowly. 'It reminds you of all the hard work, the good times, aye, and the bad times too. An' all the friends ye had.'

She could see he was short of breath, but was quite untroubled by the fact. He simply took his time.

'If yer father had been alive, Clare dear, I'd have given him this. I tried to make no favourites with my family, but he was my namesake and truth to tell, I always knew what he was thinkin' as well as I knew m'self. He an' Ellie were a joy to me. They worked in one with the other . . . ach . . . if only there were more like them. Like you an' yer man, Andrew,' he added with a short nod.

He paused again for breath and she could see how tired he was, his bright eyes drooping now as he looked at her. 'You're like your mother, Clare, for all you're dark an' she was fair,' he said with an effort. 'Keep that by you for them an' me. Come rain, come shine, it'll mind you of the best, like it has minded me these last lock of years.'

She stayed only a little longer, stroking his hand until his eyes closed and he dozed off. Then she slipped away, escaped Dolly as quickly as she could and let Andrew drive her home, tears streaming unheeded down her face, the small box clutched firmly in her hand, as if she feared someone might try to take it from her.

Five

Unlike the twenty-first of June 1961, two years ago to the very day, when Sam Hamilton was laid to rest in the green space surrounding the Friends Meeting House in Richhill, full of cloudy skies and sudden heavy showers, the twenty-first of June 1963 promised to be fine and dry, the sun already beaming down on Drumsollen long before the smell of cooked breakfasts wafted up from the basement.

Clare walked out to the garage with Andrew, wished him well for a court hearing in Belfast and turned back purposefully into the silent house. She collected a bucket and secateurs, caught the front door back on its chain and ran down the steps to begin her favourite Friday morning task, choosing roses for the tall, cut glass vase that sat all summer through on the polished oak table in the centre of the entrance hall.

As she moved slowly round the flourishing rosebed, Andrew's parterre, she breathed the cool morning air and listened for the distant sounds vibrating in the stillness. There was a tractor on a neighbour's farm, a milk float, its crates of bottles chinking as it passed their own gates, and then the heavy throb of an Ulster Transport bus making the first journey of the day with people going to work in Armagh.

As she leaned over and felt the warmth of the sun on her back she remembered the quiet September evening she'd had to search the small bushes for enough blooms to make a wedding bouquet for herself. All the ones with long stems were already in the church, but she had managed to find the few buds she needed. She'd mixed them with sprays from the honeysuckle up by the summerhouse and tied them with ribbon. After the wedding pictures had been taken, she'd walked round the side of the church and left the little bouquet on Granda's Scott's grave, the buds now open in the sunshine.

When the time came, as she knew it would, she had made a similar bouquet for Granda Hamilton. She'd picked white roses for him, but she chose only those with a touch of pink on the outer petals. White flowers were considered very suitable for a wreath and white lilies the most suitably sombre of all, but Granda Hamilton did not approve of such demonstrations. Death was part of life, he always said. He was not troubled by its coming, nor by his own going. That was why she'd not worn black at his funeral.

She wondered why she should miss him so very much when she'd not seen him all that often over the years. But, then, she'd always known he was there, going about his work in that steady, unhurried way of his. Often these days, when she got agitated herself, upset by the problems that descended upon her like falling leaves, she would sit at her desk and stare at the face of his gold watch. Its tiny rhythmic tick comforted her and reminded her that whatever the problem was, it would pass in time, as all things passed. It was she who must learn how to keep steady through the bad times and make sure she took the good of whatever pleasure and achievement the better times might bring.

She moved carefully between the flourishing bushes and found there were plenty of blooms to choose from. Despite the harsh winter that got going immediately after Christmas, the spring and early summer had been kind to the roses. There were more in bloom this year, at this time, than she'd ever seen before, the opening buds more vibrant than usual. 'No, not yellow after all,' she said quietly, as she looked down into her bucket, 'more gold than yellow.'

As she came in through the front door and moved across the entrance hall, she thought of Ginny and smiled to herself. Ginny had covered herself with glory in the months she'd spent with them, working with a will and setting her hand to anything she saw in need of attention. She began by solving the problem of the bleak, bare spaces the missing ancestors had left on the walls when Andrew had been forced to sell them.

On her first day 'at work' she'd walked round the public rooms and proposed they move the remaining pictures out of the entrance hall, redeploying them to cover up the spaces in the dining-room and on the stairs. She then suggested that she use a colour wash on the pale bits in the entrance hall till she got a match with the remaining faded, but warm-toned wallpaper. She'd spent hours mixing paint and applying it, layer on layer, working in small patches so that the ancient, time-darkened paper didn't bubble or peel off. Having greatly improved the light level, she then tackled the handsome flock material below the gold-painted dado with stale bread.

Clare would never forget the look on June's face the first morning Ginny raided the bread bin, but June was the first to say what 'a real good job' she'd done. The total effect was splendid, so much so, that when Ginny went on to suggest having the chandelier professionally cleaned, Clare couldn't bring herself to say *No*. She felt sure they couldn't afford it, but at least they could go as far as asking for an estimate. It was as intimidating as she'd expected, but in the end she and Andrew agreed they would find the money. It would be an act of faith to make so grand a gesture, the one single, extravagant thing they'd done to set against all the hard work and careful budgeting.

When the chandelier was rehung after the cleaning, the effect was stunning. Not only did it sparkle as if it was made of cut diamonds, but freed of the grime of almost two centuries the glittering pieces of glass now rotated in the currents of air from the open door, making tiny, delightful tinkles. Every newly-arrived guest caught the sound, looked around them for its source and smiled with delight when they found it glittering above their heads.

The telephone was ringing as Clare strode across the hall towards the small room, once the estate office, where all the cleaning and gardening equipment was kept. She almost laughed aloud as the telephone stopped abruptly. What a relief it was not to have to stop whatever she was doing and dash for the receiver lest she missed a precious booking. Probably Helen had answered it. June hated the phone, but Helen, who was helping out for the summer while waiting for her exam results, had no such problem. Now there were phones down in the basement and on the landings of both the upper floors, as well as in Headquarters, it made life easier for everyone.

She wondered if the early caller might be Harry, ringing before he opened the gallery, following up on things they had spoken about last evening. Then, as she thought about his most recent visit, she realized her real concern was Jessie. Harry had taken to visiting them regularly, on his way back from buying trips. He was always so welcome, so full of good stories about the extraordinary things that turned up at auctions and house clearances, but although their meetings were always easy and lively, she'd grown increasingly anxious because he had so little to say about Jessie. *Fine, just fine,* was all she ever got now in answer to her questions about her and the children.

Last night, she'd asked him if he wanted to phone Jessie to tell her where he was and when he'd be home but he'd only laughed and said that she wasn't expecting him till she saw him.

Remembering how distressed Harry was when Jessie had been seriously depressed before the birth of their son, Clare made a point of telling him how sorry she was she couldn't get up to Belfast to see her at this high point in the holiday season. To her great surprise, he had nodded abruptly and said he'd thought about that. He'd offered to buy Jessie a small car for her birthday, but she'd refused, saying she'd no need of a car, *for sure didn't the bus run past their door.*

Shortly after, he'd got up to go and they'd walked out with him into the warm, golden dusk. They stood on the steps and waved till he was out of sight. To her surprise, it was Andrew who spoke first.

'D'you think Jessie's all right?'

'No, I don't, but I can't see what to do. I *do* phone her, but either she isn't at home or she doesn't answer,' she said sadly. 'When I do get her, she tells me nothing, makes some excuse about something she has to do, or says: *Sure you know I don't like the phone anyway.*'

'Perhaps I should just call when I'm next in court and see if I can get any idea,' he suggested, as he put an arm round her. 'If she wasn't expecting me, I might find out more. If she knows you're coming, she'll be all prepared, won't she?'

The morning was busy. Four couples and a commercial traveller came to pay their bills. The couples all said how much they had enjoyed their stay and three of them assured her they would be coming again. Two of the husbands said the local literature and notes on places of interest they'd found left out for them had been most useful. One of the wives commented on the tea tray with fresh scones brought to their room when they arrived, another asked for details of the formidable gentleman in ermine trimmed robes hanging on the bend on the staircase. As for the young man, he simply said: 'See you again soon.'

She enjoyed talking to guests, but she was glad enough when they went and she could get back to the week's accounts. She had just got started when a good-looking young man with dark hair and eyes and a pair of brown overalls tapped at her half-open door and handed her a crumpled invoice from the Fuel Oil Depot in Armagh. His colleague, he said, had just pumped their delivery into their tanks round the back. They were pretty low, like she'd said on the phone, but that was a good thing for she'd get the summer reduction on every gallon over the first hundred.

The postman arrived next, needing a signature on a book Louise Pirelli had sent her from Paris. She sorted the rest of the post quickly, set aside the brown envelopes, almost certainly bills, looked at the postmarks on the white ones with handwritten addresses, which might be friends, or family, or even a returning guest. One envelope was neither white nor brown. It was gold and she guessed immediately what it was. She was just about to open it when there was another tap at the half-open door.

'Helen, come in. Did you give the two Matts a lemonade?'

'We did indeed,' Helen replied, parking herself comfortably against the door frame. 'Aren't they a right pair? One old, one young, one fat and bald, the other dark and good-looking. And *both* of them Matthew.'

'And one Catholic and one Protestant. Did you know that?'

'Yes, Ma told me. She said she wished there were more like them. But maybe things would be better now Brookeborough's gone.'

'Yes, that's what Andrew says too. Any change has to be good news. I take it *you* haven't had any news yet?'

'No, I'd have come and told you *first thing*. The suspense continues. Ma sent me up to ask if you want me to go to the Ulster Bank.'

'Oh goodness, I forgot,' Clare gasped, catching a hand to her mouth. 'And there *is* a lot of cash this week. But I haven't made up the lodgement yet. If everyone that's going has gone, I might get time to do it now,' she said laughing, as she reached down into the deepest drawer of her desk for the cash box.

'Will I bring your coffee up here then?' asked Helen helpfully.

'Good idea. But give me ten minutes' start to get the lodgement sorted. Will you go on the bike or will you take your Da's car?'

'I'll use the bike, if it's all right with you. Car *looks* quicker, but it's sometimes hard to get parked anywhere handy on a Friday morning.'

'Bike's fine by me. I was only going to remind you that if you use the family car you're to make a note in the Petty Cash book for mileage. Only fair. Your petrol costs money.'

'Fresh scone and butter?' Helen asked, raising her eyebrows.

'Yes, please. Breakfast feels as if it was a week ago,' she replied, as she drew a lodgement slip from one of the pigeon holes in her desk and turned the cash box upside down in front of her.

As Clare stood on the steps saying a few friendly words to the delivery man who had brought a case of wine from Robert Lafarge and had carried it cheerfully all the way down to the basement, she saw Helen come round the side of the house and cycle off down the drive.

She smiled as Helen disappeared from view, remembering the outcome of just such a similar journey to the Ulster Bank made by Ginny while she was staying with them. She hurried back into Headquarters, took up the gold envelope, opened it carefully, took out the oblong of stiff card and beamed.

Mr and Mrs Moore of Sea View, Rostrevor
request the pleasure of the company of Mr and Mrs Andrew Richardson
at the marriage of their daughter, Virginia, to David Midhurst.

The story of how Ginny met her husband-to-be was one of her happiest memories of the time Ginny had worked with them at Drumsollen. It was the first Friday morning in 1961 when there was enough money in the cash box to merit a journey to the bank. On her return, Ginny had burst into Headquarters, radiant with excitement.

'Clare, Clare, you'll never guess what's happened,' she gasped, pushing wide the half-open door so fiercely that some small receipts on the desk fluttered to the floor in the breeze she'd created. 'I'm going riding this afternoon . . . if you can spare me, that is,' she added hastily.

'But of course I can spare you, after all the work you've been doing,' Clare expostulated. 'That's wonderful. How did this happen?'

'Well, I was turning out of the gate and I heard hooves,' Ginny began quickly. 'I didn't believe it at first. Then I looked over my shoulder and there was this lovely chestnut, just like Conker, my beloved Conker. You remember Conker, don't you?' she demanded, as if she had totally forgotten that it was on Conker she had taught Clare to ride. 'I thought I was hallucinating. But I wasn't. I rode on very slowly wondering what on earth I was going to do. I knew I just had to do *something* before the Mill Row and the Asylum Hill,' she went on, collapsing breathless into one of the fireside chairs.

Clare abandoned her desk and came and sat down opposite her.

'Well, finally, just before the end of the trees, I just stopped and put my bicycle against the hedge bank and waited,' she went on. 'And then as they came up to me I said quite politely: *Do you think I could possibly say good morning to your horse.*'

'So there was *a rider* on the horse?'

'Well, yes, of course there was, silly. She was being road trained. But he didn't seem to mind stopping too much and I stood and talked to her and stroked her nose. Oh Clare, she is lovely, just lovely, and she seemed perfectly happy with me. He actually said: *She seems to like you*, so I thought I'd better explain that I'd had a chestnut very like her and at times I felt heartbroken at having had to part with her and he said he was sure it must have been difficult but why did I have to do that.'

'And you told him?'

'Well, yes, I did, sort of. And then I asked him if he was a Cope or a Cowdy and he laughed and said, *How did I know that?* and I said they were the only horsey people around these parts except for some farmers who kept horses for competing in ploughing matches. He said, *Yes, my mother is a cousin of one of the Cowdys.* I've forgotten which one. He's over from England.'

'And did this gentleman give you a name?'

'Oh yes, he did,' she said beaming happily. 'She's Princess Tara of Ardrea by Prince Connor out of Lady Grannia, but his cousin calls her Blaze. She has the loveliest little white bit on her nose. He said his cousin thought it looked like that mark on Superman's vest.'

In the remaining two weeks of his visit to Loughgall, Ginny *did* manage to register David Midhurst's name. In fact, as she transferred her attention from Princess Tara to her rider, she rather made up for her initial indifference by deciding she was in love with him.

'Yes, Clare, I admit it, you're right,' she agreed, as the final days of his stay slipped away. 'He's the man for me, but I'm not going to marry him. At least not yet,' she added, hesitating. 'I made such a nonsense last time.'

'Has he asked you to marry him?' Clare asked, somewhat surprised at the speed with which events had moved.

'Oh yes, he asked me last week and I said no. So he said that was fine, he'd ask me every week on Fridays until I said yes.'

Clare propped the wedding invitation on her desk and turned gratefully to the tray Helen had brought. She poured her coffee and munched her scone enthusiastically.

Some months after David went back to the Cotswold village where he was setting up a riding school, specializing in cross country trekking, Ginny admitted sheepishly she was pining for him even more than for Princess Tara. Would they mind if she went off to join him? She'd asked Ginny then when she had actually said *yes* to David, but Ginny couldn't remember. She was already absorbed in the details of cross-country trekking and the prospect of a whole new life in England.

After the excitements and activity of the morning, the afternoon hours remained quiet and uninterrupted. Apart from Andrew ringing to tell her he'd be back by six, the phone was blissfully silent. At lunchtime she asked Helen to deal with any guests who might turn up in the course of the afternoon. It wasn't very likely anyone would appear until much later on such a splendid day, but having alerted Helen meant she could shut her door and make a start on the end-of-year figures.

The thirtieth of June still felt the most unlikely of times to have a financial *end of year*, but the reason was simple. July the first, 1960, was the day she and Andrew had set up Drumsollen House as a limited company. Even though she was still in Paris, by doing so, Andrew could get his hands on the money he so badly needed for the most urgent repairs. Now, there were only nine days till the end of the month and the end of their third year of trading. Today's crop of bills had been deducted in her ledger, the cheques already in their envelopes for the post. There was a predictable amount coming in from next week's bookings, but even if the amount she'd pencilled in proved to be an overestimate, a few pounds either way wasn't going to make any difference to what she had in mind.

The afternoon grew steadily hotter as she entered up the monthly figures and collated them with the Ulster Bank lodgement book. As she worked away steadily, she thought of the last time she'd met their accountant. He'd told her his senior clerks were experimenting with automated calculating machines. The sooner the better, Clare thought, as she totted up a huge column of figures. She looked at the result, then did the sum all over again, because the figure was so encouraging she had to be sure she'd not made a mistake.

She paused, got up and stuck her head out of the window. The sun had moved round, so the side of the house was now in shadow, but there was no coolness anywhere. Her face prickled with heat and she could feel her thin, cotton print blouse sticking between her shoulder blades.

She took a deep breath and went through the figures yet once more, sure there must be something she had missed, even though she knew her records were right up to date. She checked the Pass books again. It all tallied exactly. All the loan repayments had been made for the year and there was no bill for repair or maintenance work outstanding. Then she found what she was looking for. It was now some five months since they'd made the last transfer of funds from Andrew's salary into the Drumsollen Trading Account to prevent it going into overdraft. The present healthy balance was all their own work.

'Hello love, how's things?' Andrew asked, as he took his briefcase from the passenger seat.

'Not bad,' she said cheerfully. 'Wedding invitation from Ginny and wine from Robert. John's arrived and says he has jobs to do at the front, so I though we'd be posh and have dinner upstairs as its Friday night.'

'Great, I'm starving. Had to use the lunch hour to consult. Someone went out for sandwiches. Cheese with some sort of salad cream,' he said, making a face, as they walked side by side along the corridor to their bedroom. 'They were horrible.'

'Never mind, we've got something nice for dinner. *And* dessert.'

She picked up his black jacket and pinstriped trousers as he dropped them on the bed, shook them and hung them up to air beside the open window.

'You won't mind if I don't dress for dinner,' he said, teasing her with his best English accent, as he pulled on some flannels and an open-necked shirt.

'Well . . .'

'I've missed you,' he said, putting his arms round her. 'A wretched day, I'm sorry to say. One more victory for the status quo. I want to forget it all as quickly as possible. Can I carry something?' he added vigorously, as if only immediate action would erase the memory of the shabby show he'd been forced to witness in court.

'Yes, it's all in the bottom of the Aga. Except the dessert,' she added, laughing, as they pushed open the kitchen door. 'That's upstairs already.'

She loaded up the tray for him to carry and wrapped two warm dinner plates in a tea cloth, leaving her a hand free to open the door of Headquarters.

'I say, what are we celebrating?' Andrew asked, as he caught sight of the small table under the window. After years of squeezing round the large and very solid piece of furniture thought appropriate when Headquarters had been the morning-room at Drumsollen, Harry had found them a customer who had offered them a remarkably good price. The new table they'd chosen together stood below the window and was laid this evening with a white damask cloth. On it were laid two place settings, a slim vase of golden roses, two silver candlesticks and a bottle of red wine in an ornate silver wine cooler.

'Food first,' she said, as he put the tray down on the sideboard and she took the lid off the casserole.

'Anything you say, ma'am. But I can almost smell good news,' he confessed, as he carried the vegetable dish to the table and poured two glasses of wine.

They were both hungry and ate devotedly, finishing off every scrap of the tasty casserole and all the vegetables as well. As they sat sipping their second glass of wine with the remaining fragments of crusty roll, Andrew suddenly spoke.

'It's *not* your birthday, nor is it *our* anniversary. I'm sure of that.' He paused and asked sheepishly, 'Is this the day we met?'

Clare laughed and looked at him more closely.

'Oh, Andrew dear, don't be anxious,' she said gently. 'I wasn't setting you a test. Anybody can forget anything if they've been as busy as we've been. It *might* be the anniversary of the day we met, but I certainly can't remember. Have *you* any idea when that was?'

Andrew claimed never to remember personal things, but to her amazement, he proceeded to give her a vivid picture of the day when he found her bicycle, parked against the low wall beside the gates of Drumsollen, the tyres having been let down.

'Dear Jessie. She really thought I'd let them down and she was very, very cross. But you said you didn't think I had,' he continued thoughtfully, his blue eyes sparkling as he put his glass down. He paused and looked at her. 'What made you say that?' he asked abruptly.

'I'm not sure now,' she began hesitantly. 'I'm amazed you can remember. I think I just looked and saw what you were like. Your basic honesty, perhaps. Robert used to ask me about clients he wasn't sure about. He always said I could see if there was any badness in people.'

'Like Charles Langley?'

'Oh yes, dear Charles, your one-time slave at school. I couldn't believe it when he told me about fagging for you,' she said, laughing. 'I wish we'd been able to go to his wedding,' she added, a little wistfully. 'But you're quite right. Charles *is* a good example. Like you, my love, he was doing a job he *had* to do. The old obligation of a family business descending to the next in line. He certainly did the job to the best of his ability, but he never *looked* quite right doing it.'

'Was that why you had to explain to Robert about Englishmen and duty?'

'Stiff upper lip and all that sort of thing,' she agreed. 'Robert was very shrewd about people. He'd read about the English Public School style and manners, but he'd never seen it in action, so he couldn't judge for himself if Charles was completely honest or not.'

'Was he?'

'*Of course* he was. As honest as you are. But *he* couldn't get excited about buying and selling fruit and needing money to expand the import business.'

'Any more than I can go along with some of what passes for normal legal practice in this province,' he said sharply. 'And now he and Lindy have a flying school in the South Downs.'

'And are coming over to stay sometime during the winter when they can't fly,' she reminded him.

He smiled wryly and Clare guessed what he was thinking. Charles and Lindy had already managed to do what they so much wanted to do. When Charles's father had died suddenly, he was free to sell up. Weekend flying had become a major leisure pursuit in the south-east and both he and Lindy were passionate about flying. Now they had more customers than they could cope with and the project was a great success.

She stood up and cleared away the empty plates and dishes and carried a domed silver dish ceremoniously to the table. Once part of the equipment for serving a cooked breakfast to be laid out on the long sideboard in the dining room, it had been redeployed for covering whatever might be a temptation to the summer flies. She removed the cover with a flourish.

'Shall I carve, or will you?' she asked soberly.

Andrew peered at the soft icing decorating one of June's Victoria sponges and looked at her quizzically. 'Did you put this icing on?'

'I added the little sugar flowers, but June did the house and the fields. She said a cow was a bit much at short notice.'

'So it *is* an anniversary, or nearly. Are you telling me we can think about buying a cow and a field?'

'Yes, I am,' she said, as she picked up the cake knife and handed it to him. 'Perhaps even two of each if we can do as well next year as we have this year. We can certainly open a new account. What shall we call it? Cows or fields? Or Drumsollen estate?'

Six

Drumsollen House,
24, June 1963

My dear Robert,

I have some wonderful news. We have done it. We have broken even. Just. Only just, but as our good friend Emile used to say, 'That my friends is a great achievement. Without that first step nothing else can happen.'

I still can hardly believe it! If you had seen me checking and rechecking the additions and not believing what they were saying you would have laughed. Had those been the figures presented by one of your clients I would have been satisfied right away.

Clare paused, shook her fountain pen impatiently, then reached for the bottle of ink. Perhaps, if she wanted to write as fast as this, she should use the typewriter, but Robert always wrote to her by hand. She was sure he felt it was more personal. Besides, there was the question of punctuation. As she was unlikely to find a typewriter with a French keyboard in one of the second-hand shops in Belfast, she'd still have to add acute and grave accents afterwards.

She wiped the excess ink from her nib with blotting paper. Immediately, she had a vivid image of the meticulous way Robert performed the same task, a small, robust figure hunched over his enormous desk, looking even smaller when set against its wide expanses of rosewood and polished leather and the tall windows overlooking the Place de l'Opéra reaching upwards behind him.

Five years ago, she stood in front of his desk for the first time and five years ago, this very month, she had made the journey to Paris, lonely and dispirited after breaking off her engagement. She had no idea where she could find a job or somewhere to live. All she had was a single suitcase and the Paris address of Marie-Claude, whose children she had cared for at Deauville for three summers in her student years. Marie-Claude had comforted her, dressed her like a Frenchwoman, and Gerard, her financier husband, had found the job with Robert and encouraged her to apply for it.

She put down her pen again and paused, overwhelmed by the memory of the vulnerable girl she had been, suddenly bereft of the love that had sustained her since the death of her grandfather. With no home to go back to in Ireland and no job awaiting her in France, she arrived in the lovely apartment in the Bois de Boulogne not knowing she was about to get a First, that Marie-Claude and Gerard would support and care for her and that Robert would take her on as his interpreter and personal assistant at a salary far in excess of anything she could ever have earned in Belfast.

Travelling with him and translating what he had to say to the businessmen who came to him for loans taught her about banking, about money, about risk and the problems of running a business.

Now it was these very skills she deployed day and daily to make Drumsollen a viable proposition, its hoped-for success the basis for all their future hopes and plans.

Running a guest house in Ireland might seem far removed from the problems Charles Langley had faced importing fruit from France and Italy, even more so from those of the good-natured Texan entrepreneur who had decided to add some vineyards to his European investments, but she had grasped very quickly that business had its own logic, its own repeating patterns, and a whole set of variables to be considered and balanced against each other. Sometimes she thought the problems were like a difficult jigsaw. You searched for missing pieces and kept finding nothing would fit. At other times the difficulties she regularly translated for Robert's benefit seemed to her more like a route march, a long, hard struggle over rough ground, littered with unforeseen obstacles to a distant goal which was just as likely to recede before you as be reached by your efforts.

She had enjoyed her work, the strangely varied people they met and the travelling together. Sometimes, listening to clients arguing their case, Robert or Emile asking for clarifications, she felt that the whole business of assessing the viability of a project was little better than guesswork. Sometimes she felt quite defeated by the sheer variety and complexity of the factors to be taken into account, like shifts in fashion, unexpected competition, the opening up of alternative markets, a sudden rise or fall in the exchange rate.

Once, in a light-hearted mood, she'd suggested to Robert that they might do just as well assessing the viability of their clients' projects by gazing into a crystal ball. To her delight, Robert had laughed, a rare thing with him. Not many men in banking achieved the equivalent of the large desk set against those tall windows. There was no question as to how successful he was and how seldom one of the projects he financed had failed. She often wondered if it was his habitual sober consideration that had all but removed his capacity for humour.

It was a rule they had when they dined together on their travels that they never spoke about the work of the day, but on that occasion Robert had taken up her light remark and reflected upon it.

'You see, my dear Clare, it is about possibilities,' he said, refilling her glass. 'You could take two situations that seem at first sight to be identical in practical terms, but then you look at the people involved. Perhaps it is a little like chemistry, of which I have no personal knowledge at all, except what I have read,' he said, with a small wry smile, 'but you will understand about catalysts, elements which enable other things to happen. People are like that. Simply by being who they are, they can cause things to happen that would not have happened without them. That is the secret of many successes.'

'And do you think, Robert, that personal qualities can outweigh brute fact?'

'But of course,' he said, nodding. 'A fact and a brute fact are two different things. It is the clear perception of a hard and unpleasant fact that mitigates its power to overwhelm.'

'So you're saying that facing facts, however unpleasant, gives you power over them.'

'Yes, I am. It's one of the many things I learnt from Emile. He is not a religious man any more than I am, but his father *was* deeply religious and Emile had the great wisdom to test in experience all that he learnt from him. One thing he used to say to me often was: *Robert, in any situation there is always something we can do. But we have to believe that is true, otherwise we won't even look.'*

'And if we don't look, there's no possibility of finding,' she'd added, remembering how often round the negotiating table Emile had seen ways of proceeding no one else had even thought of.

'That is why your crystal ball has its limitations,' Robert continued. 'It can show you a future, good or bad, but it cannot show you the resources of the people who will make that future, or indeed remake that future should circumstances move against them.'

Clare was still sitting at her desk, pen in hand, lost in her own thoughts, her letter barely begun, when Helen tapped at the open door and told her that some guests had arrived and would like to see her.

'Oh yes, fine,' she said hastily, her mind and her memory still lingering on a flower-lined terrace in Northern France. 'Is there a problem?' she went on more steadily as she gathered her thoughts. Helen was normally able to deal with new arrivals quite unaided.

'No, no problem at all,' she replied, laughing, 'except that their name is Hamilton and they've just come from Annacramp.'

When Mary and John Hamilton chose the dining room for their welcome tray, Clare asked Helen to bring an extra cup and led the way, a sense of excitement bubbling up as she responded to their easy manner and friendly comments.

'Now Hamilton *has* to be good news,' she said, as they shook hands and exchanged Christian names, 'but Annacramp is somewhat special. I sense a story to tell.'

'Yes, you're quite right,' John Hamilton replied, grinning broadly as he draped his jacket over the back of his chair. 'The single word *Annacramp* brought my father back from Canada. One word, held in a child's memory. That and his name pinned to his jacket on a luggage label was all he had of his life on this side of the Atlantic.'

'My goodness, this *is* wonderful. You must be Uncle Alex's son,' Clare said, beaming at the smiling faces of her guests. 'Granda Hamilton told me how your father came back and went looking for his family. And he *did* find them,' she went on happily. 'Or rather, he thought he had found his uncle, and that pleased everyone, but then, later on, in Manchester, he found out how he'd come to be sent to Canada in the first place. He also found out that the John Hamilton he'd thought was his uncle was actually his cousin. Their fathers were brothers, Tom and Lofty, and they both lived at Annacramp.'

'Poor Mary,' said John taking his wife's hand. 'She's had to put up with the tangle of Hamilton family history for years now. She's so good about it, and it's quite unfair as she's as orphan herself and the Hamilton tribe has more branches than an apple tree.'

Clare looked at the warm smile on the kindly face of the dark-haired woman opposite her and thought what a happy couple they were, for Mary was taking such delight in John's pleasure.

'I'm an orphan too, Mary,' Clare said quietly, 'and so is Andrew, my husband. Like John, I'm fascinated by family history, but Andrew couldn't care less. He seems to me to be doing his best to forget his family entirely,' she went on, laughing at her own frustration. 'The awful thing is that *his* family were all excessively literate and were once wealthy, so there's masses of information about them, letters and genealogy, leases and deeds and all the rest of it. I'd give so much to have even a fraction of what he could have, but my lot were mostly ordinary working people. Apart from Granda Hamilton's stories, I don't know much about them at all. My mother's father, Granda Scott, was a dear man but he was very quiet and self-contained and hardly ever told stories and never about family. If it weren't for a friend of his, Charlie Running, I'd have nothing at all on that side.'

'Did you know your parents, Clare?' asked Mary, as Helen arrived at the table and began spreading round plates of scones and cake.

Clare laughed as she glanced at the laden tray and introduced Helen to Mary and John. 'I see you've already worked out that these Hamiltons really *are* family.'

'Oh yes, when they told me a "Mister Charlie Running" had sent them, I knew they qualified for cake,' she replied cheerfully.

'Yes, I *did* know my parents, Mary,' Clare went on, as she poured for them all. 'They both died in 1946 in a typhoid epidemic in Armagh. I was just nine, but I do remember them well. Sometimes I can almost see my father walking about, or wheeling his bicycle, but it's my mother I can still hear *saying* things. She was very loving and gentle, but sensible with it and as they say in Ulster, she had *hands for anything*. Very practical. What about you, do you remember your parents?'

'My mother died when I was born,' said Mary steadily. 'My father left me with my grandmother and went away. Even Granny didn't know where he went. But he never came back. She died when I was seven and that meant Dr Barnardo's for me.'

'But at least by the 1930s they'd stopped sending children abroad,' interrupted John hastily. 'And they *were* good to you, weren't they?' he insisted, turning towards her, his face shadowed with anxiety.

'Yes, they were,' she said promptly. 'And I still went to the same school just outside Norwich. Some of the teachers there were very kind. I still have friends from those days,' she went on, smiling, 'but I always felt lonely. Till I met John that was,' she said, looking Clare straight in the face.

Clare nodded, suddenly unable to speak, as tears jumped unbidden to her eyes. Mary's look, one of complete and trusting honesty, was totally endearing. Clare would never forget it, nor the moment that followed when she asked herself if it was always like this for children who had lost their parents, or was it just coincidence that both she and Mary had felt such loneliness until they had found someone they could love, someone who would return their love and make a life with them.

'I know Uncle Alex and Aunt Emily live outside Banbridge, but where do you live?' she asked. 'I can tell Mary isn't from Ulster. Are you living in Norfolk?'

'Yes, spot on, Clare,' replied John. 'I ended up on an air base there at the end of the war and we met at a camp dance. Married in 1947. We have two boys, fifteen and thirteen.'

'And you've left them behind?'

'Oh yes,' replied John vigorously. 'We've always wanted to come and visit Annacramp, but we couldn't while the boys were small. By the time we could afford it, we'd decided we'd like to come on our own. First time, at any rate. We only have a week, so the boys are staying with our next door neighbours. We'll return the favour when we get back.'

'But what about Aunt Emily and Uncle Alex?' Clare asked abruptly, suddenly aware she had no idea what had happened to them. They hadn't been at Granda Hamilton's funeral two years ago and she couldn't even remember him having spoken of them on her few visits to Liskeyborough from Belfast and then France. Surely they hadn't died and she hadn't even known.

'Dad retired in 1955 because his health wasn't too good. Chest problems. He'd been having a bad time every winter and Ma was really worried about him. Doctor suggested moving to Spain or Italy if they could afford it, but neither of them felt happy about that. It was my sister Jane who solved the problem. She married a German prisoner of war. Lovely man called Johann. They'd tried to set up a small business outside Banbridge and found there was such ill-feeling towards Germans that it would never thrive, even though Johann had actually flown to Ireland to *escape* the Nazis, but no one seemed willing to believe it. So Jane suggested they all go to Australia.'

'They came and stayed with us before they went,' said Mary, breaking in, 'so I did finally meet them. And Australia has been a great success. For all of them. Johann started a nursery and garden centre, which is pure delight to Emily. She and Jane work with him. There are two little girls now, both at school. They take it in turns to keep an eye on them. It's a small town in an area called the Hunter Valley and it does sound quite lovely,' she went on. 'Alex is working on what he calls "An Orphan Project". Having found out the story of his own past, he's been studying the records of children sent to Australia, *as well as*, those sent to Canada and the United States. He says we "don't know the half of it", but one of these days he'll have enough information for a book. Emily encourages him and tells us about some of his discoveries. And about the country too. We've learnt such a lot from her. She's a great letter writer and she says that out there no one appears to know or care where you've come from. Australia is all about here and now. She wishes it were like that back in County Down.'

'And doesn't she miss County Down and her garden and the rain and all her friends?' asked Clare anxiously, thinking how awful it would be living half a world away, weeks of travel by sea to get home or costing a fortune should you think of coming by air.

Clare noticed how Mary and John looked at each other when she spoke of '*missing County Down*' as if this was something they often talked about. She wondered, too, how John felt about making a new life in Norfolk. Not as far away as Australia, but still a journey to make and an expense they hadn't been able to afford until now.

'Yes, she does,' Mary said quietly. 'Even John here admits he misses Ballydown and Corbet Lough and the view of the Mournes from the back garden of Rathdrum, the house where he lived as a boy, even though he knows he *can* come back. Not every year and probably not to live, not yet anyway, but at least to make sure the places he loves are still here,' she said, glancing sideways at him. 'Emily and Alex can never come back, at least not together,' she added sadly, 'but Emily says it is different when you're old. If you've lived and loved in a place, then it is part of you and you have it forever, so long as you choose to cherish it. She says Australia has been kind to them. It's given Alex back his health and a new project. It's given Jane and Johann a fresh start. They all have work and there's a future for the two girls and a different kind of beauty surrounding them.'

'So you haven't been back here since the war, John, and this must be your first visit, Mary?'

Mary nodded and smiled back at Clare but it was John who took up the story.

'I've been back once. I wasn't demobbed till the end of 1945 so I waited till the summer of 1946, the summer you lost your parents, Clare. Mary and I were engaged and I hoped by waiting she could come with me, but she was nursing and I'm afraid military hospitals were very overworked at that point. I stayed with my parents at Rathdrum but I did actually come to Armagh. Jane borrowed Da's car and insisted on showing me the tree on The Mall where she and Johann got engaged while he was on a working party. Then we visited both cathedrals. If Da had been able to get away, we might have managed Annacramp then, but he couldn't, so Jane and

I went to see the Hamiltons at Liskeyborough on our way back to Ballydown . . .'

Clare listened carefully as John talked about the visit to her grandparents, his meeting with her grandmother, Martha, and Aunt Dolly and the time he'd spent with Granda Hamilton out in his workshop, sitting on the same two empty oil drums where he and his father had once discussed what they would do if war came in 1914. Uncle Jack was away working in Belfast, but her grandfather had told John where each member of the large family was, what they were doing and how they had fared. He'd mentioned her parents, of course, said they had a girl and a boy and were doing well.

How strange to see such an important part of her life through the eyes of someone older and more experienced, someone coming from outside the known places. She found it hard to believe how much she simply didn't know about all these people who would have been so important a part of her parents' world.

Andrew was home later than usual that bright, sunny evening. Tired and dispirited from a day in court when one more of his clients had suffered a raw deal, he parked the car at the back of the house, tramped along the basement corridor, found the kitchen empty, dropped his briefcase in their bedroom, then headed upstairs to find Clare. Surprised to hear laughter from the dining-room, he stopped at the top of the stairs just at the moment she appeared, a smile on her face, her eyes shining.

'Andrew, we heard the car and were waiting for you. We have guests. Real guests. Come and meet them,' she said, giving him a kiss and leading him into the dining-room.

'Andrew, this is Mary and John Hamilton from Norfolk. John is Uncle Alex's son. You remember Uncle Alex, don't you?' she added, a hint of anxiety in her voice.

'Of course, I remember him,' he said evenly. 'Small boy in big ship. Exported to provide labour for colonial development. But he got away, came home and proved to be a true Hamilton,' he said, managing a smile as he shook hands with Mary and then John.

Clare relaxed as she saw the two men size each other up. There was instantly an ease between them more commonly seen when men talked about cars or golf. Mary was watching them too, as Andrew sat down wearily and looked hopefully at the teapot.

'Andrew, the tea's stone cold,' Clare said firmly. 'But June has put a casserole in the Aga for us. If you and John would take the cases up to Number Two, Mary and I could clear away tea and lay dinner. It's *our* night off, remember,' she said encouragingly. 'John Wiley isn't here yet, but I'm sure he won't be long.'

'Would you like me to fetch some sherry from Headquarters?' Andrew asked, beginning to look more cheerful.

'Yes, please. But *please* do the cases first. Mary and John have had a long day. We've been talking our heads off ever since they arrived and suddenly they're going to want to go to bed.'

'What time *did* you get here?' Andrew asked.

To his surprise everyone burst out laughing.

'What's the joke?' he asked.

'It *was* early afternoon,' Mary replied, smiling. 'But we got into family history, and there seems to be an awful lot of it on the Hamilton side. Don't be anxious. When we heard the car, we promised Clare not to say another word about it for the rest of the evening.'

That evening was one of the happiest Clare and Andrew had spent for a very long time. It was like some of the good times they'd had with Harry and Jessie, helping to do up the house on the Malone Road when they'd just got married and Jessie, who swore she was only learning to cook, produced wonderful meals to share at the end of their long working days.

Over their meal, they shared talk about their respective jobs. Mary worked part-time in the orthopaedic department of the Norfolk and Norwich Hospital, while John ran an electrical business in Holt, the small town in North Norfolk where they now lived. Andrew said very little about being a solicitor in Armagh, but spoke enthusiastic-ally about their plans for buying land and rearing pedigree cattle when they could afford for him to stop working as a solicitor and have some managerial help with running Drumsollen.

'Can't always do what you want, can you?' said John sympathetic-ally. 'When the airbase closed, I had nothing to turn to. I'd left school and joined up the moment I was eighteen. I could have applied for a grant to go to university, but I'd already met Mary. Oh, she did offer to support me, and she would have, but I'm afraid I was too stubborn. One of the electricians on the base was going into business and offered me a job. I'd no electrical skills whatsoever.

Flying Spitfires and Mosquitos doesn't qualify you for much else,' he commented wryly. 'Happily, it worked out well. I picked things up very quickly and night-school helped. But actually, it's boats I love. If I had lots of money I'd take up sailing, perhaps do half-crown trips to take visitors out to Blakeney Point to see the seals, or something like that,' he ended laughing.

'And have you any experience of sailing, John?' Clare asked.

'Only in a Mosquito,' said Mary soberly.

There was a moment's puzzled silence and then both John and Mary began to laugh heartily.

'I ditched in the Mediterranean when we were delivering planes from North Africa to Italy. Mechanical fault. But it could have been the end of me. Parents got the usual *Missing* telegram. Poor dears, it was hard on them. Aunt Sarah got her Foreign Office husband to pester someone in the Air Ministry he'd been at school with, but even then there wasn't much they could do. My chum had seen me go down, but that was the last I was heard of.'

'So what happened?' asked Clare, horrified at the thought of poor Aunt Emily and Uncle Alex thinking he was dead.

John grinned ruefully.

'Well, I kept afloat and nothing ran me down or spotted me for quite a while. I could have been picked up by a ship or even an enemy sub. Being run down was much more likely. Not much protection on a plane made of light metal and balsa wood and designed for speed.

'So what did happen, John?' Andrew said quickly.

'I was picked up by a fishing boat, a Greek caique manned by very loud, noisy, bearded Greeks. At least, that's what I thought at the time,' he said, smiling. 'It's actually rather funny looking back now, but that's what made it all so difficult. You see they weren't Greek at all, they were British and it was a special ops job. They couldn't risk giving the game away in case I was a German spy deliberately planted in a ditched Mosquito. They made me take off all my wet clothes and I wondered then why they wouldn't give them back. They had to stick to their plans, so they couldn't put me ashore till their job was done. They also had to make sure I didn't hear them speaking English or using their radio.'

'But how on earth did they manage that on a small boat?' demanded Clare.

'There *was* a cabin. Someone used the radio in there, while the rest made a noise. Sometimes they sang. Occasionally they did PT exercises, or hammered pieces of the rigging, and they shouted at each other all the time. I knew there was something funny about them but I couldn't figure it out. The boss-man spoke "a leetle Englessh" with a thick American accent, said he had "sister in New York". I think he decided I was genuine, but he still couldn't put me ashore. Once I had to ask for help to get back to my unit, someone would be bound to ask how I'd got there in the first place. I found out afterwards, years afterwards actually, that they were all Oxford and Cambridge men and only one of them spoke any Greek at all and that was Classical. But they certainly did manage to fool me on that one.'

'And after all that, you still think you'd like a boat?' asked Clare.

'Yes, I would. It was a very odd experience but I loved being on the water with all that space and sky. A strange longing for a real landlubber, brought up among the little hills of County Down, don't you think? Must be a hand down from some ancient ancestor,' he said lightly.

'Maybe it is,' said Andrew promptly. 'My mother was so good with animals, especially horses, but she wasn't from a country family. I've had no real experience with animals either, but I just know working with them is what I want. It's the way I feel when I'm with them. I feel more myself in some strange way,' he added, looking slightly foolish.

'We're certainly going to try it,' said Clare, 'if we can make a success of Drumsollen. How about you?'

'Oh yes, there is a *Grand Plan*,' Mary smiled. 'We've bought two derelict cottages a little way back from the coast. Baconsthorpe, the village is called. Very small, just church, pub, general store and a few houses. We're working on them, so we can let them as holiday cottages, or perhaps sell them.'

'And buy a boat?' asked Clare.

'Spot on, Clare,' said John grinning. 'Then you and Andrew will have to come and visit us. Do either of you know Norfolk at all, or do you think it's very flat, as they say in *Private Lives*?'

'I've been a few times,' said Andrew easily. 'I had two aunts, one lived at Wiveton and one at Cley, my mother's aunts actually. The elder one, Auntie Bee, died some years ago but her younger sister,

Aunt Joan, still lives in Wiveton. She's in her seventies now and keeps asking me to come and bring Clare. I haven't been over for a while. When was it, Clare, when I painted Auntie Bee's kitchen after the floods?'

'Must have been 1954, or 1955. The floods were 1953, weren't they?' Clare said slowly.

'What's your aunt's name, Andrew?' Mary asked quietly, while Clare was still trying to remember exactly when it was. She'd been so worried about Andrew because he had to cross the Irish sea in winter when the weather was very stormy.

'Well, she had three names and I'm not sure which she uses. Her family name was Ayton, but she married a doctor called Everett, who died, and then a man called Pye who bred donkeys. They were terribly happy together, but he died too, quite suddenly, and she's been on her own for a long time now. She's rather poor but doesn't let it bother her. She has a holiday flat attached to her cottage and she grows old-fashioned plants and flowers and sells them in summer to the visitors.'

Mary and John looked at each other and shook their heads.

'You're not going to believe this, Andrew,' said John slowly. 'When the base finally closed and we had nowhere to live, my Commanding Officer said he had a friend who might be able to help, a Mrs Joan Pye at Wiveton. We lived in Joan's holiday flat for two years till Sandy was well on the way. Your Aunt Joan is our son's godmother.'

'And you're not going to believe this either, Mary,' said Clare laughing. 'This is the first time in living history I have ever heard Andrew say anything about any member of his family without it being prized out of him! Now what do you think of that?'

Seven

When Mary and John Hamilton said their goodbyes on the steps of Drumsollen on the last day of June, the sky a perfect blue, the breeze warm even at the early hour of their departure, they had secured a promise from Clare and Andrew to come and visit them in Norfolk at the first possible opportunity. It was a promise happily given. After three days in which they'd shared every hour they could spare with their 'family guests', they felt they'd made a friendship that would extend far into the future.

'My goodness, can you believe all that's happened in six months?' Clare said, turning to Andrew as the little car disappeared round the bend in the drive. 'Have you time to walk up to the summerhouse with me? I'm not on breakfast duty this morning.'

'Fine. Nothing waiting for me that won't wait a bit longer,' Andrew replied. 'Besides, it's only eight o'clock. Charles never gets in before ten.'

'I was thinking of how awful it was in January,' Clare went on, 'those frozen pipes we thought might burst and the awful chill of the empty bedrooms and corridors. Do you remember how dangerous the car park was and how we slithered and slid and worried about the few visitors we did have?'

'I seem to remember you consulting me about our proprietor's liability, which I had to go and read up. Not my department at all,' he said, looking at her sideways. 'My dear, beloved Clare,' he began, shaking his head. 'Can you please tell me why, on this glorious morning, you are thinking about the most God awful winter anyone in these parts can ever remember?'

Clare laughed and nodded.

'I'm not actually being negative, you know. I'm celebrating the way things can come good even if they've been grim. Oh, I suppose it goes the other way too, but I keep thinking of this last week. First the good news about breaking even, then Mary and John arriving and all the splendid talk we had with them. Like the sun coming out, suddenly life is brighter and easier and it's wonderful. Don't you think?'

When he didn't reply, she assumed he was just as much out of breath as she was. In their enthusiasm to gaze out over the luxuriant green countryside and scan the mountains of Tyrone and Donegal, they had climbed the steep steps far too quickly.

'Andrew?' she prompted.

'Do you really think we can make a go of it?' he asked. 'I mean, like we had planned.'

The tight tone and the tell-tale creases at the corners of his mouth, sure signs of anxiety, warned her to tread cautiously.

'Well, yes, I do. Weren't you happy with the figures when I showed them to you?'

He made a visible effort to collect himself.

'Oh yes, absolutely,' he said quickly. 'I just haven't taken it all in yet I suppose. You really think I could give up the job in another year or so?'

'Unless the situation changes markedly,' she replied. 'There are no signs of that at the moment. So we have to proceed on the assumption that it won't. If it does, that'll be the time to take stock and think again.'

'What shall we do to celebrate?' he asked, suddenly sounding more cheerful.

'Bit early in the day for champagne,' she said, keeping an absolutely straight face and hoping to make him laugh.

To her delight, he did. She breathed a sigh of relief. Whatever dark shadow had moved up towards consciousness it had vanished as quickly as it had come.

'I was taking a more long-term view,' he said, successfully mimicking their accountant, who was full of his own importance and inclined to be pompous. 'What about the other half of the parterre, or the left-hand rose bed by any other name? I'm sure it's not the right time for planting roses but they come in containers these days which must make a difference. I've seen them in the market in Armagh. Could we afford fifty? If *you* bargain for them I'm sure we could.'

'What a lovely idea, Andrew,' she replied, beaming at him. 'Like the chandelier,' she went on. 'A gesture, a palpable gesture. Let's do it. We can plant them ourselves, this time, now there are two of us.'

'And then we'll have a weekend away,' he added, glancing at his watch. 'No. I'm *not* joking. I have *a plan*. Tell you tonight,' he said, kissing her quickly and setting off briskly down the steps, a smile on his face as he disappeared round the side of the house.

Throughout the arc of the summer, days of bright sunshine and brilliant blue sky alternated with days when heavy clouds piled up on the green hills, the air grew thick and oppressive, before giving way to sudden drenching showers accompanied by the occasional rumble of thunder.

According to Charlie Running, the regulars at his favourite pub in Loughgall had been predicting a summer as extreme in its sunshine and warmth as the winter had been in its snow, ice and bitter cold. They were wrong and their disappointment was obvious.

'Shure there'll be no good stories out of a summer like this,' Charlie explained on one of Clare's regular visits. 'What ye need for these boys is the apples so thick the branches are near breaking, the hay three feet high, the dahlias the size of dinner plates and the roses like wee cabbages.'

Whatever the disappointment for Charlie's drinking companions there was none for Clare and Andrew. Whether it was rain or shine, the weeks of that summer *were* memorable, filled with a pleasure and delight they were sure they would never forget.

However long and demanding the day had been and however late it was by the time they'd completed the day's tasks, evening after evening, they walked down the front steps and round their garden in the lingering dusk. Ostensibly, they were keeping an eye on the newly-planted roses, but what they were really doing was celebrating all that had happened to so encourage them in their hopes and plans for the coming year.

'But how can we go away, Andrew, even for a weekend, never mind a week?' she protested, when he first spoke about the possibility. 'You know we're understaffed. If we're not here to fill in the gaps evenings and weekends, goods and services break down.'

'Absolutely true,' he nodded, looking pleased with himself. 'But you would agree there's nothing we do that is highly skilled, apart from you masterminding our finance. Anyone can make beds or run the washing machines or clear out the drain when it blocks. June and Helen could cook a full house of breakfasts, if ever we were to need it.'

'But they can't do all the jobs we do as well as what they do already,' Clare protested.

'Of course not. But if we take the first week in October, Helen won't have gone back to Queens, nor will Jennifer have started and John has two weeks due to him from Robinsons' farm. He's saving up to change his car. He says he'd be well pleased to do a whole week here.'

'So we'd have FOUR Wileys instead of two and a bit,' said Clare thoughtfully. 'Well, we do advertise ourselves as a *family* business. We don't have to say *which* family runs the place.'

'So you agree?'

'Well, I can now see it is possible, but where did you think we could afford to go?'

'A small but stately home in Fermanagh, with its own extensive gardens, woodland and a lake. With a boat. And Great-Uncle Hector who has been pestering me for three years now to bring my beautiful bride to Killydrennan.'

'Killydrennan, what a lovely name,' she said, her eyes lighting up. 'What does it mean?'

'Mean? I haven't the faintest idea. I thought it was just a name. But you would like it, I'm sure you would. And Hector is a good sort. Bit of a ladies' man in his youth, married three times apparently, but he's been a widower for thirty years.'

'Andrew,' she gasped. 'What age is he now?'

'Getting on for ninety as far as I know, but he's got all his marbles,' he added reassuringly. 'I'd love us to go.'

To her surprise, Clare caught a distinct hint of wistfulness in Andrew's tone. She remembered he'd visited Fermanagh several times while she'd still been at Queens, because there'd been some complicated dispute over land. Whether it was his uncle's land or a neighbour's, she couldn't now remember. She had no idea either who Great-Uncle Hector was and how he fitted in to the Richardson side of the family but Andrew had got on really well with him.

'Right then, we'll go. What do I have to pack for a stately home?'

'Anything you like by day,' he said, smiling, 'and we'll need weather gear for the paths down to the lake and the boat, but I do have to tell you Hector still dresses for dinner. I'm sure he'd love it if you dressed up for him.'

'Shall I take *the emeralds*?'

'Why not,' he laughed, 'and that short dress that matches them so well. Maybe your wedding dress too, if you've done what you planned to do to it. Pity not to wear some of your lovely Paris creations. I'm afraid I don't provide many opportunities for dressing up, apart from the Hospitals Dance in Armagh every New Year.'

'Once a year does very nicely, thank you, until we're further on. Going off together is such a lovely thought. The more I think about it, the better I like it. I'm looking forward to it already.'

★　★　★

Once Andrew had cleared the outskirts of Dungannon and picked up the good main road to Ballygawley, Clare unfolded her map.

'I do actually know the way,' he said helpfully, as he glanced briefly down at her lap.

'Of course you do,' she replied, laughing. 'But I don't. And if I haven't got a map I'm sure to miss some place whose name I heard long ago, or I've met in my reading.'

She paused, while she carefully consulted the next fold in the sheet she was holding.

'We are now in Tyrone,' she declared. 'Did you know that Tyrone is known as *Tyrone among the bushes*?'

'Does your map tell you that?'

'Of course it doesn't, silly, but it does have many old Irish names and they always tell you something about the land. Most of the names about here, though, seem to be Scots or English.'

She pointed to a signpost they were passing.

'Fivemiletown, you see. One of my uncles is the station sergeant there. He was posted from Moy just recently. We passed his old barracks just before the egg packing station. I was going to point it out to you, but you were stuck behind that ancient tractor and trying to pass.'

'How do you know all this about place names?' he asked, without taking his eyes off the road.

'Charlie is working on a place name project. He says it's a way of keeping up his Irish. No one now speaks it round the Grange. He told me the old names describe features of the land. Like Inishbane. That's *Inish*, an island, and *bane*, white. So, white island. Probably white with blackthorn. So if you study thousands of names you keep up a lot of information about the past.

'Isn't your Uncle Alex doing some research as well?'

'Oh yes. He's got two strings to his bow,' she replied, laughing. 'The export of orphans, like himself. You know about that. But he's working on family history as well. Mary and John told me he's been contacting Hamiltons all over the place and then he writes to them and tells them what he's found out. All kinds of fascinating things turn up.'

'So you get your family news via Australia?'

'And America. Via Dublin. Aunt Emily has a friend in Dublin, a bookseller called Brendan McGinley and he's in touch with the

New York McGinleys, the nephews and nieces of Rose, my great-grandmother . . .'

Clare broke off as the road narrowed and they found themselves driving between tall hedgerows. Overhead, the mature trees met and almost touched. The sunlight splashed down through the canopy they created and threw bright, shimmering patches on the road ahead.

'Oh Andrew, aren't these trees marvellous? The chestnuts here are far further on than ours at home.'

She looked up through the arching branches into the clear blue of the early October day. At last they were on their way, just the two of them, driving south and west to Fermanagh, for a week, a whole week with nothing to do but be good guests at Killydrennan. She felt her spirits lift yet further as if this memorable autumn day were a sign that all would be well and their best hopes come to pass.

'I though you said it was *small*,' Clare protested, as they emerged from a driveway that ran between mature trees and dense shrubbery. Ahead of them lay a wide gravelled area in front of a handsome house, the main part Georgian, but with later additions sprawling untidily to left and right. It stood on a slight rise and overlooked parkland with clumps of trees and a distant view of mountains.

'It's small enough, as these things go around here. Think of Castle Coole or Florence Court,' he said, glancing round as they slowed to a standstill. 'It has only twenty bedrooms or so. You should have seen the one that was burnt down,' he added wryly, as he switched off the engine. 'It had fifty or sixty, I'm told. I think this one was built originally as a dower house but added on to in the last century to accommodate a proliferating family. Hector lived here with his first wife and he never liked the big house. He didn't shed any tears about it when it went up in flames, but he'd had good warning which gave him time to move out all the stuff that really mattered to him.'

Clare stared at him in amazement.

'Do you mean the big house was deliberately burnt down?'

'Oh yes. During the Troubles. Lots of the big houses were torched, but as Hector was well-liked and had Catholics as well as Protestants on his staff, someone tipped the wink to a parlourmaid

Anne Doughty

and the family got out with their valuables . . . and their lives. Not everyone was so lucky,' he added, as he got out and went round to open the boot of the car.

'Andrew, there's someone watching you,' Clare whispered as she came to join him, her hand poised for the nearest suitcase.

'Is that Uncle Hector?' she asked, as Andrew glanced towards the small, dark figure who'd strode out of the pillared entrance and was now standing firmly to attention at the top of the wide stone steps.

Andrew looked up, smiled and raised a hand in greeting.

'That's Russell, Hector's butler,' he replied. 'He's getting on a bit too. Don't touch the cases. If he's come out, he'll send a boy,' he said quietly. 'Just take your handbag.'

'Russell, how splendid to see you. Keeping well, I hope,' said Andrew as they climbed the steps to meet him. 'This is my wife, Clare.'

'You are welcome to Killydrennan, ma'am,' said Russell with a deep bow. 'My Lord sends his apologies that he is not here to greet you. He had an early morning engagement and is taking a short rest before dinner. I have ordered tea to be served in Lady Rothwell's sitting-room. I shall lead the way.'

Clare murmured her thanks and noted that a young man had descended upon the car and was now disappearing round the back of the house loaded with suitcases and grips. She had never in her life travelled with more than one suitcase, but then she'd never in her life been greeted by a butler and addressed as ma'am.

Russell marched them briskly through the entrance hall. The sunlight poured down from a domed cupola high above, the walls were hung with spears and guns, the gleaming marble floor spread with richly coloured rugs. He strode ahead, swept open the door to the sitting room and stood holding it in place until they caught up. A log fire blazed in the hearth. On a low table between two pink and gold armchairs an array of gleaming silver covers suggested there were scones *and* cake to welcome *family guests*.

'Should you require anything, sir, the bell is to the right of the fireplace. Dinner is at eight o'clock and the dressing bell is at seven thirty.'

With a small bow, Russell disappeared, leaving Clare amazed and delighted as she gazed round a room entirely decorated in toning shades of deep pink offset by the gold of mouldings and massive, carved picture frames. It was filled with paintings and objets d'art that would leave Harry green with envy and longing to acquire them for the gallery. As they walked together towards the welcoming fire she saw their reflection in the huge gold overmantel. It was a moment she was sure she would never forget.

Despite the picnic lunch they'd enjoyed under a tree in a quiet side road overlooking one of the many small loughs not even named on Clare's map, they were grateful for the generous spread. Andrew appeared to be ravenous, ate appreciatively and then jumped to his feet, his long legs stiff from the drive. Clare found herself watching him as he stood in front of the fire, teacup in hand, now appearing very much at ease.

'You look as if you owned the place,' she said, half serious, half teasing him.

'The next Lord Rothwell, you mean?' he said soberly, as he put his cup down, picked up the teapot and poured more tea for both of them.

'Where did the name Rothwell come from?' she asked. 'I know Hector is a Richardson but I'm puzzled as to how Lords get their labels. Do they choose them? Oh, I know they get handed down, but somewhere in the mists of time there must have been a first Richardson who became Lord Rothwell. How did he get the Rothwell?'

'Yes, there was a first one. A Richardson from Yorkshire, that is. As far as we know, he came over with Cromwell, was given land in payment for services rendered, then made a lot of money. I don't know exactly how he did it, investing in merchant venturing, I suspect, but it takes a lot of money to get a Lordship. Clearly, he managed it. Rothwell is a village in North Yorkshire. Perhaps it was his old home. Seems unlikely that was where he made his money. His son made *his* money in Kenya, hence all the wild beasties in the hall. The Richardsons have had a Kenya connection since goodness knows when.'

'Andrew, why have you never told me any of this?'

'You never asked.'

'Andrew, that won't do,' she retorted, trying not to be cross. 'I have tried to find out about your family, but the first time I ever heard ANYTHING very much was when you told Mary and John about that nice Aunt Joan in Wiveton. I knew you had an aunt, because you went over once and painted her kitchen, but that was Aunt Bee who died and you'd never mentioned Joan. I know I made a joke about you and family history when Mary and John were with us, but there's something here that isn't funny. It's important, Andrew. I want to know properly why you've never talked about your family.'

As soon as she'd spoken, Clare regretted it. In a moment, his ease had vanished and so bleak an expression came over his face, he looked stricken. They'd had such a splendid day. They'd been easy and happy, talking about everything and anything, delighted to have time to do just whatever they felt like. And now her words had brought on a familiar distress, like a sudden dark shadow over the day.

To her great surprise and relief, he smiled briefly, nodded and sighed. She saw the dark cloud dissolve.

'You're right. You always are about me. Well, about the things that really matter, that is. Do you remember when I was at Cambridge, how you put up with me sending you postcards, because I couldn't face writing letters?'

She nodded and watched him carefully.

'Being asked to write a letter home the day after my parents were killed *was* traumatic. You understood that, but no one else ever seemed to. I thought it was just up to me to get over it. In the same way, there are so many things I can't face and my family is one of them. I try not to think about them, unless I'm forced to, but Hector is different and so was Aunt Bee, and Aunt Joan, of course . . .'

He broke off and came and sat beside her, his shoulders drooping, his lips pressed together.

'There are things I've been thinking about that I should have told you, but I haven't,' he confessed. 'I didn't want to think about them in the first place. But I will. I promise. But not now. Don't let's spoil today, or our holiday. If it's waited this long, it can wait a bit longer.'

She put her arm round him and kissed his cheek.

'No, we won't spoil our holiday. Don't worry about it. Whatever it is, we'll find some way of making it better. Remember what Charlie always says: *You can't fix the past, but you can grow past it.* We've sorted out some nasty things about the past between us.

There's no reason to think we can't do it again. You ended up writing very good letters, if you remember.'

'I told you you'd like Hector,' Andrew said, beaming at her as he shut the bedroom door behind them. 'But I didn't realize what a fancy he'd take to you. I'll have to watch out if he offers you a conducted tour of his trophies. I'll never forget the look on his face when you complimented him on the wine.'

'It was most extraordinarily generous to open a bottle as good as that,' she replied, kicking off her shoes and collapsing into a comfortable armchair. 'But he is such a generous person. He gives so much of himself. I've never known anyone tell such good stories, even when they were not to his credit,' she went on, smiling to herself. 'I just never knew what he was going to come out with next. *When I was in Mafeking . . . There was this lioness none of us had spotted . . .* Honestly, Andrew, I can't quite believe the experience he's packed in, even if he is nearly ninety. Africa, royalty, rich American wives. Did he tell you the same stories when you came down five or six years ago?'

'I've heard the one about the lioness and how his cousin lost his leg, but most of the others were new to me. He's never mentioned Kenya before. I certainly didn't know he and Galbraith Cole both fought in the Boer War and then went to Kenya and watched the flamingos on Lake Elmenteita. Wasn't it sad about Galbraith's arthritis? That would have put an end to his flamingo watching,' he said sadly.

'And he chose to be buried overlooking the lake,' Clare added, looking up at him. 'So many of the people Hector talked about are long dead. It must get very lonely if you live as long as he has,' she added thoughtfully. 'Andrew, who is Nancy? He seems to admire her very much, but who is she?'

'Nancy is Lady Enniskillen,' he said, dropping his dinner jacket and black tie on the bed and sitting down opposite her. 'She and the sixth earl lived up the road at Florence Court, though the fifth earl gave the house to the National Trust. There was a bad fire there in fifty-five. Hector has always said if it hadn't been for Nancy the damage it did would have been much worse.'

He paused and began to laugh.

'What's the joke, Andrew?'

'Actually, there is a story he might have told about the fire, but he was probably being polite on your first night,' he began, grinning at her. 'Apparently, when the fire broke out Nancy took charge and organized everyone. But at some point she decided she'd better contact the Ulster Club in Belfast and break the news to Lord Enniskillen. The story goes he was not pleased at being interrupted and was overheard shouting down the phone: *Well, what the Hell do you expect ME to do about it?* There are different versions of what *exactly* he said. Some of them even more explicit!'

Clare yawned and shook her head. 'I am not bored, my love, but suddenly I just can't keep my eyes open. Are you really going off at dawn with Hector?'

'Oh yes,' he replied enthusiastically. 'The first few white-fronted arrived yesterday and Hector says the main group might well arrive overnight. I've never seen white-fronted geese. They come all the way from Greenland and don't usually pass east of Fermanagh, but they might move on from the lake here. You don't mind, do you?'

The first days of their holiday passed very slowly and peacefully as they adjusted to the leisurely pace of life at Killydrennan. They went for long walks, sat talking under the trees down by the lake, drove to Lough Navar Forest and stood on the edge of the Cliffs of Magho surveying the whole of Lower Lough Erne with its brilliant blue water and scatter of islands.

Crossing to White Island by boat, they stared at the strangely carved figures lined up against an old stone wall. On Boa Island they walked round a Janus-faced figure about which nothing whatever had yet been written. As always, they puzzled about what they saw and wondered from what period in history such remnants had survived.

The remains of the old wartime airbase at Castle Archdale was not a puzzle, however. John Hamilton had told them all about it and said that Hugh Sinton, Aunt Sarah's son by her first marriage, had worked there, improving the design of the Sunderlands used for anti-submarine patrols off the Irish coast. It was these flying-boats, developed or modified at Castle Archdale, that had been so successful in hunting the U-boats lurking off the coast to intercept the stream of convoys carrying vital war supplies from America.

Hector had breakfast with them each morning, but he seldom appeared for lunch. With great tact, Russell indicated to Clare that his Lordship spent a great deal of time in the Library during the day, but he would always join them for dinner and look forward to hearing of their day's adventures.

True to Russell's words, Hector appeared, evening after evening, his tiny, emaciated figure moving briskly, his eyes bright with delight when they told him where they'd been and what they'd seen. One evening, he did admit that he'd always been a night bird and indeed it was Clare who sometimes found she was flagging as it drew close to midnight and Hector was still in full flight.

As the days passed, she was intrigued by how much information he had managed to acquire about her life and about Andrew's. His questions were perceptive and detailed, yet she never felt he was being intrusive. His interest was so genuine that by the end of the week she'd told him about her time in France and even about her life with her grandfather. She was touched when he began to refer to Charlie Running or June Wiley as people who were now as familiar to him as Viola, Duchess of Westminster or Lord and Lady Enniskillen.

He insisted they were free to do anything they felt like doing, but at the same time he was anxious they shouldn't miss anything worth seeing. To Andrew's great amusement, he was so determined they view Florence Court, he made them promise that should they arrive and discover it was not one of the Trust's official opening days, they would go straight round to the kitchen door and ask for the Housekeeper.

'Tell Mrs What's-her-name Hector Richardson sent you. She's my Mrs Watkins' sister, but I'm dammed if I can remember her name. The pair of them married a couple of soldiers billeted here during the last war.'

Florence Court was officially open, however, on the wild and blowy afternoon they drove over and they returned triumphant having taken the guided tour, seen all the public rooms and studied the magnificent plasterwork ceiling Hector had particularly wanted them to see. It appeared there was a story to tell about that very ceiling.

'You can thank my friend Viola for that ceiling,' he said, as they sat down to enjoy one more splendid meal. 'Great girl, Viola. Flying Officer in the Women's Auxiliary Air Force during the war. Mentioned in despatches. If she hadn't got on the phone to the builder chappie during the fire and got him to come and drill those holes in the ceiling, the weight of water in the room above would have brought the whole lot down. Quick thinking, that was.'

Suddenly, and quite unexpectedly, it seemed time had foreshort-
ened. Days disappeared as if someone had set the clock running
more swiftly. As Clare sat at her dressing table on the Friday morning,
she could hardly believe their last day had come.

She found herself suddenly so sad she wondered how she would
get through breakfast. She was even more upset when they went
down together to find that Hector wasn't there. Russell himself was
serving and reassured her that his lordship was quite well. Before he
left them to themselves, he presented her with a note on a silver
tray.

She unfolded the single sheet and looked at Andrew doubtfully
when she registered the large, scrawling hand.

'Hector wants me to have tea with him in Lizzie's sitting room
at four o'clock,' she said slowly.

'Hmmm,' said Andrew, raising an eyebrow and then grinning at
her. 'You won't mind if I go and have a last look at the geese, will
you?'

Tea was already laid when Clare arrived at just before four and sat
by the fire in the room the former Lady Elizabeth Monn had
furnished after her marriage to Hector in 1899. An American woman
with style and taste, Clare reflected. Clearly wealthy to have been
able to choose such beautiful decoration and objects. Suddenly, she
realized with a shock that in all Hector's talk, he had never spoken
of her. It was only looking at an old photograph album that gave
her a name and a birthplace in Connecticut.

'Ah, there you are, my dear Clare. Glad to see you've despatched
that husband of yours. I want you all to myself,' Hector said briskly
as he breezed into the room. 'Would you mind sitting in this other
chair. This is where Lizzie always sat,' he explained. 'Said she could
see my face better if I was here. Then she'd know what I was up to.'

He settled himself comfortably, took the cup of tea she handed
him and then piled up his plate with sandwiches.

'Slept through lunchtime again. Russell knows better than to
wake me when that happens. Something I wanted to say to you.
You remind me of Lizzie. She was the only woman I ever loved you
know,' he began abruptly. 'Met her in Mombasa when I hadn't a
penny to my name. She didn't give a damn. Said she'd marry me
anyway if I'd just get on and ask her. So I did. She always knew

me better than I knew myself. We were so happy together,' he went on more slowly. 'The only thing that bothered her was not having a son. We had the four girls you know and she so wanted to give me a boy.'

He shook his head sadly and demolished a whole sandwich before he went on.

'It *was* a boy too. But it was Lizzie I wanted, not the boy. And I got so lonely, I married this girl I'd always known, but it didn't work out. Then the other one married me when I wasn't paying much attention. In the end, she got bored and went off. Couldn't stand Fermanagh. Said it gave her rheumatism. Used to send me a Christmas card every year, but she's been dead now for years.

'There was only one woman in my life, whatever anyone says. I like women. Far more interesting than most men. Women like Viola, or Nancy, or you. I only saw Andrew a couple of times when he was a boy. That wretched woman at Drumsollen would never let him come here. She kept him as far away from Ireland as she could, though I have to say Adeline's family did give him a good education. But that's not everything,' he said firmly, holding out his teacup.

'He's mad about you, like I was about Lizzie, but one of these days you're going to have to tell him what to do. He's just like I was. I *never* knew what to do. When my brother died and Killydrennan came to me it was the last thing I wanted. But we had the four girls by then and a lot of friends around here. I would have gone back to Kenya to get away from the whole Lord Rothwell bit, but it just didn't make sense. So here I am,' he said flatly, filling up his plate again as she handed him the sandwiches.

'You're right about Andrew,' she said slowly, as he munched his way through them. 'He's always had difficulty making up his mind. I thought it was because no one had ever asked him what he really wanted, they just assumed he'd do what was *suitable* for a Richardson, even one with no money. But maybe I'm quite wrong about that.'

'No, you're not far wide of the mark. My brother was the heir to the title and he was trained up for it. Great chap he was too, I liked him. But my father didn't think much of me and he didn't like Lizzie, didn't like Americans on principle, in fact, so when he thought poor old Charles might not inherit he set up a trust. I got the estate all right, but nothing was mine. Entailed everything so I could never leave. Or if I did I'd be penniless. Lizzie had an income, but that went when she died and I had the four girls to bring up.'

He stopped abruptly, leapt to his feet and passed her the cake.

'You've eaten hardly anything. Come on, this is Mrs Watkins' seed cake. You have some of that and I'll shut up. I've told you it all anyway. I wanted you to know why I can't leave anything much to you and Andrew, possibly even nothing at all. All I own is what's in this room, what Lizzie left me and that's how I'll provide for Russell and the staff. Except for one thing.'

Clare ate her cake slowly, watching him as he hunted through his pockets. She was surprised when he took a matchbox from his waistcoat.

'This *is* mine and it's for you,' he said firmly. 'Lizzie had it from her grandmother and we used it as her engagement ring. Unlike your pretty emeralds, this *is* the real thing,' he added, with a little laugh. 'Sorry about the box, it went in the fire.'

Clare put down her plate, took the matchbox from his bony, long-fingered hand and opened it. Inside on a piece of dusty cotton wool lay a most beautiful sapphire ring.

Eight

'Well, it's still here,' said Andrew quietly, as they rounded the curve in the drive and saw Drumsollen laid out before them.

On the west side of the house a small area of stonework still reflected the pale sunlight of a rain-streaked October day, but the rest of the facade was in deep shadow. The blue grey cloud piled up above wet, grey slates had already begun to throw large, random spots on the windscreen.

Clare picked up the flatness in Andrew's voice and wondered if he was feeling the same sudden dip in spirits she had felt as she glimpsed the chestnuts on the main road. Already branches were bare but for a few pink and gold leaves, ragged and tattered. The message was clear: summer was well over and winter lay ahead.

'Did you think it might have disappeared?' she replied, glancing at him, her tone as light as she could manage.

'We've still got roses in bloom,' he went on, without taking his eyes off the leaf-scattered driveway.

She watched him as he gazed around. He was trying to sound enthusiastic about having arrived home but she wasn't deceived by his effort. She knew how tired he must be after the long and difficult drive, the villages and towns on their route congested with Saturday shoppers and slow moving farm vehicles, but even allowing for that he had seemed very preoccupied on the journey and unusually silent. When she'd offered to drive after each of their brief stops, he'd said he'd rather stay at the wheel because it kept him occupied.

'*Back to porridge*,' he pronounced, as he stopped the car.

It was one of her grandfather's favourite sayings. If anyone had been away it was always pretended they'd been living *in the lap of luxury*. Now they were back it was all over. There would only be porridge for breakfast. Whenever she'd been away in her schooldays, he'd make her laugh when he said the words next morning. But in Andrew's flat tone, there was nothing to laugh about.

'I'll park here and get John to help me with the stuff. Easier than trying to get it all down through the back door,' he said, as he got out, the wind blowing his hair, his eyes tightening against a scud of rain.

'Right. Let's just dash in and find everyone and wait till this squall passes,' Clare replied, as she struggled against the force of the wind.

They ran up the steps together and shut the glass doors behind them. The hall was empty and dim as they stood shaking large drops from their shoulders. Except for the tinkle of the chandelier, its glass diamonds set in motion by their sudden arrival, the house was completely silent.

'Where is everyone?' he asked, looking round anxiously. 'There are no cars outside. Surely there must be *someone* staying?'

'It's only half past three, Andrew. If there *are* guests they'll be out. Come on downstairs,' she said quickly, 'June's bound to be there.'

The kitchen was very clean, very tidy and completely empty. There was no trace whatever of June. As Clare turned to speak to him, the ominous cloud dashed its mixture of sleet and rain against the basement windows and drowned out her words. The room became so dark, they could hardly see each other. She hurried over to the light switches, turned them all on and caught sight of his pale face. He looked as if he had been struck by lightning.

'Andrew, love, what's wrong?'

At that very moment, June came hurrying in, followed by John. They were both dripping wet.

'Now there's a nice welcome for you,' said John quickly, as he shook their hands, 'the pair of us down on our knees beside the drain and not a soul to put the kettle on.'

June made tea and they sat round the kitchen table eating fruit cake. By the time they'd heard the story of the overflowing drain and the other highlights of the week at Drumsollen, Andrew's face had regained some colour. The cloudburst eased, then stopped abruptly; a few gleams of sun returned as John and Andrew went to bring in the suitcases.

June explained there were, in fact, no guests booked for that night, though there were bookings for Sunday and a few for the coming week. The drain in the back yard was now beyond John's capacity, so Helen had taken the car and gone into Armagh to see if a plumber John knew would be willing to come out tomorrow.

'Yer man's a big shot in the church,' June said, raising her eyebrows, 'but if he goes an' prays in the mornin' he can slip roun' here in the afternoon an' no one a bit the wiser. He's always keen on wee extra jobs, but he'll expect cash,' she warned. 'We thought it might go that way when it overflowed the first time, so we've put the week's takings in the cash box instead of Helen takin' them to the bank. I hope that was all right,' she added, suddenly looking anxious.

'Of course it was, June. It was very thoughtful of you,' Clare said reassuringly. 'You know perfectly well we never carry much money, even if we had it,' she added laughing. 'I think we've still the price of some fish and chips for tonight. Last night of the holiday,' she added wryly. 'Then it really is *back to porridge*. But we had a *wonderful* time. All thanks to you and the family. Bless you. I'd forgotten what a holiday was like.'

'Aye, you haven't had much time off, these last three years, bar Friday nights,' said June, looking at her sharply. 'D'ye think ye might get it a bit easier over the winter?'

'Can't afford it to be easier, June dear. If there are no bookings, we'll have to look for events. Weddings, conferences, or whatever. It might actually be harder work, at least for Andrew and me. I wish I could afford to pay someone like Helen, she's been so good over the summer, but that's because she uses her brains. We can't really afford brains, just a modest measure of competence, or in this case neither, just do it ourselves!' she ended laughing. 'You're really going to miss your girls, June. *Both* of them at Queens from next week,' she went on, 'and *wee Caroline* not so wee now. Do you think she'll want to go as well?'

'Ah don't know, Clare, I really don't know,' she replied, shaking her head. 'She's different from the other two. I never know what she's goin' to come out with next. We'll just have to wait and see.'

'We both will, June,' Clare replied, holding out her teacup for a refill. 'Some days, I think I can see what's in the wind, other days I'm not so sure. Things have a way of changing in ways you don't expect. You've always said that to me and to the girls,' she went on. 'Strangely enough, it was something Andrew's uncle talked about often. He had such marvellous stories, some happy, some sad, but so many of them were full of the unexpected. He's quite a character. I wish I'd known him sooner,' she added wistfully. 'June, do I remember you once saying you'd met him or am I imagining it?'

'No, you weren't imagining it,' June replied, shaking her head. 'But it was only the once. He came up here for a reception for Andrew's parents when they came back from their honeymoon. They'd married over in London, of course, so the Senator and The Missus had a big do here to let Adeline meet the local gentry and so on. I was only a housemaid then, but I remember His Lordship asking me for water.' She paused and laughed to herself. 'When I brought it up to his room, nothin' would do him but I'd sit down and talk to him. It was more than my job was worth if The Missus had found out, but he said nobody would notice for a few minutes and he'd take the blame for keepin' me back if I was caught. He wanted to know all about workin' here and what it was like. Listened to every word I said. And then he gave me half a crown,' she added, wrinkling up her face as she laughed her small, infrequent laugh. 'That was a lot of money in 1932. No wonder I remember him!'

'June dear, its half past four,' Clare said quickly as she caught sight of the kitchen clock. 'Here am I keeping you talking when *we* made the effort to leave after breakfast so we could send *you* home early. *And* I haven't given you your little present either. This won't do, will it? Now go and put your coat on,' she added firmly.

'Not much point when there's no car, is there?' June replied, without moving a muscle.

'Goodness, I forgot that as well,' Clare said, putting her hand to her forehead. 'But look, Andrew will drop you and John home and Helen can follow when . . .'

'Hi, Clare, welcome home,' said Helen cheerfully as she strode into the room and peeled off her anorak. 'Any tea left, Mum? Sorry it took so long. Got held up by the police.'

'Were you robbing the bank?' June asked dryly as she picked up the kettle and refilled it.

Clare giggled, suddenly remembering how difficult she had found June's flat-faced comments when she'd first got to know her.

'No, it was a demonstration of some sort,' Helen replied, as she collapsed gratefully on to a kitchen chair. 'Somebody told me they were protesting about the message to the Pope. Whose message I don't know. I thought the poor man died in the summer. Anyway, they were saying O'Neill's a traitor and the Queen Mother and Princess Margaret are disloyal, so I couldn't get through Marketplace. Someone was bawling their head off to a big crowd and the police had just cordoned it off as I came back up Thomas Street. Then we all had to wait till they'd stopped the incoming traffic on The Mall, so they could send us down Scotch Street and out of town that way. It was absolute chaos.'

Clare sighed and shook her head.

'I think I know who was bawling his head off. For goodness' sake don't mention it to Andrew. He's been following the antics of the not-so-Reverend Paisley since he started stirring up trouble on the Shankill. He's convinced that gentleman is an unholy disaster.'

'You think it was him?' asked Helen quickly. 'Do you think Andrew's right?'

'I think he might well be right,' she replied slowly. 'I've only seen Paisley once on television but he reminded me of those old newsreels of Hitler, the light in the eyes and that pointed finger. He certainly frightens me.'

'Why's that, Clare?' June demanded, as she brought the fresh pot of tea to the table. 'There's not a lot frightens you.'

Clare shook her head, surprised at June's words. She'd never thought of herself as brave.

'Shure, look at the way you went off to France all by yourself,'

June demanded, as she poured tea. 'No job. No money to speak of. That takes a brave nerve.'

'It does indeed, Mum,' said Helen quietly. 'But I don't think that's what Clare means about being frightened. Am I right?'

'It's not the man himself,' Clare said nodding. 'It's what I think he's doing and the way he manages to pull out the worst in people. Just when things were looking brighter now that Brookeborough's gone.'

'And do you think O'Neill really has plans for a better future for everyone?' Helen asked sharply. 'Catholics *and* Protestants?'

Clare nodded vigorously.

'Yes, I think *he* means it all right, but I've never been much good at politics. Andrew says I'm too honest, so I don't know where I am with politicians. Unless I can watch their eyes, of course, like I can with O'Neill or Paisley. Charlie Running says he'll believe change when he sees it. There's too many leopards would have to change their spots . . .'

'Right, ladies, taxi at the ready,' John announced, pausing at the door, his arms full of coats and wellington boots. 'Finish your tea and then we're off home. Boss here says we've been given time off for good behaviour.'

Andrew grinned broadly. He nodded down at an armful of well-wrapped plants from Hector's garden.

'Where do you want these, Clare?'

'Garden shed, please,' she replied, getting to her feet. 'Can you put them in buckets of water, please? Have you found the striped bag yet?'

'Already in the Wiley taxi.'

'I'll miss you on Monday,' Clare said, as they all went out together. She paused and gave Helen a hug. 'You've been great company over the summer, it's going to be very quiet without you.'

'I'll miss you too, Clare. I've really enjoyed working here. Not sure I'm really cut out for teaching after all, but don't tell Mum. Not yet anyway.'

'*Mum's the word*, as they say,' Clare replied, smiling warmly. 'Good luck. Make sure you drop in when you're home,' she added, leaning forward as Helen settled herself in the back of the elderly car. She stood and waved as they drove off, gave a big sigh, and turned resolutely towards the house.

*   *   *

While Andrew drove back into Armagh for the fish and chips they'd promised themselves on their return journey, Clare lit the fire in Headquarters. It protested, the chimney damp from lack of use over the summer and the recent rain. She coaxed the smoking firelighter with dry twigs from the basket, then began to add small logs one by one, wanting a bright blaze for Andrew's return.

It was a strange feeling to have the house completely to themselves when they weren't expecting it for some weeks to come, but she was not sorry. Tired as they both were, she would have to discover what had been going on in Andrew's mind to make him so downcast and distraught when they arrived back and thought the house was empty.

Despite the warm glow from a pair of converted oil lamps, the room had grown dim and shadowy while she'd been coaxing the fire. She got up, crossed to the window, began to draw the curtains, then changed her mind. She would leave them open till she heard the car go round the back, the light from the window a welcome for Andrew in the gathering dusk. The overcast sky had made the shortening of the evenings very obvious and this further forerunner of winter reminded her of her own sudden drop in spirits as they came into the driveway. She had to admit it hadn't just been Andrew who'd not been quite himself on their return.

She sat looking into the smoky flames, wondering what she could say to him, how she could encourage him to share his thoughts and feelings, something he still found difficult, despite all his efforts to overcome his ingrained reticence. Nothing came to her. She went on sitting, hoping for inspiration, and found her mind full of images of green hills ribbed with winter ploughing, hawthorn hedgerows dripping with red berries, leaves blowing in the wind, the sky opening and closing with alternate rain and shine.

She jumped up with a start, aware time had passed. She added more logs to the fire, now producing proper flames, and looked first at the clock, then at her watch. She couldn't quite believe it was now after seven. Andrew had gone into Armagh as soon as they'd unpacked. That was nearly an hour ago and Fortes was just opposite the Post Office, barely a mile away.

She peered anxiously out of the window and told herself not to be silly. There must be some simple explanation. Perhaps he'd had a flat tyre and couldn't find a phone. She tried to remember if there was a phone-box in Railway Street. There certainly wasn't one beyond the level crossing and the little stone houses in Gillis Row certainly wouldn't be able to help.

'Perhaps there's a long queue, because it's Saturday night,' she said aloud, as she switched on a light in the entrance hall and headed downstairs to make coffee for the Thermos jug.

The coffee was long made, the tray set up and the plates put to warm for their supper before she caught the distant sound of a car slowing on the main road. Moments later, a reflection of the headlights flickered briefly on the barred windows of the basement. Even before she'd put down the old newspapers she was sorting, Andrew strode into the room and dropped two well-wrapped parcels on the table.

'Sorry, love, they'll be stone cold,' he said hastily. 'It was that bloody man. I'm sure it was,' he went on angrily, as he pulled off his coat and came and put his arms round her.

She hugged him and felt him clutch her in the way he sometimes did when he simply couldn't tell her what was wrong because he didn't know himself.

'Right now, my love, you need your supper,' she said firmly. 'Supper will heat up perfectly well, but it will take a wee while. Would you like some coffee? Or a drink?'

'No, nothing. Just you. It's about the only thing worth having.'

'All right then, me *and* fish and chips. I'm starving,' she said, kissing him. 'Now, come on, whatever it is we'll manage. Reach me out a roasting tin while I unwrap these and we'll go up to the fire while they reheat. It's not the first time we've had to reheat a fish supper, is it?'

She was grateful for his small, bleak smile as she arranged the almost cold food evenly in the tin he'd handed her. She covered it with silver foil, put it in the Aga, shut the door and took him by the hand.

'Upstairs. Fire. I *think* we have some sherry,' she said steadily. 'Worth a try,' she added, as they moved back through the silent house.

Headquarters was now warm, but he shivered as he held out his hands to the lively blaze.

'Riot,' he said matter-of-factly. 'Apparently Paisley had a gathering in Marketplace this afternoon. His supporters didn't go home, they went out looking for trouble. Catholics rather, to be absolutely precise. There were police Land Rovers everywhere. I think there was trouble on Banbrook Hill and Cathedral Road, which was why I was delayed, but the only officer I managed to speak to said they hadn't enough police to cope. All they could do was search for weapons in any vehicle that wasn't local.'

'Weapons!' she repeated, horrified.

'Only one hand gun, thank goodness. Sharpened scythe blades, metal piping, chair legs . . . What can we do, Clare? This man will destroy everything, for us and everyone else.'

'No, he won't, Andrew,' she said firmly. 'No matter what he does, we have *some* choices. He's only one man and there are so many good people trying to make things better. You mustn't despair.'

'But that's the problem, I *do* despair. I always have done. I started to despair during the war, reading the headlines with no one to explain them to me, no one to sympathize or comfort the fear. And now I *can't stop*. I'm never going to be any good to you or anyone else,' he burst out, close to tears. 'When we got back and I saw Drumsollen and thought of all the hard work you'd put in to try to keep the place for us, I just felt so useless, because I knew I could never play my part as I should,' he went on, shaking his head sadly. 'Oh yes, I can cook breakfasts and do chores and I used to be able to clear that drain, but I just haven't got what it takes, Clare. I'm no good to you,' he ended, almost choking on the last few phrases before dropping his head in his hands.

Well at least he's got it out, Clare said to herself as she knelt on the floor beside his chair and put an arm round his shoulders. This wasn't the first time things had fallen apart for Andrew, but it was the first time a public event had set it off.

'Why do you *think* you can't do your part?' she asked quietly. 'Have I complained?' she asked quietly.

'No, you *never* complain.'

'Oh yes I do,' she responded vigorously. 'I get fed up with lots of things. I'm always complaining about not getting good drying when we've loads of sheets, or not even having time to go out and spray the roses when they get greenfly . . .'

'That's not what I mean by complaining,' he retorted. 'You *could* complain that I can't make a go of being a solicitor, but you don't. And I'm no good with money. Neither getting nor spending. You're far better at both.'

'Well, what's wrong with that? As long as one of us can do sums and keep an eye on the outgoings. There are other things you can do.'

'Like what?' he demanded bitterly.

'Like pour us some sherry and see if there might be a bag of crisps in the back of the cupboard.'

He got up, poured the sherry, and meticulously divided a bag of crisps between two wooden bowls. When he turned back towards her, she could see her effort at lightness had done nothing to ease the tension she read in every line of his body.

'Andrew, have you forgotten what we've said about no one ever asking you what you wanted to do?' she began again, getting up and sitting in the other armchair, her back already aching from kneeling on the floor.

He handed her a glass of sherry and a little bowl of crisps, sat down opposite her and fidgeted with his own glass.

'I think I know now what's done it,' he said, at last. 'When I went down to the lake with Hector yesterday, he asked me what I really wanted to do and I told him. He went on then and asked me why I'd said *yes* to mother's family. Eton and Cambridge and doing Law and all that.'

'And did you tell him?'

'Yes I did,' he said wearily. 'He's the only member of my family who has ever listened to anything I've ever said, except Grandfather, and I didn't see much of him, not if The Missus could help it.'

'And what did Hector say?'

'Said it was a crying shame he couldn't leave me the estate. He'd never had the slightest interest in farming. What he'd really wanted to do was overland exploration, but he'd finished up immersing himself in good works in Fermanagh, because he couldn't go anywhere else and he couldn't bear being idle.'

'Good works?' she asked, not quite seeing Hector in what sounded suspiciously like a religious context.

'Oh, the usual run of offices open to the local gentry. Magistrate, Justice of the Peace, Charity Commission,' he replied. 'Rank didn't allow him other options, so he did what he could. He had a spot of bother with the Orange Order to begin with when he refused to join, but he spun the local Grand Master a story about his Quaker ancestors and got off with it on conscientious grounds.'

'And were they Quakers?

'I expect some of them were, but Hector has no time at all for any sort of religious stuff.'

Clare couldn't help smiling at the thought of Hector manoeuvring his way out of joining the Orange Order. To her great relief Andrew smiled too.

'If Hector's wife hadn't died, they could have run away,' she said quietly.

He looked at her for the first time.

'Not a very brave or responsible thing to do,' he said harshly.

'Doesn't that depend on what choice you've been given?' she retorted. 'Wouldn't you try to escape from a Prisoner of War camp?'

'Yes, I would.'

'Life, liberty and the pursuit of happiness,' she said quietly. 'Every one of us has a right to make as good a life as we can, and *we* want to make that life together. I can't do it by myself, I've told you that, and you can't do it either. Just like Hector, you need someone to help you make a go of it. Do you think Hector is *no good to anyone* because he didn't manage to do what he wanted?'

'No, of course not,' Andrew replied vigorously. 'Hector made the best of things when he lost his wife. He's the one relative I have that reconciles me to being a Richardson.'

'Do you need to be reconciled?'

He hesitated for a moment and she thought uneasily that she might have pushed him too far.

'Yes, perhaps I do. It was being a Richardson that meant I was sent away. It was The Missus who sent me away, Clare. Away from Drumsollen. Away from my home, which I loved, so now I'm almost a stranger here. People think I'm *English* because of my accent and the *good class* way I speak. Oh, not the Wileys and our real friends, but clients and colleagues. I see a wary look in their eyes as if to tell me they know I'm not one of them. And it's true, isn't it? I don't fit in and perhaps I never will. I don't think I can really forgive the Richardson family for that.'

By the time they'd talked it all through and agreed they could make things better if they worked at it and that they *did* have each other, the fish and chips were a bit dried up, but they were so hungry they hardly noticed. When they brought the coffee tray back upstairs, the fire was glowing red and gold and the room was full of the smell of the apple wood logs.

'It's still hot,' Andrew said, surprised, as he poured for them. 'Are you exhausted?'

'Yes, I am. But if you actually mean, *Will coffee keep you awake?* the answer is *No.* I could sleep on a bare rock or a wooden board,' she said, yawning hugely.

'What about a nice, warm bed instead?'

Nine

'Easter Cards?' said June, as she looked down at the neatly stacked bundles covering the surface of Clare's desk. 'You're in good time.'

'That's what Andrew said when they arrived last week,' Clare replied cheerfully. 'It was snowing then. Not much I admit but it *was* snow,' she added, laughing. 'Do you recognize the daffodils?'

June put her tray down on the sideboard and peered at the card Clare had been about to sign. 'Are those here?'

'Yes,' Clare nodded. 'Don't they look good? Andrew took the photos last year and I found a firm that makes cards by the hundred. They're not too expensive if you need a lot. I'm sending them to all our former guests. Personally signed, of course,' she added, flourishing her pen hand. 'Details of booking discretely included.'

'I don't know where you get all the ideas from,' June said, shaking her head. 'First it was candlelight wedding receptions, then it was office parties . . . I must away on, I've a cake in the oven. Enjoy your coffee.'

Clare smiled to herself. She loved the daffodils at Drumsollen. Left undisturbed for years, there must be hundreds of them by now. Plain, old-fashioned ones, with glowing gold trumpets and nodding heads. She loved them and she loved their message too. Once there were daffodils the worst of winter was over. In this first week of March they most certainly weren't in bloom, but the vigorous grey spikes were growing fatter day by day.

After the record breaking snow and exceptional cold of 1963, this year had been mercifully mild, but it was still an enormous relief to see the first hints of spring, an even bigger relief to know the heating bills would soon grow less dispiriting.

She made a space on her desk for June's small tray, picked up her coffee cup and took a bite from the buttered scone. Even after all this time, one of June's still-warm scones seemed the greatest of luxuries. She took a few minutes rest, then returned to the three hundred Easter cards still to do. Despite the effort she'd made to be as efficient as possible, it was still going to take a long time. If there was one thing she had learnt running Drumsollen in the last four years, it was that patience paid off. Large jobs could be done, even by one person, if you broke them down and kept at them, but it didn't stop the job being as tedious as it was tiring. She had to admit there were times when she did lose heart, times when she felt *cabined and confined* though she did her best never to let it show.

One of her worst ever weeks had come immediately after their October visit to Fermanagh. The plumber had come to look at the blocked drain on Sunday afternoon as agreed, but he'd discovered the drain was the least part of the problem. While Drumsollen did have a mains water supply, it did *not* have mains drainage. The septic tank had been adequate for a large family home, but clearly could not accommodate the needs of a guest house. Besides that, the land drains serving it had become cracked by the movement of cars and service vehicles round the back of the house. Some of them had caved in and no longer took away waste water into the adjoining fields. Given the distance from the house to the nearest main drain the only option was a new and bigger septic tank.

The pneumatic drills that hopped up on down on the concrete like demented creatures had shattered the silence, driven away the birds and landed an enormous bill on her desk. She still didn't know how she'd managed to keep the final amount a secret from Andrew who would certainly have panicked had he laid eyes on it.

Time passed, the pile of cards grew taller, and it was almost noon when she caught the swish of tyres. Expecting a parcel of tourist literature and feeling in need of a break, she got up, stretched and headed for the front steps to exchange a friendly word or two with Ernie, who'd been doing this postal round since they'd first opened. The wind was cold and blustery but not unexpected as she stepped outside; the vehicle parked at the foot of the steps was a different matter.

Where the original bodywork paint remained, it was blue, but well dappled with rust. Even the most disreputable of the vehicles parked at the back when the men were working on the septic tank looked positively new compared with this one. The car's driver looked equally disreputable. A pair of oil streaked dungarees, also once blue, but now alternately oil-streaked and worn pale, had been pulled on over a crumpled tartan shirt and battered leather boots with wedge heels.

'Hi, Clare,' the figure greeted her, as he finally managed to close the driver's door after several hefty bangs.

Clare's heart sank. For a moment, she couldn't remember when she had last seen her younger brother. He had not appeared at her wedding, nor at Granda Hamilton's funeral, but she was unlikely to forget that in the past he only bothered to turn up when he wanted something.

As he tramped up the steps, a broad grin on his face, she did remember the last time they'd met. It was when she was working in Paris and came to visit her grandparents after staying with Jessie and Harry in Belfast. That was when he'd asked her for money to buy a car. Having previously broken his leg riding his uncle's motor bike without permission, she'd refused to give it to him.

'Hello, William, how are you?'

'I'm great. How are you . . . and Andrew?' he added, as an afterthought.

'Fine. Working hard,' she replied, as she turned and led the way back into Headquarters.

'I say. Real posh,' he enthused, trailing behind her to look up at the chandelier. 'Granny says you're doin' great. This your office?' he asked abruptly, his eye lighting on the bundles of cards. 'What's all this?

'Advertising,' she said briskly, as she cleared the chair beside her desk so he could sit down.

'I hear you were *very* busy last summer. Granny said you had advertisements in all the papers, Armagh *and* Portadown.'

'How is Granny?'

'Oh, she's fine.'

'What about her legs?'

Clare knew well enough that William hadn't the slightest interest in anyone but himself but she accepted that she would probably always go through the motions of normal behaviour with him because she found his indifference so hard to accept. She paused, waiting.

'Clare, now that you're doin' so well, I thought I'd come an' see if you could give me a job.'

So that was it. Clare was torn between relief that she now knew what she had to deal with and irritation that he appeared to have made no progress at all as he grew older. He was now twenty-four and was still behaving just as he had at eighteen.

'What sort of job?' she asked coolly.

'I thought I could do some drivin' for you. Collectin' and deliverin' stuff. And I could look after your cars, yours and Andrew's. And the visitors'. Keepin' them smart.'

'Sorry William. We have only one car and we do our own fetching and carrying.'

'What about the visitors?'

'What about them?

'Who cleans their cars?'

'They probably do it themselves before they come on holiday. Besides William, I'm afraid we can't afford extra staff.'

'But you must be rolling in it,' he protested, casting his eyes round the room.

'No, we're not,' she said firmly. 'We just, only just, break even.'

'You're mean, that's what you are,' he spat out, jumping to his feet. 'You always have been. You wouldn't give a body daylight, you and that fine English husband of yours,' he went on, his face screwed up in a nasty leer. 'Well, I'll be able to tell Granny all about you and how nice you were to me.'

He spun on his heel and made for the door, pausing only to turn and make a rude sign. She heard him stride across the hall, throw open the glass doors and run down the steps. By the time she'd reached the open doors, he'd driven off in a cloud of fumes, his tyres squealing. She shut the doors behind him, but not before the stiff breeze had blown the smell of burning engine oil into the entrance hall to linger there long after he had gone.

'How go the daffodils?' asked Andrew, dropping his briefcase and coming over to kiss her. 'I left the car out front in case you wanted us to go back into town and post them.'

'Thanks, love, that was kind,' she said wearily, as she pushed another bundle into a plastic carrier bag. 'I think they'll *have* to go to the Post Office. Too many for a pillar box,' she continued, nodding to the pile of carriers already stacked beside her desk. 'How was today?'

'I had a letter this morning making enquiries about my wife,' he said sharply. 'I'm trying to be amused about it and not succeeding. In fact, I think I'm furious and I am about to write a very sharp letter, icily polite of course, and wrapped up in impeccable legal language, but actually saying, *Piss off.*'

'About your wife?' she repeated, bursting out laughing. 'Andrew, what *are* you talking about?'

'You may well laugh,' he said more moderately, 'but I was so cross I had to go and walk briskly round The Mall in my lunch hour so as not to bite the head off poor Thelma. Do you want to see it for yourself or shall I give you a synopsis?' he asked, his tone softening a little. 'I'm good at synopses, or *synopsisis* as Thelma calls them.'

'This I must see,' she declared, overwhelmed by curiosity as she got up from her desk.

The text of the letter was brief, but the engraved and illuminated heading was most impressive and the sheet of paper she held in her hand the thickest she'd ever met.

'*It is incumbent upon us as executors and administrators of the Rothwell estate to ascertain the religious proclivities of both the potential contenders themselves and of their spouses . . .*' She broke off, quite overwhelmed.

'What on earth do they mean?' she asked, sitting down opposite him, the document still in her hand.

'Simple,' he answered, amused by the look on her face. 'No Taigs here. Only good Prods need apply. Check out the wives as well. Make sure they're kosher,' he added, just to make the point quite clear. 'Just what our late unlamented Prime Minister used to recommend: *Don't have one of them about the place.*'

'But what on earth has it got to do with us, Andrew?'

'Oh, it's just routine,' he replied dismissively. 'I must be somewhere in the line of succession to the title, every male Richardson would be. In the legal business, we always assume death and disaster, you know that. I suppose if Australia sinks into the Southern Ocean it might kill off a few of Hector's grandsons.'

'But I thought Hector only had daughters,' she protested.

'By his first wife, remember. The second one produced a son, then upped and went taking son with her. Hector told me way back that he was raising sheep in Australia. He's a bit older than me, married very young and has several sons and daughters.'

'So if Australia sinks, as you put it, you could be in the running for Killydrennan?'

'Theoretically yes, however unlikely in practice. There can't be all that many male Richardsons around. Maybe one's just died and that's why they've got the wind up. So they are checking out to make sure *you* have not converted to the Catholic faith.'

'Honestly, Andrew, I *am* sorry. I think I've not been as sympathetic as I should have been over your family. It's such a nonsense in the twentieth century, all this business about male inheritance and religion. I think you're quite entitled to tell them to mind their own business.'

Andrew laughed, the ominous shadow lifted, and he looked a whole lot happier than he had since he arrived home.

'Except, of course, my beloved, it *is* their business, and very lucrative it must be too,' he said, taking the letter from her. 'Just look at their notepaper and the engraving of their premises in London.'

'Let's leave the Post Office till the morning, Andrew,' she said quickly, as she picked up the edge come back into his voice. 'One day isn't going to make any difference. You can do the post on the way to work,' she went on, the weariness of the day now printing out in her own voice. 'How about opening one of Robert's more modest bottles? It's a beef stew with dumplings and mashed potato. Are you hungry?'

'Ravenous. And wine would be lovely. Shall we drink to their confusion?'

'Who's confusion?'

'The gentlemen in the Inner Temple with the posh notepaper.'

She laughed and nodded vigorously, bent down and put a match to the fire. At some point in the evening, she would tell him about her contact with her own family, but certainly not till a glass or two of good red wine had softened the edges of the day's vexations.

March continued to blow in vigorously, bringing with it the first scatter of guests, but it was the end of April before there were enough to require regular wash loads of sheets each morning. Clare was especially grateful for a small number of commercial travellers who had become regulars. They were happy to drive a mile out of town to a relaxed and friendly atmosphere and avoid the problems of trying to park in the city centre.

They were also happy to chat about their own concerns. Listening to them Clare noted both the changes in their work and the changes they'd observed in their usual customers. Most of them, it seemed, were heartened by the positive tone of government pronouncements about attracting new industry and reducing unemployment. Whatever their own particular line of business they all agreed that new invest-ment from abroad at a time when Ulster's traditional industries were visibly fading was just what the Province needed.

Clare had always hoped they could eventually offer evening meals to their guests, but the cost of employing a chef and the provision of choices of food when bookings were so light argued against it. One evening as they sat over coffee she was turning over the problem in her mind once more, when Andrew came up with an idea.

'If June cooks something for us or leaves us a cold meal on a tray, she could probably do the same for our regulars, couldn't she? She used to do it when we had those two surveyors when we first started.'

Clare had to suppress a smile at the thought of adding one more job to June's long list, when she spent her time trying to ensure they didn't exploit her endless goodwill. Nevertheless, she reckoned Andrew had pointed the way to a solution, but only if she could find the money for an extra pair of hands. Within the week she'd found a young woman urgently needing part-time work in the afternoons.

When she arrived to be interviewed, Bronagh had such a lively, easy manner that Clare took to her at once. Sitting opposite her, the dark eyes that looked out from under a mass of dark hair met hers so candidly as she explained the situation and the needs of the job. It was agreed she begin work the very next day. Clare would be able to offer a buffet meal on a tray to any guest who didn't want to drive out to a local hotel, or go back into the city for dinner that evening.

Bronagh turned out to be an even better idea than she had seemed at first, for she was willing to tackle whatever work was needed when her own work was done, and she was good enough to satisfy even June's rigorous standards. Clare overcame any reservations she might have had over creating another addition to the wages bill when she saw how Bronagh's unforced gaiety, her way of laughing suddenly at little things had made June smile more often. The burden of cleaning and maintenance which Clare and June had previously shared between them now seemed a good deal less than before.

But despite the success of adding Bronagh to what she and June laughingly called *The Staff*, adding up the figures at the end of April was not encouraging. Back in October, after meeting the cost of the septic tank, she'd made an extra effort to recover their position by advertising for the coming season and promoting Drumsollen as a venue for special occasions. Looking at the figures, she had to accept that those efforts were certainly not yet making a significant difference to their overall position. In fact, as if that were not disap-pointing enough, there were fewer bookings for the months ahead than at the same time the previous year, or the year before that. The critical summer months, in which the takings would normally be at their highest, were looking very flat indeed.

Using all her skills, she looked for anything that might have caused such a falling off in bookings. They might yet pick up, of course, but if they didn't, then their plan for Andrew to start buying land and farming at Drumsollen would have to be delayed another year.

She studied the advertising and pricing of all the guest houses in the immediate vicinity, identified possible competitors and looked carefully at the detail of their publicity material. She listened to the comments of departing guests, read the local and national papers, as well as her regular copy of *Le Monde*. She had still found no clue until, in the course of May and early June, she received a handful of friendly notes from guests who had been delighted with her Easter card.

Most of her replies came from couples or families, a mixed group, people of different ages and from different parts of the country, Scotland, the North of England and Southern Ireland mostly. There was a picture postcard from Florida and a proper letter of thanks from some Canadians who had come over especially to research their family history in and around Loughgall.

They all said how nice it was of her to write, what a pretty card she'd sent and how well they remembered her lovely roses. Expressed in different ways in each of the notes, however, was the critical piece of information she had been looking for. They were dropping her a line because they would *not* be coming to Drumsollen this year.

That was no surprise with the Americans or Canadians, but what emerged as she read and reread the notes from those nearer at hand was a dramatic shift in holiday plans. Several former guests were visiting sons or daughters overseas because airfares had now dropped low enough to make it thinkable, but most admitted, slightly sheepishly, that they were going to try one of these *package holidays*, because they really did want the promised sunshine, despite being faced with *foreign food*.

'*Trends and fashion,*' Emile used to say, to clients of the bank. '*These are unpredictable in their appearance, but if you see the signs of either you must be prepared. Positively or negatively. The goods or services you are offering may become more desirable. On the other hand they may be superseded by some new offering that catches the eye of the market.*'

His wise words exactly fitted her present situation. New offerings of cheap air travel and sunshine holidays certainly seemed to have caught the eye of the market.

As the burgeoning spring moved towards full summer, bringing blue skies and longer evenings, Clare decided to keep her observations to herself at least till the end of June. If she told Andrew of her concerns now and there was a sudden rush of bookings at the beginning of the school holidays, he would have been worried unnecessarily. If there wasn't a rush, it would have become quite apparent to him by then.

In the event, it was Andrew who came home from work on the last Friday of June with the really bad news.

The last day of the month was always busy for Clare. As well as sharing the domestics with June, as she did every morning, when they stripped and remade the beds, tidied the rooms and checked out the soap and towels, she had the bills to pay, the lodgement to make up for the bank and the accounts to balance.

She was often still at her desk when Andrew came home. Today, for once, she wasn't. She'd felt so tired and so frustrated by five o'clock that she abandoned the remaining paperwork, took up her secateurs and went to deadhead the first faded blooms on the roses.

The sun was still high and warm on her shoulders as she worked her way round the two large beds. The month had been kind, ideal for the garden, the weather sunny by day, but with cool nights that brought either heavy dew or light rain. The roses had thrived and had produced enough blooms for the hall table as early as mid-month.

Soothed by the warmth, the fresh air and the vibrant colours after being shut up all day in Headquarters, she was miles away in her thoughts and had her back to the driveway when Andrew arrived somewhat earlier than usual. Only when he banged the car door and startled her did she spin round and see him, a tall figure in a dark suit, his face so pale she thought he must be ill.

In her haste to reach him, she dropped her bucket of prunings and nearly tripped over it as she hurried through the rose bed.

'Andrew, are you all right? Whatever's happened?'

He pressed his lips together, gazed silently round the garden, then put his arms round her.

'Clare, I'm sorry, so sorry,' he said, dropping his face into her hair. 'I think I knew something was brewing, but I couldn't be sure. I've lost my job.'

She opened her mouth to say something just as a car drove briskly past and stopped by the stone steps.

'Andrew, I'll have to go. Get out of your suit and make us tea. I'll come just as soon as I can.'

'Love, I'm sorry it took so long,' she said, as she hurried into Headquarters and shut the door firmly behind her. 'They wanted to chat and I was so through myself I took up the wrong tray the first time . . . I just can't believe this. How can a partner lose his job?'

'Quite easily, if the term is no more than a courtesy title,' he explained. 'When Charles set up in Armagh, I had no money to put in to the business. He did it all. He paid all the expenses and offered me a share of the profits. He guessed at a monthly figure to give me a regular salary and he wasn't far wrong. Now he's decided he has to move to Belfast. So no more salary.'

He looked so woebegone as he paused and drained his cup, his tone so flat and dispirited, she longed to jump up and take him in her arms, but she knew there was more to come.

'Fairly, he did invite me to Linen Hall Street,' he went on wearily, 'but he knows perfectly well I still have no money, not for the sort of set-up he wants. I think it's all Helen's idea and I should have seen it coming. Maybe I did and couldn't bring myself to admit it. You always said she was a social climber and her father is rolling. I think he's stumping up, probably offloading for tax purposes, so Helen's pushing him.'

'But you're not penniless any more, Andrew. What kind of money are we talking about?' she asked quickly.

For a moment she thought Andrew might be frightening himself, as he often did over money, but when he named the figure she shook her head in amazement. He was quite right. Of course they couldn't produce that sort of money. She picked up her cup and took a mouthful of the tea he had poured ready for her. It was stone cold, but her mouth was so dry she drank it anyway.

'Why is it such an enormous sum?' she asked.

'Well it's Linen Hall Street for a start,' he began, 'as if I ever wanted to work *there* again,' he added sharply. 'Listed building three stories high, thick carpet and leather volumes in the bookcases. Portraits of the former incumbents and the *Titanic* on her sea trials in large gold frames. Very upmarket and fees to match. Would you want me commuting to Belfast every day?'

'No, of course I wouldn't,' she said vigorously. 'I remember how you hated it when you were articled to those three old boys when I was still at Queens. But you *did* seem happier in Armagh, given it's not what you'd choose to do in the first place.'

'I've tried, Clare. I *have* tried, but I've failed. I've let you down,' he said, looking the picture of misery.

Clare took a deep breath and poured herself more tea.

'If I told you Drumsollen was back to only breaking even at the moment, would you say I'd failed, that I had let *you* down?' she asked coolly.

'No, of course not,' he replied, his head jerking up, his startled blue eyes focusing upon her. 'I know how hard you work, but even you can't invent bookings if they don't appear.'

'And you can't stop Charles investing his father-in-law's money in a Belfast practice. Andrew, it is not *us* who fail, it is *our plan*, or

our project that fails. *We* only fail if we don't face up to what happens
and then let the failure come between us.'

'Look, Andrew, the notice has gone,' she said, as she untied the
string on the gate at the foot of the curving slope of Cannon Hill.

'What notice?' he asked, as he pocketed the car keys and took
her hand.

'Trespassers will be prosecuted.'

'*Or persecuted*,' he added, laughing.

They walked up the steep slope in silence, grateful for the
warmth of the evening, for the gold of buttercups and the calm
that had followed Andrew's bombshell. It was Clare who suggested
leaving the moment John arrived, but it was Andrew himself who
suggested they go to Cannon Hill.

'The right place, at the right time,' she declared, as they reached
the tall stone obelisk on the top. 'Clever you,' she added, kissing
him.

'This was where it all began, wasn't it?' he said quietly, as they
leaned against the rough stonework. 'We came on bicycles on our
first date and you promised to write to me in Cambridge.'

'We should come here oftener,' Clare replied thoughtfully, gazing
out over the lush green countryside, the shadows now beginning to
creep out from the hedgerow trees and invade the yellow-green of
pasture and the gold of ripening corn. 'It lends perspective,' she went
on. 'There's you and me and there's the world out there. We can't do
a lot about what happens, the world will do its own thing, but we
can do *something* about how we manage to respond to what happens.
We can always change us, if we have to.'

'Yes, you've finally managed to teach me that,' he said wryly. 'I've
been a bit of a slow learner.'

They fell silent. Clare saw him scan the patchwork fields. She
remembered how once, up here, he'd confessed that what he really
wanted to do was farm. Another time it was she herself who'd
admitted freely that this countryside of little humpy hills was where
she really wanted to be, but she'd be sorry if she never managed to
travel beyond it.

So where did that leave them now, she wondered, standing here
in the midst of warmth and sunlight, the sky a blue arc above them,
at the mid-point of the year, their arms around each other.

Ten

By the time Clare and Andrew arrived back at Drumsollen to let John get off home, they were in need of a second supper. Too tired to go into Armagh to fetch fish and chips, they made scrambled egg and toast and sat down at the kitchen table, daylight still filtering down into the shadowy room at almost eleven o'clock.

They were still sitting there as the clock struck midnight. By then, the sky had finally darkened enough for a scatter of stars to appear. Reluctant to put on the overhead lights, they went on talking, the kitchen lit only by the concealed lighting over the work surfaces and the tiny stars of red and green on large appliances that hummed and whirred quietly.

By the time they finally made their way to bed, they'd managed to call up a small spark of possibility. It might come to nothing, but it was worth a try. They already had a plan for the morning.

'Going to be hot again, June,' Andrew said, coming to collect the shopping bags. 'We've done the Laverys' breakfast and they're just settling up. We've a wee extra job we need to do in Armagh,' he explained, as he took the list she handed him. 'Is it all right if I take Clare with me and leave you to hold the fort? She says you're not to bother with the upstairs, and we'll be back in good time,' he promised.

June nodded abruptly, gave that short, sharp laugh that used to disconcert him, and said; 'Aye, away on the pair of you.'

The city was busy, the streets so full of traffic and shoppers they had to park on the far side of The Mall. The air was still cool under the trees, but the light was dazzling out on the cricket pitch where the groundsman was inspecting the crease for the afternoon's match.

They moved briskly across The White Walk, crossed the road, and walked up Russell Street on the Hartford Place side to the tall, terrace house opposite the Police Barracks where Andrew had worked since he'd come to Armagh.

It was a long time since Clare had been to Andrew's room.

The idea of referring to it as Chambers had always made them laugh. As she climbed the stairs ahead of him, she thought sadly that running a guest house when they were half *The Staff* didn't leave much time to do things together. Even at weekends they had to work separately to get all the jobs done. Someone had to be available in Headquarters, unless, like this morning, June had agreed to cover for them.

'A poor thing, but mine own,' said Andrew, as he unlocked the door of his room and she walked over to his desk.

'Do you really think Charles owns this house?' she asked, running her eye over the tall bookcases and the faded wallpaper in between.

'I'm fairly sure he does,' he replied. 'I could ring and ask him now,' he offered, nodding to the phone on his desk.

'Let me have a better look first,' she said quickly. 'I can't remember the kitchen, but I know there is somewhere you brew up. And there's a bathroom on this floor too. I do remember that,' she said, laughing. 'It has a huge bath with claw feet and brass taps exactly the same as the one in Gosford Row when the High School was still there. We used to keep our hockey sticks in it.'

'I think you'll find this one full of box files,' he said easily, as he followed her on to the landing and watched her continue her inspection.

'What about the top floor?' she asked.

'Haven't been up there for ages. Papers, I should think. I used to see Thelma passing my door with the odd armful.'

Their feet echoed on the uncarpeted stairs which did a sharp twist and ended at a minute landing. There were two doors standing open, revealing two smaller rooms with sloping ceilings. Brilliant patches of sunlight reflected back from the bare boards, but apart from dust and cobwebs both rooms were entirely empty.

'Looks like Charles has been busy,' he said sharply.

'But wouldn't he be responsible for storing or destroying the firm's documents?' she said gently.

'Yes, I expect so,' he agreed, striding across the larger of the two rooms and looking down into Russell Street. 'Must be hot,' he declared, 'the policemen have their sleeves rolled up. Did you know there's a regulation number of folds when they're on point duty?'

'Well, what d'you think?' he asked, after she'd looked through the dusty sash windows and checked they did still open.

'I think it's worth a phone call,' she said steadily, after they'd stepped carefully down the worn stairs and sat down again in his room.

'Do you remember when we had the flat over the Gallery after Jessie and Harry started working on the Malone Road house? It wasn't any better than this, but we managed. We didn't even have a bath, we had to wash in the kitchen. We could make this place quite nice with a lick of paint and some remnants of carpet.'

'So do we move in and live poor but happy ever after?' he asked with a large grin. 'Very handy for the shops and we can walk round The Mall together every day.'

She laughed, grateful to see how his mood had changed since the bad moment upstairs when the empty rooms spelt out the fact that Charles must have been preparing for this move for some time.

'No, I think we can do better than that,' she replied soberly. 'If we can rent the house from Charles and let these rooms to some young couple like we were, we've got something towards the overheads. You'd have Charles's room on the ground floor with Thelma . . .'

'Then all I'd need is clients knocking at the door,' he interrupted, sounding much less easy.

'But, Andrew dear, you've been dealing with clients here in Armagh for six or seven years now. You *are* known. Not all of Charles's clients were the great and the good, though that's what Helen would have liked, I know. You've come home pleased often enough and told me that you've been able to help someone who'd had a raw deal. Not as often as you wanted, I know, but it's a start, until we see how things go at Drumsollen.'

'Yes, that's true. There *are* people I've helped,' he admitted slowly. 'Though what earned my salary was probably doing the donkey work for Charles's briefs. That's gone.'

'Yes, of course it has. And we don't know how it will all work out, love. But do let's see if we could set you up on your own. If it's possible without breaking the bank, would you give it a try?'

'Yes, of course I would. Anything to help to keep us solvent. Am I going to complain about sitting here trying to drum up business when you're doing exactly the same thing in Headquarters? Fair's fair, Clare.'

'Why don't you give Charles a ring,' she suggested. 'I doubt if Helen's out of bed yet, but he will be. You mustn't blame him for what's happened, Andrew,' she continued. 'He's done what he's done because he's had to, but I don't think he's changed in his feelings towards you. I'm sure he'll do what he can to help, but you must give him the chance.'

By the time they'd carried the heavy bags back to the car and loaded them into the boot, they were both hot, sticky and longing for a drink.

'There are tins of soda water in one of these carriers,' Andrew said, rummaging around in the nearest one. 'Can you drink from the tin?'

'Don't have to. Picnic mugs in the glove compartment,' she replied, opening the passenger door and reaching down into the warm and steamy car. 'Somewhat dusty, but technically clean,' she added, blowing on them, as she brought them out. 'Let's sit on the wall for a few minutes till the car cools off a bit.'

'Oh, that *was* good,' she said, pausing, mug in hand after a long swallow. 'Mine was still cool from the chill cabinet. How was yours?'

'Wonderful,' he said. 'Marvellous things bubbles.'

'Poor man's champagne,' she said cheerfully, feeling a lift in spirits that told her something of great significance for the future had been resolved between them.

'You were right about Charles,' Andrew said, sheepishly, as they went on sitting side by side in the heavy shade of a chestnut. 'He does want to help. Said he'd ring with a figure this afternoon. Can't ask for better than that, can you?'

'I know it was a dreadful shock for you, love, but just think how hard it was on Charles. You've worked together for all this time and never an upset between you. Oh yes, I know you've had disagreements, but so have we. What's important is that there's never been any bad feeling between you any more than there's been between us. Perhaps Charles is not as happy about this move as he pretends to be.'

'You're probably right,' Andrew replied. 'I think he *was* upset yesterday when he told me. He boomed a bit, like he does in court when he's on a sticky wicket, but I was in such a bad way myself I wasn't thinking about him. Mea culpa.'

She held out her hand for his picnic mug and the empty tin. 'Love, we mustn't forget June. You told John you'd run her home and I promised we'd not be late.'

'So did I,' he said jumping up and pulling out his car keys. 'Have you home in two shakes of a lamb's tail,' he added, as she dropped the empty mugs and tins on the back seat.

'Make that three, would you. I think I'm feeling a little fragile,' she said, as she leaned back in her seat and fluttered her eyelids. 'Rather a lot has happened this morning.'

He laughed and manoeuvred in front of the museum with meticulous care.

With the exception of one phone call just before they'd arrived back, June said she'd had a quiet morning. She said she'd done everything she wanted to do and had left them a casserole for Sunday.

They never asked June to cook for them, though sometimes Clare did add their name to the list of buffet meals being prepared, but June had a mind of her own and if she did make a casserole for them they knew better than to protest.

'Who called, June?' Clare asked, after she'd thanked her for Sunday lunch and Andrew had picked up her basket.

'Yer man Charles,' she replied, turning towards him, as she took off her apron. 'Yer Boss at work,' she went on, waving her hand in the air. 'He said he'd pop in this afternoon. He has to take his wife to see her mother in Loughgall. I think he'll be glad of the excuse if the mother's the woman I've heard tell of,' she added, as she hung her apron on its hook. 'He chose a good day to come for I've baked for the week. There's three different kinds of cake,' she announced with satisfaction.

The moment they'd gone, Clare sat down gratefully at the kitchen table. It would take only ten minutes or so for the round trip to Wileys at Ballyards, but it was just what she needed. Charles taking the first opportunity to come after Andrew's call this morning could only be good news and she needed time to think before he arrived back.

★   ★   ★

By the time July made a spectacular end with a rainstorm that blew the door off the garden shed and left the tarmac covered with sheets of water, many things had changed.

From the point of view of running Drumsollen as a guest house, the month had been a disaster. They had not even covered their costs. The intermittent wet weather was certainly a cause for the fall in bookings, but it was hard to avoid adding on the effects of the regular outbursts of sectarian violence in Belfast which hit the headlines, day after day, and were extensively covered even by foreign television channels.

Riots and reprisals in what were now known as *sensitive* areas were sparked off by demonstrations both before the Orange processions on the Twelfth of July and on the day itself. With the same predictability that high humidity leads to torrential rain, all the regular marches brought trouble in their wake. While Ulster people themselves knew how local such violence might be, you could not expect guests, either old or new, to know that Drumsollen was quite untroubled by any such disturbances.

At the end of the month, Clare was forced to move money from Andrew's account, the one in which they had saved towards their Grand Plan, to prop up the Trading Account. Without that withdrawal, she could not have paid the wages or the normal monthly bills. What made making the withdrawal even harder was the knowledge that his July salary would be the last predictable figure she could count on in this account.

It would take the year ahead to give any clue as to how successful Andrew's new venture might be. For the moment, she had to admit there were modest grounds for hope. It began when she caught sight of Charles's elegant new car parking in the front of the house on Saturday afternoon. When the tall, well-rounded figure disappeared into the boot of the car and emerged with a large and splendid bouquet of flowers, she felt sure she was right. Whatever his wife might want, Charles had no intention of losing Andrew's friendship or the easy relationship he had always enjoyed with them both.

Charles had indeed come bearing gifts. The sum he named for the rent of the house in Hartford Place was as low as it could be without being too obvious. He had planned to have the place decorated before letting it, so he insisted they should instruct the decorators themselves and send him the bills. He had no objections at all to sub-letting the upstairs as a flat and almost apologized for wanting to leave the current furnishings where they were for them to dispose of as fitted their needs.

'He's been more than generous, Clare. I'm really a bit ashamed of myself,' Andrew said, after Charles had suddenly looked at his watch, remembered what time he was to pick up Helen and disappeared with the hastiest of goodbyes.

'I think perhaps you were so upset yesterday, you didn't give him a chance to offer any alternatives,' Clare said tentatively.

'I as good as walked out and just managed not to slam the door behind me. I shall apologize on Monday when I see him on my own. It was Charles who saved my skin when Edward died and I inherited all the family debts. If it hadn't been for him, I'd have ended up in jail. I just didn't know where to turn.'

He stopped abruptly, his face suddenly pale and taut as the memories came flooding back.

'And I had walked out on you too,' she said bleakly. 'Yes, I know, we've talked about it,' she added hastily, as she saw him about to protest. 'In the end it *was* for the best, I know, but it will always make me sad, thinking of you coping on your own.'

'I'm not very good at that.'

'Neither am I, my dear love,' she replied firmly. 'You still confuse practical skills with overall coping. I'm good at other people's problems, I admit, but you've seen me lose hold of myself, just the way you do. Remember what happened after Edward died and all our plans fell apart and I thought everyone else came first. I didn't cope at all, did I?'

'I suppose you're right, but I confess I've never seen it that way.'

'And how often do I say the same thing to you?'

'Well, yes. Sometimes I do have the odd idea.'

'Very odd,' she agreed, teasing him. She laughed as she began to clear up the tea things. 'Aren't you pleased with your present from Helen?'

'Helen!'

'My beloved Andrew, who do you think gave the thumbs down to that lovely old desk of Charles's and the entire contents of the two offices? *My dear, how could you possibly take this old furniture to*

Linen Hall Street?' she asked, mimicking Helen's over-refined accent. 'What do you think she'll choose for the new one, Louis Quinze or traditional Harrods' mahogany?'

'I hope it works out for Charles,' Andrew said fervently. 'He's very good at the job, but he's straight. No pulling strings just because a client's got money or a title. No brown envelopes for Charles. But Helen has no such inhibitions. She'll have Charles meeting the *right* people, however wrong they might be for Charles. I think I'd rather be poor and honest myself, but it's a bit hard on you,' he ended, putting his arm round her shoulders.

'I agree with the honest, but we might not have to go on being very poor. We've got a bit of time yet,' she said encouragingly. 'What's a brown envelope, Andrew? Is it what I think it is?'

'Probably,' he nodded. 'In the kind of plain English those using them would go a long way to avoid, it's a bribe. Often reciprocal. You know the phrase: *You scratch my back and I'll scratch yours.*' He paused and went on dryly, 'I suppose brown envelopes are less conspicuous than white. You can slip them into the hand on Lodge night, or at a Council Meeting. It's more generally known as *greasing the palm.*'

'That is certainly *not* Charles,' she said, standing up with the loaded tray. 'Any more than it ever would be you.'

August was very quiet in Andrew's new practice, just as they both expected. They'd promised they wouldn't be upset if there were no cheques to bank at the end of the month, provided the decorators had been supervised properly and the new flat was furnished and equipped. Even if they were not doing the decorating themselves there was a great deal else be done. Moving Andrew's files and papers to Charles's room and reorganizing Thelma's meant a lot of legwork up and down stairs, most of which Andrew did, but furnishing the new flat meant acquiring carpets, furniture and basic equipment. That was Clare's department.

She began by going through all the cupboards and drawers at Drumsollen to see what duplicates they might have that could be spared. Then she deployed the skills she'd acquired in locating and bargaining for items when they'd first set up the guest house. Charles had left Andrew a pile of non-urgent briefs to finish, but he declared that getting the place going properly before the Law Term began was much more important than being tidy-minded over briefs. He set them aside and turned his attention instead to fitting cupboards and curtain rails.

The Wileys were on holiday, so they had to take it in turns to work in Russell Street because they couldn't leave Drumsollen unattended, even when there were no guests in residence. When the Wileys returned, however, and gave them back their *Friday night off*, they spent it at the flat. Sitting having a tea break in the tiny, freshly-painted kitchen, having vacuumed the new carpets or polished the old bookcases, they admitted to each other that the thought of having a home of their own, however small, a place they didn't have to share with anyone else, was suddenly very appealing. It reminded them of how happy they'd been living together for the first time in Harry and Jessie's flat over the Gallery.

By the end of August, the flat was ready. There was a real twinge of sadness as they walked round for the last time, every-thing fresh and bright, before the advertisement went into both the *Armagh Gazette* and *Guardian*. They were inundated by replies. It seemed that Armagh was still so short of housing that young couples were forced to live with in-laws. Anne and Adrian, one of several young Catholic couples who contacted them, both teachers at local primary schools, had been engaged for two years. As they put it so honestly when they viewed the flat one Friday evening, having to live with either family would probably have split them up.

There were indeed no cheques to bank at the end of August, but the rent of the flat, paid monthly in advance, did cover Thelma's salary and, to their great delight, Anne and Adrian asked them to come to their wedding party. '*The one with our friends, as opposed to the reception after our marriage,*' as Anne explained emphatically.

'Ach sure I've missed you these last weeks, Clare,' Charlie Running said when she arrived on his doorstep on the first Wednesday in September. 'I know you've been desperate busy, and I suppose you couldn't leave wee Bronagh to mind the shop, as the saying is, when June was on her holidays. I hear you've got Andrew all organized and the wee flat let.'

Clare followed Charlie into his front room and sat down in the space he'd made ready for her. She'd missed Charlie too. It was one thing writing letters to Robert and Louise and Marie-Claude in France, and phoning Jessie and Uncle Jack, and Mary and John in Norfolk, and a few other friends from schooldays, but Charlie was something quite different. He was not only a mine of information and a wise counsellor but also her only remaining link with Grandfather Scott and her life at the forge house.

'Now, Charlie, I did send you a wee note about Andrew's move, but how did you find out about the flat? It was only let last Friday,' she said, laughing.

'Ach well, I got regular bulletins about the whole process, the decorating and the way the two of you rearranged the place and made it look so homely. My nephew Ronnie was one of the decorators,' he admitted, grinning. 'He fancied the place himself, but decided it was a bit too near the Police Barracks. He has a wee habit of drinking one too many and jobs aren't that easy to find these days, are they?'

'I thought the O'Neill government had been doing quite well on job creation,' she said, surprised. 'I keep reading about new factories.'

'Oh yes, Clare, so you would,' he acknowledged. 'There's some good developments, sure enough, specially these synthetic fibres, Enkalon and what have you, but nobody is writing articles about the losses in the old textile industries, cotton and linen and hemstitching and suchlike. If you actually do the sums, as some of us are inclined to do, there's no net gain. Even more to the point the jobs aren't evenly spread through the Province. When have you read anything about new factories west of the Bann?'

Clare couldn't think of anything, but she assumed that was her fault. Sometimes there just weren't enough hours in the day to get as far as reading the newspapers. They'd given their fourteen inch television to the Wileys when they found they never had time to watch it. She might well have missed a report of something major.

'Absolutely nothing, Clare,' he said flatly, before she had time to reply. 'All the new development is east of the Bann. Antrim, Down and Armagh. A very one-sided picture you might say. However, I will not ride off on my hobby-horse or even mention the word *discrimination* until I've heard all your news,' he said, collecting himself. 'Now what about you and Andrew and the Grand Plan. Is this setting up on his own in Russell Street part of it? And what sort of a summer did you have at Drumsollen? Did the riots affect you, never mind the weather?' he prompted, settling himself comfortably in his battered armchair.

'Well, I can't say it was a good summer for Drumsollen,' she began honestly, 'but I can't judge whether it's a trend or what the business analysts call "a local blip". Bookings were well down, especially in July, and some regulars wrote and told me they were going to Spain or Italy.'

'Aye, I think that's the coming thing,' he said, nodding sharply. 'I've a wee niece works in a travel agents in Belfast. She says they were powerful busy with people wanting to get away for The Twelfth. I'm beginning to think there's people here wanting to see a bit of the world. We've been very turned in on ourselves here in Ulster, and then there's the small problem of those who would have us back in the Dark Ages if they could get away with it. Wee Jeannie told me that the guy from the Tourist Board who comes in to see them and check out their figures said some hotels and guest houses were closing for The Twelfth fortnight, for it wasn't worth their while staying open.'

'It certainly wasn't worth our while,' she admitted. 'But you can't know till afterwards, can you? Sometimes I wonder whether choosing what to do by sticking a pin in a list might equal all the thought, talk and discussion Andrew and I put in.'

'That's the sad thing about life,' Charlie agreed. 'You can't gain experience if you don't risk making mistakes, but if you make too many mistakes then you've not the wherewithal to capitalize on the experience you've gained. But don't forget you and Andrew have a gift many business people don't have.'

'What's that, Charlie?'

'You have hopes and dreams to be sure, but just as important, you have no illusions,' he said quietly. 'If something doesn't work out neither of you will go pretending that it *is* working out, nor that it only wants more money putting in to make it work, or more demand, or an upturn in the economy. I worked for years with companies who were within a week's wages from trading while insolvent, but would they listen? You only need one man or one woman in a position of power to put a company at risk. They cling on to what they *want to see happening* as if that would *make* it happen. You wouldn't do that, now would you?'

'No, Charlie, we wouldn't. We know what we'd like to happen, but it's touch and go at the moment. Andrew going it alone was making the best of a bad situation. It's only because Charles has moved to Belfast. We've no idea how he'll do on his own. He's as dependent on customers as Drumsollen is.'

'Has he bought any land yet?'

'No, not yet. He says there's no point having land till he can stock it and engage the help he needs. It would only be sitting idle. Better to let the money earn what interest it can.'

'Aye, I see his point. Though I suppose if you had extra money available to invest, buying up the bits of land would be a good way of starting. Have you them mapped out?'

'Oh yes,' she said smiling. 'All the fields he knew as a little boy, before the war came and the Richardson's money ran out and they had to sell off to the local farmers.'

'And he'll be hoping to buy it back, will he?' he asked, nodding to himself as he lit a cigarette.

The way he blew out smoke and avoided her eye told her that something was wrong. Charlie, normally the most open and direct of men, was hiding something and he wasn't doing a very good job of it.

'What are you not telling me, Charlie?'

He blew a smoke ring up to the tobacco-stained ceiling and sighed.

'You know that field that runs alongside your drive from the house down to the Loughgall Road?'

'Yes, of course. That's one of the fields used to belong to the house.'

'It was sold by Private Treaty last month to a man from Portadown. Do you know how much he gave for it?'

He named the figure and she gasped.

'But it's only fit for grazing, Charlie. Andrew says it's never been improved. It's certainly not best arable.'

'But it has frontage on the main road, Clare, like most of the Drumsollen land. And isn't there a shortage of houses around these parts? It doesn't matter to yer man if it's grazing or arable. Yer man's a builder.'

Eleven

When Andrew arrived home from work on the last Friday in September and saw the table by the window in Headquarters laid for supper, complete with a small arrangement of roses, he thought for a moment he'd been so preoccupied with his own affairs, he'd missed some important event. Then he reminded himself that Clare didn't play games like that. If there was a birthday or an anniversary coming, she'd simply ask him what he thought they might do, if anything. She was quite likely to say, *Look love, I know it's our anniversary, but how about we celebrate on the first available Friday? We're fully booked and we'll get no peace even to have a proper meal.*

'I thought we were going to the pictures,' he said, as he came to put his arms round her.

'So did I,' she said, laughing wryly. 'Do you really want to see the most horrifying monster ever to threaten the earth?'

'Can't say I do,' he replied, looking yet more puzzled. 'I thought it was a Jack Lemon comedy.'

'So did I, but that was *last* week and I only got to last week's newspaper yesterday.'

He laughed and peeled off his jacket, hung it over the back of his fireside chair and stretched out his long legs on the hearthrug.

'So what *are* we celebrating?' he asked, feeling suddenly quite glad they weren't going out after all.

'Oh, I've managed to think of the odd good thing,' she said promptly. 'Ask me later and you can decide if they're worth celebrating,' she said with a broad grin. 'But right now we need to have our meal, so we can be finished and tidied up before John comes to take charge of Headquarters, even if all he does is read the newspapers. If you want to go and change, I'll come down and bring up the tray,' she added, as he stood up. 'I *have* managed to cook our dinner for this evening, but I haven't been out of the house all day, lovely as it's been. I thought we might do an inspection of the Drumsollen estate before the light goes. It could have been taken over by Triffids for all I've seen of it this week.'

The evening was fine and still warm for this late in the year as they set off round the back of the house to the small remnant of what had once been the home paddock. Andrew's mother had kept her horse there, together with a small, shaggy pony, which he remembered because he'd thought him very large at the time.

Early in the year, Clare had been studying the flower catalogues, hoping to create a border of perennials alongside their driveway at the foot of the hill, when she'd discovered Andrew eyeing the pages of a wildflower catalogue with equal enthusiasm.

'I didn't think you could *buy* wildflower seed,' she said, surprised, as she picked up the one he had just put down. 'Some of these I've never even seen.'

'Those grow on chalk or downland, not right for this part of the world at all, but there are plenty of others that would be happy enough if one provided the right conditions. The soil in the old paddock was never cultivated, so it's pretty poor. Do very well for most of these,' he added, producing yet another catalogue. 'I'd thought of seeding a couple of patches and perhaps planting some buddleia against the garage walls over at the far end, to attract the butterflies,' he continued, his face brightening, the weary lines of his day's work dissolving completely.

'Don't think I've ever met a buddleia either,' she said slowly, surprised and delighted at how animated he had become.

'People call it the Butterfly Tree. Wonderful spikes of purple or mauve with tiny orange nectar guides. It'll grow almost anywhere that's dry,' he began. 'You'll even see it growing out of brick walls in railway stations. Euston, for one. There are sites in London that haven't been redeveloped still covered with buddleia and rosebay willowherb. Now that's one of my favourites,' he went on vigorously. 'It's tall and pink and seeds in the wind like dandelion. Fire weed, they called it after the war. It grew everywhere the bombs had dropped.'

It was the fire weed she thought of as they went through the space in the open-planked fence of the paddock and walked slowly along the grass path he'd left between his two lengths of seeded meadow, now a mass of tall, swaying grasses with points and patches of colour. There had been rosebay willowherb in the late summer and she'd watched the curved seed carriers float in the light winds, caressing other plants before coming to land. Some of the tall, pinkish stems were now part of an arrangement of dried flowers she'd made for one of the upstairs landings.

'Andrew, what's that one?' she asked, pointing to a vigorous yellow bloom.

'Corn poppy,' he replied, looking pleased. 'I've never actually seen one growing here in Ireland,' he confessed. 'But that's no reason not to encourage it. Especially as it's been disappearing over the other side of the Irish sea.'

'Why's that?'

'Because of the way farmers are using chemicals to spray margins instead of cutting them with a scythe or a sickle.'

'But why do that?' she asked. 'Aren't chemicals expensive?'

'Yes, they may be, but labour is *more* expensive. Hasn't Charlie told you the way the numbers of agricultural labourers have dropped since tractors became common?' he asked, as they paused and looked at a patch of purple vetch twining up the stems of nearby grasses. 'England is far more mechanized than Ulster. Hardly surprising with their pressure of population. When John Hamilton was here and I took him round the place, he was telling me about the grain harvesting in Norfolk. He says the way it's moved in the last ten years it reminds him of something you'd see on the prairies.'

'And that's not a good thing?'

'It might be all right on the prairies, though I'm not sure about that, long term,' he replied, frowning. 'Treating land as if it were an exploitable resource without looking at all the factors involved seems short-sighted to me. You dig out coal, or minerals, and you have a space, a hole in the ground. Something has gone for good, you *can* perhaps create a lake, or a rubbish dump, or a building site, but agricultural land and forest and bog and mountain is part of our landscape. You have to take care of it, replace what you take out, or you end up living in a desert.'

'Like *Silent Spring*?' she asked, remembering the book that had sat by his chair throughout the previous winter.

'Yes, you're right. I may not agree with every word Rachel Carson writes – she really does go right over the top at times – but she's right to sound the alarm. If we don't treat the land with respect we lose our birds and our animals, our flowers and our trees, and once they are gone, there's no replacing them, so we've destroyed a part of ourselves.'

Clare made no immediate reply, for she was thinking Andrew had just revealed a part of himself he'd never shown her so clearly before. That he'd wanted to farm she'd known since that magical summer at Caledon when he'd declared that if he had lots of money he'd spend it on buying cows. Now she grasped that his commitment to the land went far beyond the activity of farming and keeping livestock.

'I thought you said buddleia liked it dry,' she queried, as they surveyed the flourishing bushes.

'Yes, that's why I dumped all the broken concrete from the old septic tank here,' he explained. 'It doesn't matter if we get too much rain as long as it can drain away fast. They like mortar, so I reckoned broken concrete was the next best thing to get them to put down roots.'

'No butterflies yet,' she observed, as she peered at the small insects creeping in and out of the fading blooms.

He laughed as she pulled on the cardigan she'd thrown round her shoulders. 'It's too cool for butterflies this evening,' he explained. 'There might have been some this afternoon when the sun was reflecting off the brickwork behind, but we may not have had very many in the first place this summer. Most of the ones we get Ireland are migrants. If it's cool and wet, they don't make it, so there are only the native ones and there aren't many of those here in Ulster compared with England.'

'You do realize, don't you, that I'm seriously underinformed about butterflies and bees?' she said, as they walked slowly back to the front of the house and made for the steps leading to the summerhouse. 'I thought I knew a bit about garden birds and my robin does come to my hand now when I call him, but I think my ecological education has been seriously neglected.'

He laughed and threw an arm round her shoulder.

'Were it not for your superior knowledge of sums, my beloved, of adding up pounds and shillings and pence, I couldn't have afforded the seeds, never mind young shrubs from the nursery. You can do a lot with very little money if you have lots of time, but if you haven't got time, then you *do* need money. I've never been able to get the balance right.'

'Yet.'

'What?'

'Yet,' she repeated. 'I said you hadn't managed to get the balance right yet.'

'Which implies, of course, that I will eventually.'

'Yes, of course you will, my love. Things take time. I'm sure you didn't know all the things you've just told me about, last year or the year before. I've seen the books by your chair. Do you think I had accountancy skills when I came back from France? I was good at high-level finance, but keeping a budget going is a very different matter. I had to learn on the job.'

They stood together on the small terrace in front of the summer-house looking out over the well-wooded landscape of small fields and low hills as the shadows lengthened and the air cooled.

'I was always *supposed* to know things,' he said abruptly. 'But they were always things that weren't important to me, so I could never hold on to them. That's what really got me into trouble, especially with The Missus. I suppose I still think I'm never going to know what I need to know.'

'Come and sit down for a minute,' she said gently. 'It's always warmer inside,' she added, taking his hand.

'My love, I'm so sorry I had to tell you about the builder and the land round Drumsollen,' she began, looking him straight in the eye. 'We've always said we'd be honest with each other. It *is* a setback, but you mustn't think buying back Drumsollen's own land is the only way forward. There are other places, other opportunities. What's really important is holding on to what you really want. We do know what we want, we'll find a way. It may just take a bit longer than we'd hoped.'

To their great surprise and delight, there were *three* cars parked in front of the house when they came down from the summerhouse and they were just in time to help John with the welcome trays. Although he was well able to do the job by himself, he always hated keeping people waiting. As he put it cheerfully some time later, 'It's like what they say about buses. You stand there waiting, doing nothin'' and then three come along at once, and there's still only one of you!'

It was after eleven when they were at last free to go into the kitchen to make themselves tea and toast.

'Honey or jam?' Clare asked, as the toaster popped.

'Either. I'll still have to wash my hands afterwards. Unlike you,
I'm not very good at licking my fingers,' he declared, pouring them
large mugs of tea. 'By the way, my beloved, you've forgotten to tell
me what we're celebrating,' he said, as he buttered his toast.

'Mmmm,' she replied, already munching devotedly. 'Well, it's like
this. I had to spend the day deciding what to do about staff holidays
and winter closing, two *very* big decisions, and I *think* I've come up
with the perfect answer.'

'But the staff have had their holidays,' he protested mildly.

'These staff haven't,' she replied crisply. 'We haven't been away
since last October and Hector keeps ringing me up and asking me
what he has to do to get us to come down again.'

'Ah, so you've been doing a line with Hector, have you?' he
asked, looking at her severely.

'Yes. It's a pity he's not sixty years or so younger,' she said laughing,
'or you might have a point. But his calls *have* concentrated my mind.
If we just keep on working and working and trying to jump over
all the obstacles that keep being thrown up in front of us, we're
going to lose heart. We need to do something on the other side.
Like seeds and buddleias, only more so. So, I've *decided* we're going
to Fermanagh again. I *will* consult you about the date, but we will
not argue about going or not going. Right?'

'Fine by me, love, and I'm sure June and John will help out, but
what about the cost?'

'Well, I think I've solved that little problem and it's mainly thanks
to Robert,' she began. 'Do you remember when we started trading
in July 1960 and we had to scrape up every penny we could find
to produce a viable balance for the bank? I had some shares in a
French company and he wouldn't let me sell them.'

'Yes, it was something peculiar, like the Saint Etienne Municipal
Waterworks, wasn't it?'

'You're not far wrong,' she said smiling at his French pronunciation. 'He promised me the shares would go up and they have. Now
he *still* won't let me sell them because he says they're certain to go
up still further in the present climate. So that's a tiny bit of income
outside the company, we can have for our very own. It's not much,
I know, but I propose a *Comforts Fund*, like they had for the troops
in wartime. Small treats and perks. Though, of course, Fermanagh
is quite a big treat, given the extra wages and petrol.'

'What a splendid idea,' he said, polishing off the last of his toast and honey. 'Do you think I could have a pond for frogs?'

She sighed dramatically. 'Yes, I dare say you could, but don't you want to know about the other big decision?'

'Sorry,' he said, composing himself and doing his best to look suitably attentive.

Clare giggled and then began to talk quietly, the weariness of the long day showing up in her voice. 'I've been arguing with myself all day, as to whether or not we keep open over the winter. We would save a lot on heating and wages if we close, but what would June and Bronagh do? And John for that matter. Besides, our commercial travellers do turn up every month of the year. We can't let them down, can we?'

'But presumably staying open would actually cost money, if we didn't have enough bookings?

'Or alternative income.'

He nodded and yawned hugely. 'Of course, but where are you going to find that over the winter?'

'That's what I'm celebrating,' she said, standing up. 'I've thought of something to keep June and Bronagh and I employed that might make enough to cover our overheads. But as you're now half asleep, I shall tell you of my new Grand Plan tomorrow,' she said firmly, pulling him to his feet and pointing him in the direction of bed.

Saturday dawned fine and dry, the forecast good for several days. It was in fact to transform itself into the loveliest weekend of the whole autumn; the following weeks of October were rain-sodden and overcast. For three days in a row, the mornings were misty with heavy dew lying damply on the lawns and the first piles of swept-up leaves, while the afternoons were warm and sunny. So good was the weather, the three couples who had arrived without bookings on Friday night decided to stay on until Tuesday. A group of friends who met up from time to time, they liked the spaciousness and informality of Drumsollen and were delighted they had the big house all to themselves.

With June coming in for a short Saturday morning only, Clare and Andrew were kept busy, providing breakfasts and buffet meals in the evening, as well as keeping up with the routine jobs they expected to do every weekend. Clare's Grand Plan was still somewhere at the back of her mind when their guests departed on Tuesday morning, smiling and well-fed, vowing to return the following year.

'Ye've had a time to yourselves,' commented June, as she and Clare stood sorting laundry soon after the three cars had driven off. 'And eight o'clock breakfasts as well,' she went on with a wry smile, knowing how slow a starter Clare was.

'Andrew did most of it,' she confessed easily, as she loaded the first wash. 'I did get everything lined up the previous night under covers, so he only had to cook, but you know I can just about make a pot of coffee before about ten. It was his own fault too,' she added, laughing. 'He told them about Castledillon lake and the three men all wanted to go out early to bird-watch.'

'They made a brave hole in the scones and cake,' June went on, as she inspected her tins. 'I'll have to start with a wee spot of baking and leave the rooms for Bronagh this afternoon. Is that all right?'

'Yes, of course. We've two doubles and five singles ready and waiting and I doubt if we'll have more than one or two of our travellers this week. But we can't be caught without scones or cake, can we?'

'Definitely not,' June agreed.

'It might not matter in France, or in England or Wales,' Clare said thoughtfully, 'but I fancy here and in Scotland having the right thing in the tin is obligatory. I suppose it's a concrete sign of welcome.'

'Aye,' said June abstractedly, as she lined up her cake tins on the kitchen table.

Clare took the hint. June always made it perfectly obvious when she wished to be left alone. Bronagh had taken no more than her first week working with her to know when to disappear. She closed the kitchen door behind her, walked briskly along the corridor and upstairs to Headquarters.

She could hardly believe that another month had ended, financially at least, even if there was one more day left on the calendar, but the sooner the bills were paid and the accounts done the better. She wanted to be free to make her weekly visit to Charlie tomorrow afternoon, start pruning the roses, and go through her clothes, ready for their return visit to Fermanagh at the end of October.

At least the figures would look rather better today than if she'd been doing them at the end of last week. There *would* be a lodgement to go to the bank tomorrow. What was much more problematic was whether the results of Andrew's first full working month in his own practice would produce anything whatever to pay in at the same time.

One look at Andrew's face as he pushed the door of Headquarters fully open told Clare that something was dreadfully wrong, but she knew he wouldn't look so utterly distraught if it were just about money.

'Have you heard the news today?' he asked, as he parked his briefcase and dropped down into a fireside chair.

'No, I haven't,' she replied, coming over to sit opposite him. 'I went outside for half an hour and missed the one o'clock. What on earth has happened?'

'Acting on the orders of the Minister of Home Affairs, whom you met at Charles and Helen's summer party,' he began, 'a detachment of the Royal Ulster Constabulary attacked the headquarters of the Republican Party in Divis Street with pickaxes in order to remove a tricolour. The said flag was aimed at *provoking and insulting the loyalists of Belfast*, when as you know, and I know, there are no "loyalists" living in Divis Street or anywhere nearby.'

'Oh no, not more trouble.'

'When the news got out, two thousand Republican supporters blocked the roadway in front of the Headquarters and all traffic came to a standstill. They only had stones and empty bottles, but the police reinforcements arrived with Sten guns, rifles, revolvers, riot batons and shields,' he went on, shaking his head.

'I haven't finished,' he said, holding up his hand, as she jumped to her feet, about to come over to him and lay a hand on his shoulder. 'Paisley had already threatened he'd lead his supporters to Divis Street and take down the flag down himself unless the police acted. He'd organized a protest march, but when the police broke in and took the flag down, he cancelled it, but he did hold a meeting at the City Hall. Opened with prayer and Bible readings. Then he read a telegram from the Ulster Loyalist Association congratulating him *on his stand against the tricolour*. Then he let fly with his usual rant. You know the stuff. *No Pope Here* and *O'Neill must go.*'

He dropped his head in his hands and for a moment she thought he might be crying, but when he looked up, he was dry eyed, his face stiff and cold with anger.

'If that man is allowed to go on stirring up hate and confront-ation on this scale, I tell you, this place is finished,' he said flatly. 'There'll be no justice for anyone, no equality, no peace, no economic miracle and no place for us. What are we going to do, Clare? What *are* we going to do?'

They'd had bad times enough before this when Andrew had lost all confidence in the possibility of doing anything sensible or just in a corrupt society. From bitter experience she knew that it was no use trying to present a more positive view of the situation. It would only bring out yet more detail as to why that wouldn't work. As she came and put her arms round him, at that moment, she had not the slightest idea what she was going to do.

'Charlie agrees with you,' she said quietly, as the silence grew between them. 'He says we'll have to go.'

'Does he?' he said, looking at her for the first time. 'Why does he say that?'

'Because he believes O'Neill's plan is to *kill with kindness*,' she began steadily. 'He's banking on the hope that making things better economically will create jobs for the Catholics and they'll forget their discontents. He says it'll never work because it's only top dressing that doesn't change anything. If O'Neill were serious about change, the new university would be in Derry and *NOT* Coleraine and the new city would be west of the Bann, *NOT* a mere twenty-five miles from Belfast. Nor would it be called Craigavon, a name seriously insulting to Catholics.'

'Perhaps I ought to go and have tea with Charlie,' Andrew replied, with a small, bleak smile.

'My love, you mustn't think you're the only voice crying in the wilderness. There are so many good people who want things to be different. You don't see June and John looking sideways because Bronagh is Catholic, do you? Or Thelma changing her manner because Anne teaches in a Convent School and Adrian at St Malachi's Primary.'

He shook his head and pressed his lips together. 'My dear Clare, you'll always see the most positive side of things. I don't know where you get it from. It's a gift you have and I certainly don't have it. Perhaps a legal training knocks it out of you. Or perhaps it's that Roundhead rationalism Cambridge is famous for. Whatever the reason, I don't see much hope. That's your department.'

Perched on the side of his armchair, her back aching from the awkward angle needed to put her arm round him, she knew the only thing to do was to get them moving.

'Well, I *hope* our supper is nearly ready,' she said easily. 'Perhaps if we had something to eat and brought coffee back up here, we could put a match to the fire and see if that sheds any light on the problem. It has in the past. Worth a try?'

'Yes, of course it is. I'm sorry I'm in such a bad way. It's not fair on you,' he said getting to his feet.

'Who said life was fair?' she replied with a little laugh. 'Besides, I'll probably get my own back,' she went on, as she took his hand and coaxed him towards the door. 'It's usually six of one and half a dozen of the other, isn't it?'

Twelve

The first week of October 1964 was one that people in Northern Ireland would remember for a very long time. The streets of Belfast appeared nightly on television, the cameras angled on burning vehicles, flaring petrol bombs, angry crowds of stone-throwers and heavily armed police. It was not only the residents of the quiet, damp and peaceful Ulster countryside that could not believe their eyes. Millions around the world now watched what the media set before them. For the first time in its brief history, Ulster was international news.

Clare and Andrew viewed the rioting only once, slipping into the back of the small television room and standing behind their solitary guest, who sat glued to the set, newspaper and can of beer abandoned by his chair. Afterwards, they made coffee in silence, took it back to the fire in Headquarters before they felt steady enough to say a word. Unlike the night Andrew brought home the news of the assault upon the Republican Headquarters there was no distress between them. The intervening days had given them time to think through what was happening. Tonight they needed but a short time to reach their conclusions.

'We're not pretending it hasn't happened,' Clare said firmly. 'And we're not pretending it's not as bad news for us as for everyone else. But we're not going to depress ourselves by watching what goes on in one small area of a large city. We'll *travel hopefully*, as you say, until we see how things go. We won't give up unless we have to. Is it a deal?'

'It's a deal, pardner,' Andrew said, managing his Wild West accent well enough to make her smile.

They sat silent for a little, Clare thinking how comforting and friendly the flames were on such a miserable wet night. She tried to push out of mind the roaring flames of a burning bus, the crash of breaking glass, the faces distorted with anger, and the violence spilling all around the wet streets of a city where she had spent four years of her life.

'You still haven't told me about the latest Grand Plan,' Andrew said suddenly, looking up from the fire after he'd added small logs to encourage the cheerful blaze.

'Where was I when I left off?' she asked, gathering her straying thoughts, determined not to let herself be distracted again by images about which she could do nothing.

'Comforts Fund, out of Robert's Waterworks shares,' he said quickly. 'I've got details of pond liners for you in my briefcase.'

She laughed heartily and shook her head.

'My dear Andrew, you have few vices, and greed is not one of them, but you only ever shift yourself to get money out of me, or rather, out of our budget, when it's birds, bees, wildflowers, or some poor wee creature threatened with extinction. Did you know that?'

'Sorry,' he said, looking sheepish. 'You *do* think it's a good idea, don't you?'

'I think it's a splendid idea,' she said reassuringly. 'You could have a whole lake in the rest of the paddock if I could find the money. But I've got to find it first. That's all part of the Grand Plan, of course.'

He sat back and listened attentively while she told him where she'd got to in her detailed planning.

'So you really do think we can stay open over the winter and not have to dip into the money we made last year?'

'No, I can't say that,' she said, shaking her head slowly. 'That's crystal ball stuff. But I think it's worth a try. Keeping a good team like June and Bronagh together is worth a lot of effort. I'd be hard pushed to find a pair as good if bookings *do* pick up next year. Just think how June would feel if I told her we didn't need her till March. She'd have to find something else and she might not be able to come back.'

'I've done some research, of course,' she continued. 'Armagh is not well equipped for quick lunches for people working in offices. A lunch box has to be easier and probably cheaper if it's delivered to your desk. But having found that out and done some costings doesn't tell me whether there will be any demand or not. That's pure guesswork.'

'Thelma brings a sandwich most days,' he said, thoughtfully. 'But sometimes she asks if it's all right to pop out and she always asks do I want anything for lunch.'

'Thelma may not have time some mornings,' she began easily. 'She has her bus to catch from Markethill. That's one of the unknown factors, isn't it? Will people pay to save time in the morning? There certainly must be wives and mothers who'd be very pleased if they didn't have to make a lunch, or several lunches,' she said laughing, as she remember her own early attempts to do everything that was needed in their first months of coping with guests.

'What about delivery? You'll need the car.'

'No,' she said firmly. 'Our car might be available on the odd day, but that's no real help. It has to be regular and besides you *have* to have it for visiting clients and going to court. I haven't solved that problem yet but I'm working on it.'

'What made you think of birthday parties?' he asked, going back to the other half of the Grand Plan she'd just outlined.

'Oh, that was Jessie,' she said wryly. 'Fiona wants to have all her little friends from nursery school and Jessie is dreading it. You know she's a good cook, but she doesn't like baking. She says she can't stand making small stuff like iced buns and she loathes clearing up the mess when children come to play. She says she'll be buying everything and hiring an entertainer, but she's still dreading it. Apparently a lot of women she knows feel just the same. But that's posh Belfast. I don't know if there are any in Armagh.'

'But you do know who could make cakes and buns in her sleep,' Andrew added with a smile.

'June will love it, providing Bronagh and I do the sandwiches. That's what June hates, always has done, ever since I was her Saturday girl, drafted in when she had *to feed the five thousand*, as she called it. Isn't it funny the things we so dislike. No logic in them at all.'

'Clare dear, I don't think I'm up to philosophical speculations tonight,' he replied yawning. 'Have I now been fully informed about all the proliferations of the Grand Plan?'

'No, actually,' she replied, grinning. 'I've spelt out all the nuts and bolts, but I've kept the best bit till last.'

'Well, come on. Amaze me,' he said, eyeing her cautiously.

'Well,' she began, giggling. 'We are *not* closing over the winter, but we *are* closing for two weeks next July, the so-called Twelfth fortnight. Next year it occupies weeks one and two on the calendar.'

'But why then?' he asked, looking bewildered.

'Market research,' she said, teasing him. 'I looked up the last four years and even the best of them has had far fewer bookings in July. I was still thinking about it when a very handsome young man from the Tourist Board came to ask if I would contribute our booking figures to their databank. He gave me rather a lot of useful information while he was having his coffee. Apparently, more and more people are going abroad in summer and the Twelfth fortnight is the peak time. So we'd do well to close and let the staff have their holiday then.'

'Mmm . . . good idea,' he said yawning again.

'Aren't you going to ask me where *these* staff are going for theirs?'

'Er . . . where?'

'Norfolk,' she said triumphantly. 'To visit your nice Aunt Joan who keeps asking us, and to see Mary and John. Mary's already booked some time off for when we come. Isn't that lovely of her?'

'How splendid,' he said, waking up considerably. 'Aunt Joan will be chuffed and it'll be lovely to see *our* Hamiltons again. *AND* we're off to Fermanagh at the end of the month,' he went on. 'What a leisured life we do lead,' he declared, grinning at her, as he put the fireguard in place.

'Now, at last, I can show you my favourite piece of Norfolk. I thought it was never going to happen. I promise you it really is *not* flat.'

*　　*　　*

Clare's twenty-eighth birthday fell on Thursday the eighth of October, but the week had been so overshadowed by public events, they decided to wait until Friday the sixteenth and celebrate by having a very nice dinner in a corner of their own dining-room, with a bottle of wine from Robert's regular birthday case and John on guard in Headquarters. In the event, that same Friday would also be the first occasion when the house would be the venue for a children's party, for it turned out there were mothers in and around Armagh just as reluctant as Jessie to put on the necessary show and affluent enough to pay someone else to do it.

Like with all first times, Clare was apprehensive. In the course of the preceding week she asked Andrew on at least three separate occasions what their liability was should a child fall downstairs or otherwise injure itself. Each time he explained patiently that you were not 'in loco parentis', technically, if the said 'parentis' had brought the said children of their own free will to the said 'loco' and had signed the usual disclaimer. Nevertheless, she still felt anxious as she stepped into the kitchen mid-morning after clearing her desk. She donned her apron, saw that June was well ahead and preparing to ice the birthday cake, while Bronagh was working methodically in the sandwich factory she'd set up at one end of the kitchen table.

Clare joined her and was halfway through her first sliced loaf when she remembered the aunt with whom she'd once made sandwiches for a whole Lodge of Orangemen, an awkward-looking woman who said little but had demonstrated a very effective way to make sandwiches. Clare was miles away, thinking of that first dance on the bare boards of Cloghan Orange Hall in the arms of her Uncle Jack, when the phone rang. June's hands were covered with icing sugar and Bronagh had just taken trimmed crusts outside to the bird-table, so there was nothing for it but to pick it up.

'Hello, Drumsollen Guest House, Clare speaking. Can I help you?'

There was silence on the line and then a cough. 'I should like to speak to Mrs Richardson, please.'

There was something familiar about the voice, but Clare couldn't place it. All their advertising said: *Friendly family run guest house. Ring Clare or Andrew.* No one ever called her Mrs Richardson, not even the Bank Manager.

She looked at the large black handset and observed some sticky fingerprints on the mouthpiece, but no further sound came to help her.

'This *is* Clare Richardson speaking,' she said clearly. She waited as the silence continued. Then, suddenly, with a stomach-turning wrench, she placed the voice. 'Russell, is that you? Is His Lordship unwell?'

'Not exactly, madam,' Russell replied, his voice sounding perfectly normal. 'I fear I have to tell you His Lordship is no longer with us.'

Tears sprang to Clare's eyes as she picked up a strange muffled sound on the other end of the line. Oh, the poor man, she thought. Goodness knows how many years Russell and Hector had been together.

'Russell, I am so terribly sorry, so terribly sorry. Can you tell me what happened? Was it a heart attack? I spoke to him a few days ago and he was in *such* good spirits,' she went on, the tears trickling unnoticed down her cheeks.

'His Lordship has been going down to the lake each morning,' he began. 'You may recall that he has an interest in the arrival of the geese.'

'Yes, of course.'

'Mrs Watkins and I became concerned when he did not return at his accustomed hour, so I went down to the lake myself,' he continued, in his usual measured tones. 'He was sitting there with his binoculars beside him, but he had passed away.'

Clare could not speak, but she was grateful for the clean hand-kerchief June pushed into her free hand before leaving her. She blew her nose as quietly as possible.

'Russell, you must tell Andrew and me if there is anything we can do to help you and Mrs Watkins. We shall, of course, come down for the funeral. Perhaps I could ring you back later this morning when I've spoken to my husband,' she said, knowing that the aching sob in her throat could not be held back a moment longer.

'Thank you, madam, that would be most kind,' he said, and rang off.

Clare dropped the receiver into its cradle, sat down at the table and laid her head on her hands among the abandoned remnants of the sandwich she'd been making. She cried as if her heart would break. She was still weeping when June peeped round the door and saw her.

June had never seen Clare so distraught. Nothing seemed to help her, though she drank the tea Bronagh made for her and nodded when asked if she could drink another cup. Finally, June suggested that she have 'a wee lie down' and more or less marched her along the corridor to the bedroom.

Clare lay there weeping silently, seeing so sharply in her mind's eye the tiny, emaciated figure so full of life. She'd told Andrew once that hugging Hector was like embracing a skeleton with clothes on. He'd teased her about their embraces and said he had not had that pleasure.

'No more hugs. No more Hector. Gone. Gone forever.'

She felt as if a light had gone out, taking with it some magic power she had been given without knowing she had it. How would she survive in a world with no Hector, with no one apart from Andrew who would let her say anything she wanted to say? She lay and wept and could not stop.

'Clare, Clare darling, don't cry. I'm here,' Andrew announced, crossing the bedroom in two strides. He sat sideways on the bed and tried to coax her into his arms. 'What is it, love? What's making you cry so? It's sad and it is a shock, but Hector was a very old man.'

'I don't know, Andrew, I just don't know. I shouldn't be so upset, I really shouldn't. I'm just being silly,' she gasped, the words rushing out between her sobs. 'And why have you come home? Have you forgotten something?'

'I came because you're so upset,' he said, as she struggled to sit up. 'June phoned me. I knew it had to be bad if June was willing to pick up the phone.'

She swallowed hard and searched for the handkerchief June had given her. She couldn't find it, took the one he offered her, wiped her face and blew her nose again.

'I don't know what's wrong with me, Andrew,' she said, making an effort to stop crying. 'I was so looking forward to going down next week. Looking forward to seeing him and asking all the questions I didn't ask last time. I was going to wear that lovely ring he gave me and take him some gloves to match the scarf I sent him for birdwatching. I only had him for a little while and now he's gone. I know I have you and I'm so lucky to have you, but for a little while there was Hector as well.' She buried her head in his shoulder and just managed to get out, 'The people I love are always taken away.'

Faint though they were, Andrew heard the muffled words. Suddenly, what came back to him was the day he'd been told that both his parents were dead. He had not shed a tear that day or in the days that followed. Not then. Then he was told to be *a brave boy*. Boys didn't cry in his world, did they? It was only years later, safe in Clare's arms, the dam gave way and he had cried like the child he had once been.

He stroked her hair and wondered what to say. Loving someone didn't make it any easier to find the words for a moment like this. Perhaps, in fact, it made it harder. He'd learnt how to say quite difficult and personal things to clients whom he barely knew, but someone you truly loved mattered so much, it made you nervous.

'Russell said he was sitting by the lake with his binoculars, but when he leant over him, he knew he was gone,' she said, speaking clearly for the first time.

'Like when Jamsey found your grandfather slipped down beside the anvil.'

She stared at him as if he had said something quite extraordinary.

'You're right, of course. Granda. Much as I loved dear Hector and always will, his going shouldn't make me feel it's the end of the world, but it *was* the end of my world when Granda died. That's how I was feeling, my love, till you came home. The end of my world,' she said, clutching him tightly. 'But it's easier to bear now I can see it,' she went on, drying her face. 'Oh dear,' she added, looking down with a small laugh, 'I've got Lancôme foundation all over your nice clean hanky. I hope you've got some more in the drawer. I can't remember when I last did any ironing for us.'

'I'll borrow some of yours if I haven't,' he said cheerfully. 'Just imagine what floral handkerchiefs would do to my practice.'

She giggled and stood up, caught sight of her face in the dressing-table mirror and laughed out loud.

'Looks like I'd better cleanse and start again,' she declared. 'Definitely beyond repair.'

'But *you* seem better,' he said gently.

'I'm all right now,' she replied steadily. 'As good as new, or nearly,' she added, kissing him. 'Can you stay and have some lunch?'

'Not if you can spare me. I've three appointments lined up for this afternoon and Thelma will cancel them if I don't ring her now or get back to the office before one.'

'Three appointments, Andrew?' she said, looking surprised. 'Is there something you have *not* been telling me?'

'Birthday surprise,' he said, brushing a smear of make-up from the lapel of his dark suit. 'Tell you tonight. Anything you'd like me to bring home with me?'

'Just you, please. But I'd like if you'd ring Russell about the funeral. I said I would, but I think he'd manage better with a man. He had a very bad moment with me.'

'Right, I'll just say a word to June as I go,' he said quickly, as he took a clean handkerchief from his top drawer.

'So your wife does occasionally get as far as ironing your handkerchiefs,' she said, grinning. 'Tell June and Bronagh I'll be about fifteen minutes. I need to change as well. Trousers, I think, for eight year olds?'

'Absolutely,' he agreed, putting his arms round her. 'Good luck with this afternoon.'

The birthday party was a great success. A roaring success, as June said afterwards, not well pleased that the young gentleman whose birthday it was chose to greet his guests by pretending he was a lion about to eat them.

When it was clear his mother didn't have the slightest idea of what to do with him, Bronagh took over. She gathered all the children round her and asked if anyone thought they could roar more loudly. After a short, sharp burst of concentrated roaring, she held up her hand for silence and then asked if anyone could whisper more softly than she could.

Clare watched fascinated as Bronagh manipulated the ten little boys as competently as the Pied Piper charmed the children of Hamelin. She was a joy to watch. By dropping her voice she managed to get their total attention till all thought of roaring had disappeared.

'Bronagh, you were marvellous,' Clare said, as they stood at the kitchen table after the roaring lion had gone off clutching a red balloon.

'I have a *lot* of experience,' Bronagh responded lightly, as Clare packed a box of goodies for her to take home. 'There are ten in my family and I'm the eldest. It came in handy when I got the job in the nursery.'

Clare paused, hesitated, and then decided to take the plunge.

'Bronagh dear, forgive me asking, but why did you give up your morning job at the nursery? You're so good with children. I'm sure they were able to pay you more than we can and you'd have had holidays with pay as well.'

'No such luck, Clare,' she said evenly. 'That's why it was mornings only. I was only part-time, so I got paid by the hour on a weekly basis. I was grateful enough for that, but then the head decided it was time to make certain staffing changes,' she continued, a strange, uneasy look flickering in her lovely dark eyes.

'What sort of staff changes?' Clare asked, already half aware of what the answer was likely to be.

'No Catholics,' Bronagh replied, her tone quite neutral.

'Bronagh! I can't *believe* it . . . except that I can . . . but I still can't get my *imagination* round the ridiculousness of it. I suppose if you'd been a Buddhist or a Muslim, that would have been fine.'

Bronagh laughed. 'My father was a Protestant, but he beat my mother up. She thought all Protestants were like him, so she insisted on bringing us up *good* Catholics . . . or a not-very-good Catholic in my case.'

'And she put up with that for ten children?'

'No. He left after three but she could never say *No* to a man. There was usually a boyfriend or an uncle, God rest her soul,' she said, crossing herself.

'She's dead, Bronagh? She couldn't have been very old.'

'She died seven years ago. She was only forty and I'm twenty-four. I had a child too when I was fifteen, just like she did. But he died at birth, which probably saved me from the life of a penitent in a laundry somewhere or other.'

Clare sat down abruptly as Bronagh placed the box of cake and buns in a carrier bag.

'How many still at home?'

'Only the four youngest,' she replied easily. 'And I've a married sister that helps me out with clothes from her ones and the odd bit of money. It's a bit of a squeeze with only two wee bedrooms, but it's better than it was. If Brendan could find a proper job, we'd manage fine.'

'What age is Brendan?'

'Seventeen last week, but he looks older. He's one of the brainy ones, he and Anne-Marie. She's at the Convent. She got a scholarship at the Eleven Plus. Brendan got a County Scholarship to Queens last August but he knows we can't keep going if he isn't earning. He says he can study in the evenings and do a degree when he's older.'

'Bus or bicycle, Bronagh?' Clare asked as they walked outside together.

'Bus, today. Brendan has the bicycle. He's doing a job for a man that lives off the Cathedral Road. *Back of beyond*, he says, no buses within miles.'

'I'm sorry Andrew's not back. If he was, I'd run you home.'

'That's *very* kind of you, Clare, but I'm well used to walking. The stop down on the road is very handy,' she said cheerfully, smiling her lovely smile.

'Can Brendan drive?'

'Oh dear yes. Been driving for years, anywhere quiet where he'd not get caught without a licence. He's a good driver. Anything mechanical just comes natural to him. I don't think I'd be any good at it at all,' she confessed, laughing, as they came round the corner of the house together.

'I hope you have a good weekend, Clare,' Bronagh said gently, as they paused by the front steps. 'I'm glad you're feeling better. It was very sad about the old gentleman, but he was a good age, as they say.'

Clare nodded. 'Thank you for all you did today, Bronagh, especially with the children. I'll see you Monday afternoon. Don't work too hard yourself.'

They parted and Bronagh walked down the long drive a small smile on her face. This was the easy part. The bus would come and she could sit for the time it took to reach the stop in English Street. Then there was the long climb up Dawson Street, on up past the hospital and down by the Gasworks into Callan Street, a street where the houses had been condemned for some years now. No action had yet been taken and none seemed likely at the present rate of going.

Thirteen

'And which of these has Madam booked for her birthday dinner this evening?' John Wiley asked with a large smile, as he and Andrew replaced the tables a little after seven o'clock.

'I have no idea, John,' Andrew replied, his sleeves rolled up, his jacket and tie abandoned. 'All I know is that the controlled riot went well, the mother was delighted, there's a cheque in the cash box and she says she has some other friends who'd be only too glad of the same arrangement.'

'It was a great idea,' John said, as they manoeuvred another table back into position. 'She's full of ideas. I don't know where she gets it from. It wasn't her grandfather, that's for sure. God rest his soul, he was the decentest man alive, but he had no imagination,' he declared, pausing to catch his breath. 'It was one of the Robinsons asked him to make a field gate,' he went on. 'He drew him a wee picture on a scrap of paper and that was what started him on the gates when the work with horses and machinery began to fall away. Great he was at it too, but he'd never have thought of it himself.'

'I only met him twice,' Andrew said regretfully, as they worked their way round the room. 'Clare took me to meet him one evening the summer before she went up to Queens and he reminded me I'd ridden over to the forge on my cousin's chestnut the previous year. We'd only spoken for a few minutes, but he remembered the chestnut all right. Of course, I'd gone over hoping to see Clare, but she was wasn't at home, more's the pity.'

'Well, she's at home tonight all right,' said John beaming, as she appeared, wearing a plain, dark skirt, an open-necked, cream silk blouse and a small scarf pinned at the neck with a gold brooch. 'You're lookin' great, Clare. I heard it was trousers this afternoon.'

'It was, John, it was. And dusty it was too, down on this carpet. You'd have thought it had never seen a vacuum cleaner. I was rather in need of a bath afterwards!'

'Well now, the pair of you, enjoy your meal. Unless six cars turn up all at once, I guarantee I'll not be disturbin' you,' he promised, leaving them laughing in the midst of the empty room.

Andrew looked around him critically. 'Not many dining tonight,' he announced. 'I was surprised when I managed to get a booking. Apparently the place has quite a good reputation, but they did say Friday night was often quiet,' he continued solemnly, as he rolled his shirt sleeves down. 'Do you want me to put my tie back on?'

She laughed and put her arms round him.

'No, I'll take you as you are. That's one advantage of having our own private restaurant. How about the table by the window? Not much light about, but you can view the site of your lake. Sorry, I mean pond.'

They stood in the bay window looking out across the remnant of home paddock to one of the former Drumsollen fields where their neighbour's cattle were grazing peacefully. The day had been chill and sodden, the kind of day when wet leaves cling to pavements and the branches of trees are black with moisture. But even as they gazed the flourishing grasses bent gently in a small breeze. The sky brightened and began to clear from the west. Minutes later, flickers of sunlight reflected off the wet roof of the garage and picked up the splashes of colour amongst the swaying seed heads in the wild flower meadow.

'My goodness, what a lovely surprise,' Clare said. 'If we hurry up and fetch supper, we'll be able to have it in daylight. It looks as if we may even get sunshine.'

June had cooked dinner for them while Clare and Bronagh were providing the birthday entertainment. By the time ten hungry little boys crowded into the kitchen, their eyes wide as they viewed the plates of sandwiches and cakes laid out on the big table, a roast chicken with all the trimmings was safely wrapped in foil and parked in the low oven of the Aga.

'Eat as much as you want,' June instructed, as she was leaving, 'So long as you leave one breast and one leg to go with the ham in the fridge. You might need that for a buffet meal if anyone comes.'

The chicken was splendid, moist and succulent, and they were both very hungry, but they reckoned they would need at least

Jessie and Harry, or Mary and John, were they to reduce the leftovers from the large bird to a mere breast and leg. They toasted Robert, the giver of the wine, and they toasted those dear friends whose birthday cards had decorated the mirror of her dressing table for the last week. It was a particularly good bottle of wine, a Puligny-Montrachet, and as Andrew pointed out, when he refilled her glass, there was no one to tell them to save some for tomorrow.

When Andrew brought the cheeseboard from the sideboard they refilled their glasses yet again.

'My goodness,' he said, 'French cheeses in Armagh?'

'Oh yes. You can get them all right. Just expensive,' she said, as she opened the biscuits-for-cheese assortment and set the tin on the table between them.

'Is there dessert?' he asked, as he chose crackers. 'I'm not sure I'll have room,' he admitted, as he addressed the Brie.

'*Tarte aux abricots*,' she said, eyeing him.

'Oh well,' he sighed. 'A short rest and a couple of circuits of the dining-room will facilitate, if not entirely renew, my appetite. You know it's one of my favourites.'

'Even more to the point, June does. But she never let's on. She just suggests it and I say *yes*.'

He laughed and thought how happy she looked. And how elegant in her simple blouse and skirt. She always said that Marie-Claude had taught her to dress like a Frenchwoman, but he reckoned she'd been a star pupil. Hard to believe now how she'd looked when he'd found her weeping her heart out this morning.

'Shall I turn on some of the lamps?' he asked. 'Or do you prefer a romantic gloom?'

'Why do you think a gloom is supposed to be romantic?' she asked, as he peered at the cheese in the dim light.

'Well, one answer is that *a gloom*, as you call it, softens the edges of what you are perceiving,' he answered soberly. 'In the absence of clear definition one could, if one were so inclined, create something different from what is actually there,' he ended, with that deliberate touch of lawyer's pomposity which always made her laugh.

'In other words, if you don't look too closely you can see what you like. And if you don't listen too carefully you can hear what you like.'

'And if you have no intention of doing anything other than what you are *currently* doing, you can save yourself the trouble of even pretending to look or listen. You just *do your own thing in dedicated ignorance*, as one of my teachers was fond of saying.'

'*There's a lot of it about, isn't there?*' she replied crisply. 'That's what Charlie would say.'

'We're being very sober tonight given how splendid this wine is,' Andrew said as he shared the last of the bottle carefully to avoid the lees.

'I don't think I could manage frivolity tonight,' she said easily. 'And not just because of dear Hector. It's more a sense that tonight is one of those nights we will remember. A marker, perhaps, so that we will look back and say: *Do you remember my twenty-eighth birthday at Drumsollen with June's chicken and apricot tart and Robert's delectable white Bordeaux . . .?* But perhaps I'm just being imaginative, which is a polite way of saying I'm being fanciful.'

'No, I don't think you're being fanciful,' he said firmly. 'I think tonight is a double celebration. It is your birthday, and we are setting out again. We said last week we wouldn't give up hope when things looked so bad, and already we've made a start.'

'Birthday parties and sandwich lunches,' she said dubiously.

'You are sometimes very literal, my dearest. What I meant was that we've had some very big disappointments this year. Together and separately. But we haven't let them overwhelm us. I've think I've managed a bit of progress too. The only reason I haven't told you is that, like your children's party, it's only come together today. Something's happened that just might be a start for me as well.'

'Oh Andrew, that *would* be a really lovely birthday present,' she cried. 'Do you want to tell me this minute, or shall we make coffee, take John a cup and bring ours back here? The walk would do us good,' she said, laughing happily.

The light had gone by the time they'd taken John coffee and a piece of tart, shared a few friendly words and moved back to the dining-room. It was not a room Clare had ever liked, its decoration over-formal, the heavy, gold-framed portraits sombre and oppressive, except for Archbishop Ussher of Armagh, who stared down grimly enough from his superior position, but looked more cheerful than the rest by virtue of his bright red robes.

'What do you know about Legal Aid?' Andrew asked, when he drew the heavy curtains and sat down again, their table now in a pool of lamplight.

'Not a thing,' she admitted honestly, as she poured coffee. 'Unless you mean Thelma.'

'Legal Aide. Not bad. Not bad,' he said, grinning broadly. 'It is, in fact, a statutory right. People who are poor and haven't the resources to engage a solicitor, or go to court, now have the right to Legal Aid, paid for by the Government in order to redress their legitimate grievances and obtain justice,' he said formally. 'The legislation has only recently been put in place. It has not been made widely known and has certainly not been advertised as it should have been on this side of the Irish Sea.'

'Why is that?'

'Just think for a minute. Who are the most deprived people in Ulster, with the highest percentage of unemployment, living in the most overcrowded conditions?'

'Well, there's plenty of poverty amongst the Protestant working-class, but there's a great deal more among Catholics,' she said, thinking of Bronagh.

'Correct. You may not remember this, but back in January there was a lot of publicity when a young Protestant woman got a Council house. She was single and there were families of six or seven who'd been on the waiting list for years. Catholic, of course. She got the house, because she happened to be the secretary to one of the ward Councillors.'

'Yes, I do remember now,' she nodded. 'Charlie told me a group in Dungannon were trying to do something about it for the sake of others.'

'Yes, they have. And they've made progress. Someone must have briefed them on Legal Aid. I had three clients today with similar problems and they actually knew about it,' he said, looking pleased. 'I advertised earlier this month. More or less the same way as Charles and I have always done. I'd changed the name, of course, but when I rewrote the advertisement I decided to offer free initial consult-ations for a limited period. It's a routine way of drumming up new business, or so I hoped. The surprise was, not so much that people came for a free consultation, but when they came, the first thing they asked was whether I would take on Legal Aid work or not?'

'But why wouldn't you?' she asked, puzzled.

'Because it certainly won't be as well paid as work covered by scale fees,' he replied promptly. 'There's probably a mass of paperwork as well,' he added wryly. 'But it means I can do something useful, even if it doesn't bring in much money.'

'Oh Andrew, that *is* good news. You've always said helping someone who'd had a raw deal was the one thing that compensated a bit for not being able to farm.'

'Yes,' he said, agreeing vigorously. 'I can't imagine you want to spend your life making sandwiches, or running birthday parties, but if there's *some* satisfaction on the way, we can give it a go, can't we? What I was really bothered about was not even *being able* to get work, boring or otherwise. Like Drumsollen not having enough bookings. But this does gives us both another start, don't you think?'

'It does, love. It does indeed. We said we wouldn't give up, and we won't, not till we've given the *New Grand Plan* a fair chance.'

'And there's more,' he said, pausing to polish off the remains of his dessert. 'Like you, I've kept the best bit for last. Charles rang me again yesterday. He's got a stack of appeals against compulsory purchases for the next bit of the motorway. Not his thing at all, especially now he's in Belfast. All the disputes are in the Lurgan and Portadown area. He's recommended me to his clients as *having expertise in land*,' he explained, raising his eyebrows. 'His clients insist the land involved is all *prime agricultural land*, which I very much doubt. It's more likely they're stout farmers hoping to make a killing by holding the relevant Government Department to ransom, but there's quite a lot of work in doing the surveys and submitting the appeals. It will be scale fees and it will mean Wellington boots,' he said, clearly delighted by the prospect.

It was midnight before they went to bed, having sat with the embers of John's fire in Headquarters, long after he'd gone home. As Clare admitted, it might be bad for the bank balance, but not having guests in residence did make for a wonderful Friday night and Saturday morning.

'So what's on the menu, Boss?' Andrew asked as they finished breakfast somewhat later than usual.

'Lots and lots of jobs, I'm afraid,' she said wearily. 'But we did have a lovely birthday party, didn't we?'

'Yes, it was great,' he agreed, pushing back his chair. 'And now it's probably shopping, defrosting the fridge, clearing out the fire, bringing in logs . . .'

She was about to say 'For a start,' when the strident ring of the phone blocked out all other sound and reminded her painfully of the previous morning.

'Andrew, would you take it, please,' she said loudly. 'It might just be Russell ringing back.'

'Drumsollen Guest House, Andrew speaking. Can I help you?'

Clare listened, but couldn't gather much from Andrew's nods and minimal responses. By the time he put the phone down, all she had established was that it was indeed Russell. He had opened Hector's will as Hector himself had long ago instructed. Beyond that, all Andrew had actually said was to assure him he would be only too glad to help, should either he or Mrs Watkins have any legal difficulty whatever with the provisions Lord Rothwell had made for them.

'Poor chap,' he said, putting down the phone. 'But he is steadier this morning. He's been with him fifty years! Do you want to know now, or later?'

'Now, please. I'm thoroughly curious. It was a long call and you said almost nothing.'

'All part of the job,' he said, his face immobile, his tone preoccupied. He took a shopping list pad from the drawer in the kitchen table. 'I'll need to make some notes as we go, in case I forget anything.'

Clare listened in silence as Andrew explained that at Hector's request, there was to be no funeral. He had long ago made arrangements with the gravedigger at the local church. He'd provided him with a map of where the grave's location was to be and details of the whereabouts of his coffin, stored in one of the outbuildings. He'd left some letters for various friends and the few remaining members of his family he had not managed to outlive. The new Lord Rothwell would be arriving shortly from Australia. Mrs Watkins would remain, if required, but Russell would not.

'There's only one Lord Rothwell in Russell's life,' said Clare sadly, as Andrew paused and scribbled on the narrow pad. 'He could never call anyone else Lord Rothwell.'

'It looks like the executors have everything in hand already,' he went on. 'They've told Russell to expect one of their staff from London on Monday to provide information for Probate. I'll do the decent thing and offer to help if he runs into difficulties. There was that complicated business years ago, when I went down and sorted out boundaries,' he went on abstractedly. 'So I do know a fair amount about the estate.'

He broke off, looking anxious. 'I've forgotten something . . . Oh yes,' he said, relief obvious in his voice. 'There's a small parcel addressed to you. He gave it to Russell to post on Thursday evening, but Russell hasn't managed to get to the Post Office. It needed to be registered, so he's sending it on Monday. That's about it. My synopsis.'

She nodded and decided to ask the question that had been shaping in her mind. 'Do you know where Hector is to be buried?'

'Yes, I do,' he said, nodding briefly. 'In fact it's the spot where he died. On the bank below the willow, overlooking the lake.'

'Oh dear,' she said, overcome with sadness and unable for the moment to say anything else. 'Do you remember his friend Galbraith?' she asked after a pause.

Andrew shook his head and looked puzzled.

She took a deep breath and began calmly enough. 'He asked to be buried overlooking the lake in Kenya where he and Hector watched flamingos together, after the Boer War.' She stopped, swallowed the lump in her throat and managed to continue quite steadily. 'They must have been such good friends for Hector to do exactly the same thing all these years later,' she added, not bothering to conceal the tears she wiped away with the back of her hand.

The weekend jobs proceeded steadily despite miserable drizzle and the dim light in the basement kitchen. While Andrew did a big shop at the Cash and Carry in Portadown, she washed up their supper dishes and worked her way down the routine chores. By the time he arrived back with multiple packs of cornflakes, washing powder and teabags, she was ironing his shirts and her blouses.

'I think we *should* have a holiday,' he said firmly, looking over his shoulder, as he put away reserve supplies on the highest shelves.

'You mean instead of Fermanagh?'

'Yes, I do. It's all set up with June and John and Bronagh, so why don't we make use of it? It's a year since we were last away and it's still a long time to next July,' he said, opening one corner of the giant pack of teabags and refilling the tea caddy.

'Where shall we go?' she asked flatly, her back now aching with a familiar pain.

'Why not Ballintoy? You know we only have to ask,' he said persuasively.

That was certainly true. Since Harry had bought the apartment in the new development overlooking the bay, they'd had a standing invitation to go whenever they could. All they'd managed so far was an overnight visit, just to please Harry and see the place.

Clare had loved the view from the tiny balcony, but disliked the apartment itself. It was very comfortable and convenient, the furniture and fittings an integral part of the design, but she much preferred the old fisherman's cottage Jessie and Harry had once had. Now derelict on the shore, they'd had their first ever holiday there, the happiest of weeks, despite a complete lack of facilities, the only running water the stream that ran past the cottage and down to the beach.

'Not perhaps a good idea if it's going on raining like this,' she said, without enthusiasm.

'But it *would* be a change. We wouldn't have to do everything *separately* all the time,' he said, a distinct hint of weariness in his tone.

'You're quite right,' she said, making an effort to respond. 'It would be lovely to do things together for a change. If you made us a mug of tea, I could finish this last shirt and then I promise I'll try to be more constructive,' she said, as she sprayed water generously on the dry fabric. 'I absolutely *hate* this weather,' she confessed, with rather more feeling than she normally admitted.

'Well then, did we make the right choice about our holiday?' Andrew asked, as they set off from Drumsollen on the last day of October, a fine dry afternoon with golden leaves flying down from the chestnuts opposite their own gates.

'Yes, we did,' she said smiling. 'I'm sorry I was so cross about the apartment, but we've had a good week at home, haven't we? Even the two days it poured,' she said, laughing. 'It's years since I've read a book in two days.'

'I thought my plan for market research on lunches rather inspired,' he said lightly, as they turned left and headed for Belfast via their own back route to Portadown. 'Great excuse, wasn't it? As if we needed one.'

'Wasn't it strange going to Drumsill again after so long and seeing all the refurbishing they've done? I think I liked it better when we went years ago and they still had those pikes hung up in the reception area. But the food *was* very good, wasn't it?'

'Somewhat too generous for what we'd planned that afternoon,' he said with a smile. 'But we did manage after our siesta. One pond, complete with selected aquatic plants. By the way, do *you* know how to look after them?' he asked, as the thought suddenly struck him. 'I've never met an aquatic plant before.'

'Nor have I, but the nursery had a rotating stand with books about everything you can think of. I bought the one on water plants,' she said helpfully. 'I nearly bought one on fuchsias as well.'

'Why didn't you?'

'I was being good,' she admitted. 'I haven't got any fuchsias and it might only encourage me to buy some when I know the Comforts Fund is extinct.'

'Never mind. One of these days, I'll acquire a long-running court case with lots of briefs and mileage expenses. I'll buy you a whole tray of fuchsias.'

'Thank you, my love. It's the thought that counts,' she said quietly. 'I often wonder if people who have lots of money get as much fun out of spending it as we do whenever we manage to afford something we really want. Like our pond.'

'Were you thinking of Harry and Jessie?' he asked cautiously, as they cleared the Saturday shoppers in Portadown and headed for Lurgan.

'Yes, I suppose so,' she said reluctantly. 'It's so long since we've seen them together, I feel uneasy. I know Harry is doing very well with the Gallery. Bless him, he never makes any secret about it, but Jessie always seems so discontent on the phone. When I ask about Fiona and James she just says, *Fine, fine*, and tells me nothing. After all, James is our godson,' she went on anxiously. 'I know we agreed to forget about the God bit, but we did make all the other promises about being there if he ever needed us. As it is, we hardly know him.'

'She used to be such a lively person, so full of fun,' Andrew responded, without taking his eyes off the road. 'Do you remember when she taught herself to cook and practised on us? I thought it was absolute heaven after the food in my digs.'

They lapsed into silence, Andrew preoccupied with the heavy traffic on the narrow main road as they approached Lisburn and followed the new signs for the motorway.

'My goodness, that went quickly, didn't it?' Clare exclaimed as they came off the eight mile stretch. 'Wouldn't it make a difference if it went all the way to Portadown or Dungannon?'

'Probably it would halve the journey time,' he said as they rejoined the traffic on the Lisburn Road.

Clare found herself growing silent as they drove slowly across to the Malone Road, preoccupied by an unease she could not identify. It became worse when they drove up the perfectly smooth drive between immaculate lawns. The former bumpy and holey approach and the whole parking area in front of the house had been tarmacked, probably after the work on the new extension: a double garage, workroom and store room at ground level and an extra bedroom and children's playroom on the first floor. It did all look rather different from the handsome but run-down old house where they'd helped paint a few rooms so Jessie and Harry could move in and work on the rest.

'Hallo, Clare. Hallo, Andrew. Great to see you.' Harry strode out to meet them, hugged them both. 'You made good time, given the traffic on a Saturday. Come on in. Jessie has the kettle on for a cup of tea. We're in here with a good fire. Hasn't the weather been awful? Did you manage to get your pond dug, or were you rained off?'

Clare looked around cautiously as Harry and Andrew began to talk. It was a whole two years now since they'd visited. There had been changes indoors as well as outside. New carpet everywhere, rather deeper and more springy than the new carpets she remembered when she visited from France. There were some lovely paintings and drawings on the walls and some new pieces of sculpture placed on small plinths. Hardly surprising, given Harry's eye for something special.

She sat down on one of the two long sofas facing each other across the hearth and found herself looking at a collection of family photos. Jessie and Harry on their wedding day. Jessie and baby Fiona. Studio portraits of Fiona and James. Harry with the children. The children with Harry's parents. Of Jessie's mother there was nothing at all, and nothing more of Jessie since Fiona was a baby, six years ago.

'I'm sure there's something I can do to help,' she said, standing up and heading for the kitchen.

'Hallo, Jessie. Can I give you a hand?' she asked, as she opened the door and saw her old friend filling the kettle at the sink.

The figure who turned to face her was certainly Jessie, but it was neither the girl nor the woman she had once known. The dancing brown eyes, once so full of mischief and mirth, and the long, wavy hair, had both lost their liveliness. Under its carefully applied make-up, the face was drawn and immobile. She'd put on weight. The attractive Jaeger outfit that strained across breast and thighs was certainly two sizes larger than the outfit she'd worn for their wedding.

'You're looking very smart,' said Clare, doing her best to absorb the shock without being totally dishonest.

'Smart? With wee'ans? Are ye jokin'?' she replied abruptly, making no move towards her. 'What d'ye think of the new sitting room?'

'Very elegant. Did you put the two rooms together?'

'Aye. He's never happy but when he's knocking down and building up or out. Did ye see the extension?'

'Yes. It must make a lovely playroom for the children. Are they up there now?'

'Ach no. Harry's mother has them. Sure, there's no peace with wee'ans when we want to hear all yer news. We don't see you that often,' she added, more than a hint of accusation in her tone.

'We don't get much time off, Jessie. One of us has to be there all the time, unless we close, which is bad for business. We'd hoped it would be easier by now and we might have a manager, but it's not. Things don't always go the way you hope they will,' she added, wondering whether Jessie was even listening to her.

'You can say that again,' Jessie replied sharply, pressing her lips together in a tight line.

'Jessie, what *is* wrong? You're not like yourself at all. Have I done something to upset you? Or are you not feeling well? What is it? Something's wrong, isn't it?'

Jessie turned away, ignoring the warmed teapot into which she had just dropped teabags. She looked as if she was trying to see something moving at the bottom of the garden. Then, in a flat voice Clare would never forget, she half turned towards her and said: 'Harry's got another woman.'

Fourteen

The long-delayed visit to Jessie and Harry was not the happiest ending to their week's holiday. By the time they'd driven home in yet one more October rainstorm, they were far too exhausted to do more than share their distress that their oldest and closest friends were now so unhappy in the life they'd made together.

They woke to soft autumn sunshine which cheered them after the sadness of the previous evening. To their great surprise, just as they were finishing breakfast, there was a phone call from Harry. He wanted to know if *either of them would be at home*, were he to come up the following day. Andrew said Clare most certainly would be and was surprised when Harry rang off immediately without further explanation.

'Do you *really* think he has another woman?' he asked, as he went back to his coffee.

'No, not for one moment,' Clare replied, 'but the alternative is actually worse.'

'What on earth do you mean, love? Surely Harry having another woman is bad enough. The situation last night was grim.'

'Yes, it was,' Clare sighed. 'But this is like the way she behaved before James was born. *If* Harry *hasn't* got someone else and she insists he *has*, then it's far harder to do anything about it.'

'I never thought of that,' said Andrew bleakly. 'What you mean is that she's being paranoid.'

'It wouldn't be the first time, though I may not have known the word four or five years ago,' she said sadly. 'We might be able to do something if it *is* an affair, but I don't think it is. In fact, I'm sure it's not,' she added, as she carried their breakfast dishes to the sink.

'Oh well, you'll find out soon enough,' he said philosophically, as he stood up. 'Can you just remind me why we're clearing out the stable today. Are you expecting a horse?'

He was pleased when she managed a laugh. After doing his best last evening to help her keep up appearances, with Jessie either sharp or actively silent, he couldn't wait to get to work and forget about the whole thing.

'No, dear. I am *not* planning to practice for next year's point to point in my spare time, but I have bought a second-hand freezer. Dobsons are replacing theirs in all their retail outlets with newer models and the old ones are going at a *very good* price. The electrician is coming tomorrow. We need a level space. No dust, straw, or cobwebs, and clear access to the garage for a new cable,' she explained. 'Failing that, it's a trench from the kitchen which will be more expensive and make a horrible mess.'

'For ice-cream?' he asked curiously, for Dobsons were one of the leading producers in the province.

'Yes, we *can* keep some ice-cream,' she agreed, knowing his weakness for raspberry ripple. 'But I'm more concerned with scones, cakes and sandwiches. If we have a run of birthdays we can stockpile and not be so hard pressed on the day. That sort of stuff defrosts very well, I'm told, but we'll have to experiment. I can't see defrosted sandwiches being as good as freshly made, can you?' she asked, as they pulled on their old anoraks and made for the stable.

The high-pitched whine of a power drill next morning told her the electrician had got started. Given he was a friend of John Wiley, and would come to her if he had a problem, she could forget about him until Harry appeared and concentrate on the paperwork that had accumulated during their week off.

There were invoices to deal with, a pile of post and an end-of-month Bank Statement. She knew how preoccupied she was when she found she'd annotated the statement, then filed it in the wrong binder. She spoke severely to herself, tried not to think about Jessie and Harry and kept glancing out of the window for the first sight of his BMW as it rounded the curve of the drive.

When a rather battered, small yellow car appeared just before eleven o'clock, she failed to recognize it until Harry unwound himself from the driving seat and strode up the steps.

'Harry, how lovely, it's stopped raining just for you,' she said, as she led the way back into Headquarters, a bright fire burning on the hearth to greet him. 'Come and sit down,' she added, picking up the phone and dialling zero. 'Coffee'll be here in a minute or two.'

'Clare, I'm sorry about Saturday,' he began awkwardly. 'Jessie excelled herself, didn't she?'

'Yes, it was bad, wasn't it? But it's not the first time she's been like that, is it?' she said steadily, pausing to smile up at Bronagh, who placed the coffee tray neatly between them and disappeared without a sound.

'Before we go any further, Harry, there's something I have to ask you,' she said quickly. 'I don't want you to be cross with me, but is there another woman in your life?'

'Apart from you?' he asked, looking bemused.

'Apart from Jessie,' she replied, relief already flowing over her.

'What?' he asked, looking amazed. 'What *are* you talking about?'

Clare smiled and shook her head. 'I had to ask, even though I thought the chances were remote. Jessie told me you had another woman.'

'Oh, not you as well?' he sighed, dropping his head in his hands. 'She's made heavy hints to my mother and told our doctor it's one of the girls at the Gallery,' he went on. 'There isn't *anyone*, Clare. I'm not sure I'd even have *time* these days.'

'I must admit I'd thought that myself,' Clare said, grinning cheerfully. 'Now, come on, eat up your nice warm scone and let's see what sense we can make of it. This isn't the first time Jessie has given you and me a bad headache, now is it?'

'No, it certainly isn't. Do you remember when she was carrying James and she thought she was going to die? I had to ask you to come home from Paris to help me out.'

Clare laughed aloud. 'Oh Harry, forgive me laughing, but have you forgotten that if I hadn't come to try to help *you*, I would not now be sitting here? That's when Andrew and I met up again and fairly, I have to say, I think Jessie had a hand in that. I'll swear she sent Andrew that message to go out to Drumsollen to meet *you* when she knew you'd dropped *me* here to spend the morning with June.'

'I'd forgotten all about that,' he said, beginning to look a little easier. 'These scones really are *very* good,' he said, managing to sound almost like his normal self.

'*Specialite de la maison*,' she said grinning. 'Now, I need to know more, Harry. Don't spoil your coffee, but tell me when you think it got going and anything that's made it worse. I'm no psychologist, but I probably know more about Jessie than anyone except you.'

Harry did his best, but Clare knew that inevitably he missed just the details that might help her because he was seeing with a man's eyes. He told her of all the things he'd done to try to please her, making the house as comfortable as possible and seeing she had proper domestic help. He'd wanted her to have an au pair to help her with Fiona and James, but she'd said she didn't want any foreign girl messing up her children.

As more and more detail emerged, Clare's heart sank. There was no doubt Jessie was rejecting all Harry's offers and ignoring his very existence when she could.

'I do feel so sorry I haven't been able to see her, Harry,' Clare said, when he'd told her all he could think of. 'That may be part of the problem. I do phone her nearly every week, but she doesn't phone me. Jessie's never been much use talking except face-to-face. Can you pinpoint any event at all that might mark the beginning of all this discontent?'

'She got very cross about the work I wanted to do on the house,' he said, casting around for an answer.

'Change,' she said thoughtfully. 'I wonder if that's part of it, Harry. Jessie's always avoided making decisions. She tends to go along with things and then, suddenly, she's had enough and pulls back and looks around for someone, or something to blame.'

Harry brightened visibly, said he felt she'd put her finger on what they were looking for. They talked for an hour or more, gathering together all they'd learnt from that earlier episode when Jessie had failed to cope so dramatically, had taken to her bed and frightened the life out of Harry who thought he was going to lose her. At least this time she was more angry than depressed, which might make changing things much more possible.

'Clare dear, you've been great, as always, and I've taken it all in, but I must get back to town,' he said, at last. 'I've an important meeting this afternoon. Is it all right if I phone you during the day from the Gallery, so we can talk properly?' he added. 'Then I can let you know how things are going. I'll see about the gynaecologist chappie and enquire about that man who was so good with Ginny. Which do you think would be quickest way back to Belfast, bus from Armagh or train from Portadown? Are you very busy or can you give me a lift?' he went on, as he stood up.

'Lift, Harry?' she asked. 'You *did* come by car, remember?' she added, laughing. 'Is *your* car out of action?'

'No, no. Mine's fine. Jessie wanted me to bring you hers. You remember she said on Saturday night, she didn't need it anymore and you could have it. It was when you were telling us about the sandwich delivery scheme,' he added, seeing the blank look on her face.

'I thought she was just being unpleasant and dismissive,' Clare replied honestly. 'I certainly didn't think she meant it. But what about her, Harry? Giving up her car is the last thing we ought to let her do. That would be very bad news?' she said anxiously.

'No problem there, Clare,' he said, shaking his head emphatically. 'I'd promised her a new car. It's on order. That one is too small. It *has* got a decent boot, but she needs something with a hatchback for the children and all their stuff. It would do for sandwiches though, wouldn't it? She thought it would. She said if you had it you might come up to Belfast more often . . .'

'Harry! Did she say THAT?'

'Yes. Yesterday morning, when she asked how soon could I take it up to you,' he replied, looking baffled.

Clare shook her head and threw up her hands. 'Harry, that's the best news yet. It means she *knows* she's in a mess and she expects me to sort her out. Come on, I'll drive you to Portadown. It'll be quicker for you by train. Give me a moment to have a word with June and Bronagh.'

As she walked on to the platform with him a short time later, he turned to her and said simply, 'Clare, what would I do without you?'

'You've helped *me* out more than once, don't forget that. It's what friends are for,' she said warmly. 'Are you sure you wouldn't like even a nominal sum for Jessie's car? I *could* manage that.'

'Definitely not,' he said firmly. 'I was about to ask you to let me pay for some bodywork repairs and a respray. Jessie can be a bit careless, though she's a perfectly good driver,' he added, as they heard the Enterprise from Dublin signalling its eminent arrival.

'Definitely not,' she repeated, laughing and hugging him quickly. 'Jessie might get the wrong idea. Not to speak of Andrew. Take care, Harry. It'll be all right if we can stick it out. Give her my love,' she added, as he closed the carriage door. She waved as she watched the express departed with a farewell serenade, satisfied that between them, once more, they'd bring Jessie back to herself.

Clare had to laugh as she watched John Wiley inspecting Jessie's battered motor car. There was nothing he enjoyed more than mending something that was broken, or upgrading something that was not looking its best. Knowing perfectly well what he was thinking, she suggested he do the job on a *time and materials* basis and insisted he charge her the going rate. He went off happy, knowing he could do a good job for far less than any garage.

So, a trim little dark blue car joined the team at Drumsollen. In it, Clare and Bronagh did the sandwich run five days a week. She drove, while Bronagh hopped out and delivered to an increasing number of offices who ordered regularly, not only sandwiches for lunch, but cakes for an office party, or a treat to take home on a Friday.

Mercifully, the winter was mild and February broke all previous records for dryness, with not a trace of snow in the whole of the month. Clare was able to get up to Belfast regularly and by the time the daffodils bloomed, she had persuaded Jessie to return her visits and to start work on a series of watercolours of the house and gardens to replace the faded prints in the guest bedrooms.

The political climate seemed milder as well. Prime Minister O'Neill entertained his opposite number from Dublin to a lunch preceded by champagne and, according to a Stormont friend of Charles, a main course accompanied by Châteauneuf-du-Pape. This gave rise to a story brought home by Andrew from the Law Courts. Apparently, some member of the very select lunch party had looked at the label before pouring the wine and said: 'For God's sake, don't tell Paisley.'

Whatever the comings and goings in high places, life at Drumsollen proceeded quietly. Clare had more time to herself and was grateful for the car, realizing as she drove off on some expedition or other just how housebound she'd become. She enjoyed her drives to Belfast and as spring moved towards summer she was heartened by the change in Jessie. She has now much less discontent, had begun to lose weight and was looking forward to a Mediterranean cruise Harry had booked as a surprise. She'd delighted him when she told him she'd always wanted to visit Florence and then asked if he'd mind traipsing round the galleries with her.

As June proceeded and Clare herself began to think of their holiday in Norfolk, she began putting together the figures for the end of the month so there wouldn't be a last minute rush before they set off for the Liverpool car ferry. With only scattered bookings in the second and third weeks of the month and Bronagh now well able to cope with callers, guest, or work person, or delivery, she shut the door of Headquarters and set out on a review of the last two years trading, summer 1963 to summer 1965.

It was a long job because she decided on a full assessment, conducted as meticulously as the team from her French bank would have done, reviewing the status and potential of a business coming to them for funds.

The picture was bleak. They were not insolvent, but they had been running to stand still. Despite their low rates of pay and their own unpaid labour, the turnover of the business simply could not generate a profit in the context of as expensive a piece of property as Drumsollen, with its unavoidably high maintenance costs. Of course, she must tell Andrew. But should she tell him now or after they'd had their holiday? In the end, she decided they should enjoy what they could, before they faced what would have to be done, and done soon.

'What are those little fellows down by the water's edge?' she asked, gazing out over the smooth, empty beach to the calm, shimmering blue sea beyond. 'The ones that run like clockwork toys,' she added, when he let his binoculars drop on his chest and gazed at her abstractedly.

'Oh those,' he said, coming back to earth, having been totally absorbed by the kamikaze dives of terns hunting along the seaward shore of Blakeney Point. 'Dunlin,' he went on. 'Lovely little fellows. Do you want to look through the glasses?'

'No thanks. I can't bear to put anything between me and them, or between me and the sky, or me and the sea. I feel as if I've been let out into the light and I never want to go back in again. What is it about the light in Norfolk? Am I imagining it, or is it only because of the sunshine and the blue sky?'

'No, you're not imagining it,' he said, moving closer on the warm sand of a hollow in the dunes. 'Think of Gainsborough, though he is actually Suffolk. But it *is* different. You'll see it in all the painting and watercolours from this area. There's an exhibition of East Anglian painters in Norwich next week. We could go when we visit the cathedral,' he said enthusiastically.

'Not sure you'll be able to drag me away from the coast,' she said, laughing. 'For a real landlubber I seem to have taken a great liking to the North Sea. Maybe it's because it looks more like the Mediterranean than the Atlantic,' she added thoughtfully.

'Don't let it fool you,' he said quickly. 'I've been here in January when the waves pounded the shore so fiercely the beach was inches deep in foam. Looked like the Fire Brigade were out on an exercise.'

'And there were dreadful storms here in 1953, weren't there?'

'When Aunt Bee had to hang out her top window with a lantern to attract a passing lifeboat,' he added, picking up his binoculars again.

Clare laughed gaily. 'Now that I've met her younger sister, the story is even better,' she responded, shaking her head. 'I expect they both acquired the same ladylike accent when they went to Cheltenham Ladies College. Joan told me they say "gels" instead of "girls" and are taught to be very polite. I can just imagine Bee hailing the boat and courteously enquiring if they could possibly fit in one more.'

'Has Joan lapsed into broad Norfolk yet?' he asked suddenly. 'I thought, given how long it takes the pair of you to wash up, or do anything else for that matter, she'd have displayed her talents by now. When she does, get her to tell you about singing the hymns in the local dialect one Christmas Eve in Cley, when she was sitting beside some very posh people from London who'd come down to visit the Lascelles.'

'What were you looking at this time?' she enquired, as he put his binoculars down again.

'A seal,' he replied promptly. 'If we were to go down and walk out along the beach, he or she would probably follow us. They are noted for their curiosity.'

'I've never seen a seal, not a live one.'

'Come on then, I'll take you to a favourite place of mine. We can leave our stuff here, there's not a soul within miles to pinch it. Besides, they don't in Norfolk. You won't need shoes,' he continued, pulling off his own and stuffing them into his rucksack.

They tramped off hand in hand to the water's edge and then paddled along in the shallow water where the sand was firmer. A few yards away, the dark head of the seal bobbed up and down, watching them out of great, soft, liquid eyes. As they moved along the beach it followed, never taking its eyes off them. Only when Andrew turned right along what appeared to be a low sandbank did their companion disappear.

'You are now walking on what will be the end of Blakeney Spit in a few years' time. It's all right, we can't be cut off by the tide, it's falling. Besides, I want you to see the point where West meets East,' he added, as he strode on ahead of her.

'Look,' he said, pointing down at her bare feet a few minutes later.

To her great surprise she saw that tiny wavelets were flowing over her feet from different directions, the ripples intersecting in a herringbone pattern which glinted and sparkled in the strong sunlight.

'That's how the whole spit was formed,' he explained, sounding totally delighted. 'The opposing currents cancel each other out and the waves deposit the beach materials they're carrying to form new land.'

She did listen, and she did follow his explanation, but what she was most aware of, here in the midst of the waves, a hundred yards or more from even the deserted beach, was a sense of space, of openness, of being able to breathe after some long confinement. It was a disturbing feeling and one she could not explain to herself, never mind to Andrew.

Arriving back in the early evening, they found an ancient station wagon parked under Aunt Joan's hedge. After he'd dropped their car in the space behind, Andrew peered at the dusty rear window, trying to read the curling garage sticker. He was rewarded for his curiosity with a paroxysm of barking from a ferocious Irish terrier who leapt to his feet and danced up and down, snarling and showing his teeth.

'My goodness,' said Clare, totally taken aback. 'I'm glad that window is only half open. I think it would like to eat us,' she said, as they moved briskly past.

'Ah, there you are, my dears,' said Aunt Joan happily, meeting them at the garden gate. 'I'll just tell Rory who you are.'

She disappeared round the back of the station wagon. Silence broke out immediately, so they turned back to see what was happening. Aunt Joan had opened the hatchback and was being greeted ecstatically by Rory.

'Now then Rory, this is Clare, and this is Andrew,' she said, passing over a biscuit which disappeared instantly. 'Say, *How do you do?*'

Rory had the most lovely brown eyes. He stared lovingly up at Clare and raised one rather dusty paw for her to shake. She had never seen such an expressive look on a dog's face in all her life.

'There now, Rory, go back to sleep,' said Joan, rubbing his ears. 'I'm sorry you can't come in but poor old Bassett is frightened of you. Not your fault, old chap, but cats are like that. You do understand, don't you?'

By way of answer, Rory lay down, put his head on his paws with a look of resignation and composed himself for sleep.

'Now, *come you on in*, as they say in these parts,' continued Joan, as she led the way up the garden path. 'Phillida is here. I must say Rory is an even better early warning system than the hinge of that gate,' she added, as Andrew closed it behind him to the sound of a high-pitched whine. 'Poor dear Rory. Bassett is quite neurotic about big dogs, but then perhaps she is suffering a trauma none of us know about.'

'I've heard a lot about you,' said Phillida, getting up to greet them as they arrived in Joan's small, overcrowded sitting-room. 'Glad to meet you,' she said abruptly, as she shook their hands vigorously.

Clare looked down at a small, robust woman with a brown and wrinkled face, whose iron-grey hair appeared to have been cut with blunt kitchen scissors. Under a green flak jacket, she was wearing a crumpled white shirt, army surplus trousers and short wellington boots. Her accent suggested that she too had been a pupil at Cheltenham Ladies College.

'How are you getting on with that dreadful man, What's-his-name, the *Reverend who Roars*, I call him. Is he going to go on stirring up trouble?'

The bluntness was disconcerting, but the candour so open and direct, Clare knew the question was meant seriously.

''Fraid so, Phillida,' Andrew replied. 'But we're trying to ignore him for the moment.'

'The newspapers and television *do* exaggerate the problems,' Clare added. 'All they need is a burning bus and they film it from every possible angle, so you'd think it was a whole fleet. It's bad for the province and bad for our business too, of course.'

'The guest house.' Phillida nodded sharply. 'Used to run one myself. After the war. The first war,' she added ruefully. 'Couldn't stand being polite to people all the time. Prefer animals.'

When they had all stopped laughing, Joan asked Phillida whether she would *now* stay to supper. 'You've had a good look at them. Do they pass muster?'

'I'll stay,' replied Phillida firmly. 'But only if supper will stretch?'

'Not only will supper stretch, my dear Phillida, but there is a very special bottle of wine these dear people brought. Assuming my fridge has not packed up again it should be properly chilled by now. I've had it in there since this morning, hoping your curiosity would get the better of you.'

'Splendid. Can I do anything to help? Or can I be idle and lie in this very comfortable armchair and ask Andrew about his pond.'

'One more marvellous evening,' said Clare, as they opened their bedroom door, crossed to the window, and squeezed into the small space from which they could look down across Joan's garden to the wheatfield beyond.

'No sign of our friend yet,' Andrew said, as he scanned the dark edge of woodland that ran along one side of the pale, moonlit field.

They stood together watching, hoping to see the barn owl that had delighted them evening after evening in the last week, its ghostly shape swooping backwards and forwards quartering the field from margin to margin. Joan had told them its nest was only a few fields away in an old outhouse and it was now hunting to feed its young.

'I think Phillida took rather a fancy to you, my love,' said Clare quietly. 'She's quite a character, isn't she?'

'Mmm,' he said, agreeing. 'One of what Uncle Hector called *a heroic generation* of women. Ten years younger than him, but then his wife and most of his friends were.'

'It must be strange to have friends you've known for fifty or sixty years,' she said thoughtfully. 'Or even seventy, in Hector's case,' she added, doing the sum. 'I wonder if we'll still have Jessie and Harry, Mary and John, Lindy and Charles, when we're old. People who know all about us and don't need to be told this or that, because they've been there all along the way, seen what we've done and know what's happened to us. Like Joan and Phillida.'

To Clare's surprise, he did not reply. His eyes were focused on the dark patch of Joan's garden just below the window. For a moment, she thought he might have spotted some night creature about its own affairs.

'Clare, there's something I have to tell you,' he began awkwardly. 'I should have told you sooner, but we had such a rush to get away and once we sailed down the lough, I couldn't bring myself to spoil it,' he went on. 'But I have to tell you before we go to Mary and John tomorrow, otherwise I'll not be able to be honest with them either.'

'What is it, love? It can't be that bad. I don't think you've had time to have another woman any more than Harry has,' she said lightly, trying to encourage him.

'No,' he said firmly. 'No other woman. I told you that years ago. It's the one thing I've ever been *sure* about. I do try, you know,' he went on quickly. 'I do try to be clear about things and to make decisions, but even with all your encouragement I still find it hard. And when I get things wrong I *still* feel I've let you down.'

'Why not let me be the judge of that, Andrew. If I feel you've let me down, I'll tell you.'

She waited, wanting to help him but knowing she must give him time to find his own words.

'I told you there would be a large lump sum coming in from all the work I've been doing for Charles and that, in the meantime, my salary wouldn't amount to very much because Legal Aid doesn't pay very well.'

'Yes, you *did* explain. What's the problem?'

'The problem is there won't *be* a large sum of money from Charles, because we've already had it. He's been paying me advances every month, so I'd still have a salary.'

'And what about the Legal Aid work? You've been so busy with that you've been bringing work home.'

'Yes, I know. It *has* been hard work, but there won't be any money from it. I probably could have guessed it wasn't going to work out. I kept hoping it might, but it hasn't. All the cases I took, except one, involved Catholics. All the requests for Legal Aid, except one, were turned down.'

'Oh my poor love, you really *should* have told me sooner,' she said sympathetically. 'But I do understand. I've something to tell you too, but *I* didn't want to upset us any more than you did when we were trying to get away. Six of one and half a dozen of the other.'

'Because your news is as bad as mine, I'm sure,' he responded, more steadily than she expected. 'Even I know that if I have no breakfasts to cook before I go to work, we've no bookings, and if we've no bookings, we're not making any money. Is that it?'

'More or less.'

'So we've failed,' he said, the familiar despair colouring his voice.

'No, Andrew, *we* have not failed,' she said emphatically. 'Our *business project* may have failed through no fault of our own, but that is a quite different matter.'

'But how are we going to pay for this holiday?' he asked, a hint of desperation in his tone.

'Perfectly easily,' she answered. 'When we did make a profit, two years ago, I put the money in a high rate, fixed interest account. It paid out the day before we left. We earned more in interest on that money than we've done by two years hard work,' she said matter-of-factly. 'But the money *is* there and it gives us time to think. We haven't *failed*. We have each other and we're happy and we've learnt a lot. That's not failure, Andrew, is it?'

'No, it's not,' he said putting his arms round her and holding her close. 'There's something else I have to tell you,' he went on, in a quite different tone. 'Don't move too quickly. The barn owl is on one of the fence posts below us. That's the nearest he's ever approached the house. Do you think he might be a good sign, like a rainbow?'

She disentangled herself very cautiously and looked down at the large bird who was scanning the grass beneath him.

'Good heavens, Andrew, I think *you* are becoming quite fanciful. Do you think it's catching?'

Fifteen

'Well then, Clare, what do you think of North Norfolk?' John asked, when they'd settled themselves in the sitting-room of their new home, in the small town of Holt where John had his electrical shop.

'I think it's quite wonderful,' said Clare honestly. 'I know people never want to go home after a holiday, but I really can't bear the thought of leaving all this sea and sky and hedgerows full of poppies and white campion. There are so many things here I've never seen before. Like seals.'

'And skate and chips too big for the plate,' added Andrew lightly.

'There you are, Mary. I told you she'd be a convert. Just as I was,' John broke in. 'Oh, it's not that I don't miss the green hills of home, like all exiles, but this is a very good place to be. It's been kind to us, hasn't it, love?'

'Yes, it has,' Mary nodded. 'And all thanks to Joan and her little flat,' she went on. 'If it hadn't been for her and that flat, we might have settled somewhere else in Norfolk. How do you like living in our *first* home, by the way?' she asked, looking from one to the other.

'Well,' replied Clare, laughing, 'we love the wildlife, the owl and the hedgehogs, and the wee birds that hop in and out through the kitchen window, but it must have been cold in winter. None of the windows or doors shut properly. Even in summer you can feel the draughts.'

John laughed heartily. 'I read recently that more interlock vests were sold in Norfolk than in any other English county. It *can* be really cold in winter, but it's much drier than dear old County Down and it is such a help to have it dry in my line of work.'

'So, how goes *your* Grand Plan?' Andrew asked after they heard about improvements to the shop. 'Is your new garden meant to be a wildlife sanctuary or was it just neglected?'

'Neglected,' said Mary grinning. 'Like everything else. The old lady who lived here nearly made her century, but nothing had been done for years. The kitchen had to come first,' she explained, looking round at the discoloured wallpaper and paintwork. 'I hate these curtains passionately,' she added, breaking into a little laugh, 'but it has to be one room at a time.'

'You did say you'd got the holiday cottages up and running, but what about your boat, John?' Andrew persisted.

'Yes. They're doing very well, I'm glad to say. And I *have* got a boat, but it's rather more of the owl and the pussycat kind than what we had in mind.'

'We had *not* thought either of our dear sons would want to go to university,' Mary said, matter-of-factly. 'They are both eminently practical. We thought technical or trade apprenticeship would be what they'd want. But no. *Electrical engineering*, says one, and, *Maybe me too*, says the other. They're both doing very well at school. Sandy is waiting for his A-levels and Johnnie for his O-level results. Johnnie *is* two years younger but he jumped a year and gets good marks in Maths. I think his teacher will nudge him towards a Maths degree.'

'So, change of plan for us,' said John. 'Little boat for fun and a bit of fishing off Blakeney Point, but the money's gone into this house to give us all more space. And Mary and I are going to have a big holiday next year. Australia. Visit to Mum and Dad and meet our nephews and nieces,' he explained. 'Now what about you two and *your* Grand Plan?' he asked, looking from one to the other.

To Clare's great relief, Andrew laughed. 'My dear wife says we have to be positive about our achievements,' he began cheerfully. 'So far, the only livestock I have raised are rather a lot of frogs in the pond we dug last October. It may not be commercially viable, but we do have a heron who seems to think we are a good idea and visits us quite regularly.'

John laughed in turn and raised his eyebrows. 'We *do* think of you very often. We could hardly forget you with the amount of publicity you're getting on the box. It must be bad for business,' he said grimly.

'Yes, it is,' said Clare nodding. 'But it's not just the disturbances. We've discovered we can't buy land because all the surrounding farmers are convinced they'll be able to make a fortune selling their land for building houses or motorways. Drumsollen itself is just not viable, as you've probably guessed. Apart from the competition from the package tour industry, it seems nowadays people expect en suite bathrooms *and* a telephone *and* television in their own room, even in a guest house. We just can't compete in that market.'

'So, change of plan?' suggested John soberly.

'That's about it,' said Andrew. 'Any ideas for the redeployment of a financial genius who speaks fluent French and passable Italian and an unemployed farmer with legal skills?'

'So that's what they look like after twenty years or so,' Clare said, as she stood gazing up at the flourishing buddleias in Phillida's garden.

'Yes, they are splendid, aren't they? My favourite is that Emperor Purple,' Joan said, pointing with her walking stick to a large bush so covered with long, flowering spikes that barely any foliage was visible. 'But they all seem to be equally popular with the butterflies,' she added, as she named the various species moving slowly over the blooms, brightly coloured wings fully open in the sunshine. 'Clare dear, your husband seems engrossed in Phillida's pond. Shall you and I leave them to it? I'm afraid my bad leg is being a bore. Do you mind fearfully if we go and sit down?'

'No, of course not. Is there anything I can do?' Clare asked, as they moved back along the garden path. 'Do you carry tablets, or a rub that I can use?'

'Tried them all. No use whatever. All *IT* wants is for me to sit down,' she said crossly, as she negotiated the French window and picked an upright armchair by the hearth. 'Oh, that's better,' she announced with a sigh, as she sat back gratefully. 'Actually, the heat doesn't help at all and I did far too much in the garden yesterday when you went to see Mary and John. How are they both? Do tell all for I haven't managed to see them for over a month. What's the new house like? Good deal larger, I expect.'

Clare gave Joan a full account of the new house and told her how welcoming they'd been. She said how vigorous they'd been in encouraging them to come and live in Norfolk and have another shot at their Grand Plan.

'We told them about our problem not being able to buy land, even if we *could* afford it now, and John assured us that green belt *is* respected here. He admitted there were always a few sharp deals going on with, what he called "back garden building", especially in Blakeney and Cley, but he said developers would never get planning permission here beyond agreed village limits.'

'I should think not,' responded Joan fiercely. 'Redevelop old property by all means, or establish a new village if needs must, but dropping houses like little boxes here, there and everywhere isn't good for the land. Isn't good for people either. At least the Parish Councils here recognize that,' she added. 'Well, they do *now*. Surprisingly, it's the incomers who work hardest to keep a sense of community going. My father was one for a start. He came here from Manchester, had a holiday home in an old railway carriage, then moved down permanently in his mid-forties. He sat on the Parish Council till he died. Dear old Dad,' she went on, her voice softening. 'If it hadn't been for that railway carriage, Bee and I would have been brought up in Manchester.'

'And if it hadn't been for keeping afloat in the Mediterranean, John Hamilton wouldn't have been posted to Norfolk and met Mary and lived *happily ever after*,' Clare said with a smile. 'Thanks to your flat keeping them up here on the coast,' she added. 'That's what they said to us yesterday.'

'Well, I'm blowed,' said Joan, looking pleased. 'Perhaps you and Andrew should think hard about what they said. I do very much fear from what he told me about the discrimination against Catholics, that he'll never be able to settle to the profession he's been trained for. Entirely his uncle's fault,' she said sharply. 'Adeline's brother, you know. Terribly responsible and generous with it, but no imagination. Andrew is his mother's son. Even as a little boy he watched *every creature that moved,*' she said emphatically. 'But when his parents were killed, all Christopher could think of was proper schooling and *giving him a good start*. Meant well, but he did get it wrong. Never asked the poor boy what he wanted. I'm afraid, my dear girl, you're the only one can put it right,' she ended abruptly. 'Thank goodness he found you.'

'I'm not sure this was such a good idea,' Clare said, as she paused and leaned against the rough inner wall of the tower of St Nicholas, Blakeney.

'Not far now, love. Joan assures me it's worth it, though perhaps a cooler day might have helped.'

They saved their breath and kept going steadily up the steep stone steps and wooden ladders until they reached the small door leading out into the open air.

'She was right, wasn't she?' Andrew said, when he got his breath back enough to contemplate the wide vista laid out below them.

'She usually is,' replied Clare, still gasping, as she came to his side, grateful for a small breeze after the warm, dusty air filling the tower.

'Bit higher than our Scrabo Tower,' he said grinning, as they moved to the seaward side.

They stood silent, looking out over the marshes to the long shingle bank defending them from the sea beyond. Light glanced off the ridge they'd tramped along days before, pausing to examine the strange shapes of horned poppy and to watch the bees burrowing into the prolific blooms on the patches of sea-campion.

The light was strong and clear; only the horizon was smudged and shimmering as they scanned the whole length of coast and looked down at the villages, red roofed and compact, built above the flood line.

Clare felt Andrew move by her side and saw him raise his binoculars. She followed his gaze over the marshes, but there was no hen harrier, or cruising fulmar, no bird at all that she could see in the dazzle of light. Then she realized he was looking down on a herd of black and white Frisians, grazing peacefully on the short, rich turf of the reclaimed marsh that ran alongside the coast road.

'Could you live here, do you think?' he asked, his studied casualness giving him away completely.

Quite unexpectedly, another time and another place flooded

into Clare's mind. The tower of a chateau in Southern France, beside her a man she'd thought she loved. Christian Moreau. He'd brought her there, high above the spread of the family's extensive vineyards, to show her his favourite view. The weekend visit to his parents had gone well and she knew he was about to ask her to marry him. Indeed, Robert had warned her he would propose to her. That was why he'd invited her. Christian was a very proper young man, of very good family, and would not speak without approval from his parents.

She had stood looking out over the rugged, dissected country-side, harsh, yet with its own kind of beauty. *You would be happy here*, he had said, taking her hand. That was the way Christian had always proceeded. He told her what she would think, what she would feel and even how happy she would be. Never once did he ask her. She had told him as tactfully as she could that it was indeed wonderful countryside but she could never be happy here, for she would always long for the little green hills of her home in Ireland.

Suddenly, she became aware that Andrew was looking down at her, waiting. She collected her thoughts, but she knew her answer, just as surely as the last time. 'Yes, I'm sure I could live here,' she said quietly, 'but only if it was with you, my love.'

Clare was rather anxious that she might cry when they said 'Goodbye' to Joan. She had taken such a liking to the older woman, had appreciated her directness, her concern for Andrew, and her warmth towards herself. As she finished their packing very early on the Saturday of their departure, she realized that, though she had many good friends back in Ulster, there was no woman in her life with the long experience and wisdom of a Joan.

To her surprise, it was Joan who shed tears. Standing by her garden gate in the freshness of the early morning, she hugged them both after Andrew had closed the boot on their suitcases and rucksacks and the plastic bags in which Clare had packed the plants and cuttings Joan had given her.

'Come back soon,' she said, as she blew her nose. 'And ring me tomorrow as soon as you arrive home. I'll be expecting you,' she added, as she turned away abruptly and left them to drive off down the twisty lane to the main road.

Despite the awkward cross-country stretch in the absence of any link between the M1 and M6 far enough north to be of any use to them, they made good time.

'Different next weekend,' said Andrew, as they swung west at last, heading for the East Lancs Highway and the Liverpool Ferry. 'English schools haven't broken up yet. Once you get families on the roads we've been using, it will be nose to tail. At least today, it kept moving.'

They made the ferry with time to spare and slept peacefully on one of the calmest crossings either of them had ever had. The early hour and the quiet of an overcast Sunday morning meant the streets of the city were deserted as they came up from the docks. It was cooler than on the other side of the Irish sea, the day without a breath of wind. As they drew away from the city Clare noted the leaves on the trees lining the motorway had darkened, the lightness and luxuriousness of early summer had now fully passed.

'At least we missed The Twelfth,' said Andrew easily, as they drove under the bunting and the massed flags in Portadown and turned off for Loughgall on their usual route home, past the old forge house, Robinsons' farm, Charlie Running's bungalow and so to Drumsollen.

'Back or front?' Andrew asked, as she closed the gates and got into the car again. 'Which would be easier?'

'Back,' she said. 'Most of the stuff in the boot is heading for the washing machine.'

As they rounded the final curve on their own driveway, Andrew braked sharply. For a moment, neither of them registered quite what had happened, but when they got out and walked towards the steps it became only too obvious. On the pale stonework either side of the front door, in the matching spaces between door itself and the adjacent window, someone with a well-loaded brush had painted matching slogans in huge letters.

'Taigs out,' it said, in red on one side. 'Brits out,' it said on the other in black.

They were still standing transfixed when they heard a car drive up behind them.

'Ach, I'm sorry I didn't get here afore you,' said Charlie, as he jumped out and came towards them. 'I didn't think you'd be home this early, but I saw you go past. John Wylie told me last night what had happened. He'll be here himself any minute now. I phoned him,' he added awkwardly. 'I only got it in last week. That's the first time I've used it.'

'When did it happen, Charlie?' asked Clare.

'We think it *might* have been the night of The Twelfth or maybe the night before. John came up to check around on the thirteenth and found the paint was dry. Otherwise he'd have started in on it then. He's been trying to get industrial solvents, but of course, everywhere was still closed for the week. I don't know whether he's managed anything or not,' he went on, pricking up his ear, as he caught the sound of an engine. 'Sure here he is. We'll soon find out.'

'Ach, what a welcome home for the pair of you,' John said, shaking their hands. 'I'm heart sorry I didn't get here before it was dry. I'd have had it away before you saw it.'

'That's good of you, John, but maybe we need to know there's somebody out there wants rid of us,' said Andrew, his eyes moving back to where the red paint had dripped down from step to step like a rivulet of blood.

Clare looked at him quickly, saw he'd gone pale and realized that she herself was feeling shaky. *How silly*, she said to herself briskly. *It's only paint. We'll get it off.*

'Did you have breakfast on the boat?' Charlie asked suddenly, as he looked from one to the other.

'No,' replied Clare. 'Just a cup of tea. We wanted to get home. But I think we could all do with some refreshments. Tea or coffee?' she asked, knowing that if she didn't get him moving, Andrew would go on staring at the gleaming paint as if someone had put a spell upon him.

They agreed nothing could be done today. Only a high powered solvent with steel wool was likely to make any impression now the paint had hardened. Even then it might take a light sanding to remove any residual staining.

John had already asked Robinsons' for a day off to come and help. Charlie said he was sorry he couldn't join them, but he was having a wee problem with his chest. Doctor's orders. No dust, says he. No heavy work. And cut out the smoking. He hadn't managed that but he'd been trying to cut down.

'Is there any way we could cover it up temporarily?' asked Clare, as they sat round the kitchen table.

'Aye, I thought of that,' said John, 'but it's two such awkward places. We can't very well drill the stone to put in hooks for dust sheets. Are you expecting guests?'

'No. There's no booking till Thursday as far as I remember,' Clare replied. 'I was thinking more of Bronagh.'

'Aye well, she's a sensible wee girl. There's many a worse thing she knows about I'm sure,' Charlie declared. 'She'll not take it amiss.'

He stood up. 'I'll have to leave you now for I've visitors this afternoon and I don't think there's room for them to sit down,' he explained, making them all laugh. 'If you need me, just give me a ring,' he added airily, presenting Clare with a small, printed card. 'I'll hope to see you Wednesday, Clare. If you can't make it, just ring that number.'

'He's terrible pleased about his phone,' said John a little later, as he too got up to go. 'I'm all for it, but June's still worried that the girls will run up the bill ringing their friends. But we'll see. We'll see,' he repeated, as Clare walked out to the car with him, averting her eyes as best she could from the messages left to welcome them home.

Andrew was sitting just where she'd left him, his half-eaten bowl of cornflakes pushed to one side, his head in his hands.

'Clare, why don't we just get back in the car and go? Go anywhere out of this benighted country. I'll get a job, any job, and we'll not have to watch what we do, or watch what we say and give offence by merely existing. What about it?' he said fiercely.

'Fine. Good idea in principle. Just one or two small problems,' she said, hurriedly collecting herself. 'There's June and Bronagh and Thelma for a start. Left without an income. And John too, though it's a lesser matter. And we do have the odd friend who might be just a bit upset. Jessie and Harry for starters, and Charlie for another. Apart from that, what's to stop us?' she said, trying to keep the bitterness out of her voice.

'What *are* we going to do, Clare? This is the last straw for me. It's bad enough we can't employ Bronagh without raising up that old nastiness, but I'm not exactly immune to being called "a Brit", as if the Richardsons hadn't been in Ireland for centuries. Wouldn't you be upset? Aren't you upset?'

Anne Doughty

'Yes, I am. But I'm afraid I may be partly responsible for this.'

'What? But how could you be?'

'Well, you remember my dear brother came looking for a job,' she began steadily. 'What he wanted was cars to play with. I told him we only had one car and we did our own fetching and carrying. No, let me finish, I'm not imagining things,' she said firmly, as he started to protest.

'I've been doing the sandwich run with Bronagh. I drive, she drops. But then I asked her if she'd like to learn to drive and she said, *Yes, I would*. I told you I didn't think we'd ever need Jessie's car, my car if you like, at the weekends because one of us always had to be here. When you agreed with me, I started lending it to Bronagh. Brendan came on the bus on Friday night, took Bronagh and car home and returned Bronagh and car on Monday morning. Before we went away she told me he's a great teacher and she'll soon be able to go solo. She's been practising in Armagh with him so she can do the sandwich run in case I'm ever ill or not be available,' she went on, taking a deep breath.

'So what you are saying,' Andrew interrupted, 'is that your brother, who hangs about Armagh and Richhill, may have seen two cars at Drumsollen. Then he sees you driving round with a Taig, as he no doubt calls them, and two more Taigs, driving in and out of Drumsollen in the second car without you.'

'I think that's just what has happened,' she admitted. 'He's always been vindictive when he can't get his own way. I don't think he's got a job. Uncle Jack said he isn't living with them and no one knows anything about him.'

'Don't you think we should tell the police?' he suggested, sounding more like himself.

'I don't think there's much point,' she replied honestly. 'We've no evidence it was him and the police have more urgent matters on their hands. Besides, the fewer people who know what's happened, the better. It would be the worst kind of publicity.'

'I'm sorry. You're quite right. I just wasn't thinking.'

'You were very upset,' she said gently. 'And it was more of a shock for you. It only took me seconds to work out what had happened.'

'Clare, I think I have a confession to make,' he said bleakly.

'They do say it's good for the soul.'

'I can't quite believe it, but suddenly I know I could walk away from Drumsollen. All my life, I've longed to be here, to live here, to make a home and a family here, but now I just want to go.' He paused and looked even more desolate. 'Clare, how am I going to manage to keep going now I know how I feel?'

She sighed and thought of the North Sea and the light over the Norfolk coast. And Joan. And Mary and John.

'Perhaps, my love, the only way for both of us is to make a private pact, here and now, that yes, *we will go*, and then get back to work so that we face up to the problems one by one and don't do anything we might regret. What do you think about that?'

'It's a deal, pardner,' he said, smiling sheepishly for the first time since they had arrived home.

Sixteen

Andrew went to the office as usual on Monday morning, enquired if Thelma had had a good holiday, went through the mail and dictated a few letters. Then he came home, got into his dungarees and joined John, who was already addressing the slogans. By the end of the day they were both exhausted, but the paint had gone, though a shadow remained on the stone that only an industrial sander could ever remove.

'Sure a man on a gallopin' horse will never notice it,' said John philosophically, as he and Andrew sat drinking tea in the kitchen, their sweat-marked faces speckled with dust, their dungarees streaked with both paint and solvent.

'And we don't get many of them around these days,' said June sharply, her Monday routine upset by the comings and goings. 'Ye can hardly believe the badness of people.'

To Clare's great surprise, Andrew got up, put his arm round her and kissed her cheek.

'But then, June dear, you have to remember the *goodness* of people. Like you and John and the girls and the way you've always helped us out and encouraged us. Clare and I will *never* forget that,' he said, pressing his free hand on John's shoulder.

'And we'll not forget the way you've worked with Bronagh. And Brendan too, when he comes to give us a hand,' added Clare. 'If only *everyone* were like you.'

'Ach well,' said John awkwardly, watching June as she got ready to go home. 'Sure life's too short to be making bad feelin',' he went on, as Clare slipped an envelope into his jacket pocket without him even noticing.

'What do we tell them about what's going to happen?' Andrew asked after they'd gone.

'Nothing at all for the moment,' she said firmly. 'I don't know where to start yet and I hadn't much time in Headquarters today. We had a huge pile of sandwich orders. Besides, I wanted to spend time with Bronagh. I was worried she'd be upset about the slogans.'

'And was she?'

'Yes, she was, but it was you and me she was upset about. She said we didn't deserve that sort of treatment from anyone. She actually asked me if it might be better for us to find another Protestant. She said she'd understand.'

Andrew sighed and shook his head. 'And what did you say to that?'

'I said, *Not likely*. Apart from the fact she's part of the team and we're glad to have her, that would be giving in.'

'It almost makes you want to stick it out, doesn't it?' he said uneasily.

'Well, it *does* remind us of the good things, as you said to June, but I'm not sure we *have* very many options. There is still the matter of bookings. I sent out a mailshot before we went away. I'll know better when I've seen the response to that.'

'I'm sorry, love, I didn't mean to sound as if I'd changed my mind,' he said quickly. 'We made a deal and I stand by that. What I was really trying to say is that I've no idea *what* to do, or *where* we go, or *when* we go. You won't think I'm not doing my bit, will you, because I'm not making helpful suggestions?'

'No more than you thought I wasn't doing my bit when I didn't get going on the paint with you and John,' she came back at him. 'I think I *am* better at planning, I'm certainly better at sums, but I'd be no use at anything much if I wasn't doing it for us and for our future. You just mustn't forget that, love. We each do what we can and confess what we can't manage.'

'Like I can't manage without a bath, right now,' he said, laughing.
'Yes, you do smell a bit. I was trying to pretend I hadn't noticed.'

As July ended and August launched itself with heavy rain and regular rumbles of thunder, Clare had plenty of time to think. Apart from the sandwich round between twelve and one from Monday to Friday and a solitary birthday in the second week, the only bookings were the commercial travellers, old friends now, and a small scatter of tourists wanting a single night so they could visit Armagh's two cathedrals.

Their income from guests at Drumsollen just about covered food and wages. That meant the monthly mortgage payments went out from their Trading Account without anything coming in to balance them. That account had had a boost in June from the return of funds she'd put into the Fixed Rate Account. At this present rate of outflow those funds would run out April, or May of next year, unless Andrew made enough for her to support it from his earnings.

Morning after morning, she studied her figures and projections, not because they could tell her anything new, but simply because she'd always found it hard just to sit and think. But as days passed she had to admit no inspiration had come. She was simply going over the same old problems and making no progress whatever.

Obviously, their main asset was Drumsollen itself, a robust, well-built house, in reasonably good condition, but to put it on the market would announce that their project had failed. Were they ready to do that now? Would the end of August be a good time to try to sell? Or would it be better to wait to the spring? If they did sell before the winter, where would they go? Most of all, there was the question of how they could earn a living. Could one or both of them find work? And if so, where?

Sometimes it seemed that every decision rested on some other decision. Did she order a full load of fuel oil before the end of August to take advantage of the reduced summer price? Or would that simply deplete cash reserves and leave a half-full tank for someone else to use, if they did go this side of Christmas?

She had just decided to confess to Andrew that she was going round in ever-decreasing circles when he arrived home early one

Friday afternoon looking more cheerful than he'd looked for weeks.

'This has to be good news,' she declared, as he strode into Headquarters and stood with his hands in his pockets in front of the floral arrangement in the fireplace.

'Totally unexpected,' he said. 'The last thing I ever thought of. Lord Rothwell's Land Agent rang me today. He wants me down in Fermanagh for three days at the end of the month. It looks like someone has managed to lose the documents on the boundary disputes my former employers supplied. The executors have been looking for them since Hector died and have finally given up. There *should* be copies of the maps and my notes, of course, but my old firm went out of business a couple of years back. Several of the partners are no longer with us, no one seems to know where, *or even if*, they deposited their records for safe-keeping. They could have ended up in a skip.'

'My goodness,' she said, totally taken aback, as he named the fee he'd been offered for his three days' work. 'That would take us to the end of June.'

'What *do* you mean?' he asked, looking totally bemused.

'Sorry, love,' she said. 'It just slipped out. I've been working out how long we could go on paying the bills on the present level of income. I'd reckoned we could stay afloat till April or May of next year, but your fee would give us enough to carry on till the end of June.'

'Then why don't we say, *Thank you nicely*, and put a ring round the thirtieth of June? It would give us something to work to, wouldn't it?'

'Yes. It would. It's a great idea. It might even stop you saying you don't have good ideas. It would be such a help to know *when* we are going. That only leaves us the HOW,' she said grinning. 'How about a small celebration?' she went on. 'It's Friday night and I have a piece of news for you too. Not quite in the same category as yours, but worth the last bottle from Robert's Christmas case.'

Sadly, they hadn't any wine left after all. When Andrew went to fetch it, he remembered they'd used it July when Harry called unexpectedly. He'd been in very good spirits. Jessie, he said, was much better since she'd been on the hormone treatment recommended by the gynaecologist. He was delighted by how much time she was now spending painting. As she was away on a weekend course, the children with his mother and he'd been going home to an empty house, it had been a perfect excuse for a celebration.

'Never mind,' Andrew said, as they settled side by side in the summerhouse and he poured their coffee from the Thermos jug. 'There's still your news to lift my spirits.'

'Well,' she said happily, 'I was hard at work . . .' She broke off and giggled. 'That's a good start, isn't it? Are you impressed?'

'I'm always impressed, but I am also consumed with curiosity. Please, *do get on with it*,' he said, appealingly.

'I did order oil last week to get the summer discount. And it came yesterday,' she began steadily. 'Usually, young Matt comes round for my signature and old Matt supervises the delivery, but yesterday old Matt arrives looking really pleased with himself. He's a rather sober character, though June says he's a good sort underneath. So, I invite him in, take a quick look at the invoice and ask him if he and his colleague have swopped jobs. *Ach no*, says he. *I got out of the way to give yer man a chance with Bronagh. He's been trying to pluck up courage to ask her out since she nearly fell off her bike opposite the Depot. And that's six months ago.*'

'Anyway, it seems the chain came off her bike. Young Matt sees her get off and goes out and fixes it. And every chance he gets, about that time of day, takes a wee walk over to the gate in the hope he'll see her again. So says Matt senior.'

'Well, I *am* enthralled. What happened next?'

'Apparently the last delivery we had, Bronagh and I were out with the sandwiches, so young Matt was very downcast. Matt senior says he was so annoyed he actually went into the Boss's office when the Boss was outside having a smoke, to see when the next delivery might be due. So here I was, trying to decide whether to have oil or not, little knowing I was impeding the course of true love,' she declared, laughing.

'How do you know it's true love?'

'I don't,' she admitted, more soberly. 'But I've my fingers crossed. Young Matt is a nice man and it's not the first time I've heard a story about someone having to wait till the chance appeared. My father used to tell me how he had to make do with one or two dances a year with my mother because there was someone else. But he used to say he waited and it all came out right, because she was worth waiting for.'

'And did Matt manage it? Did he ask her out?'

'June says *Yes*. She got out of the way as well, but she says when they left Matt was smiling all over his face.'

'That's just great,' he said, looking really pleased. 'I do hope it works out too. Somehow it would make it a bit easier to go, wouldn't it?'

Clare found it easier to concentrate as August proceeded. It was a month she always loved, strong hints of the coming autumn mixed with the last fine, warm days of summer. She now had time to spend a day with Jessie every few weeks and she found she was indeed much more like her old self. She continued her regular visits to Charlie and discovered to her amazement one afternoon that he was tidying his sitting-room.

'Good Heavens, Charlie, are you moving house?' she said, teasing him, as she viewed a whole empty sofa for her to sit on and far fewer piles of books on the floor.

'Ach, it's the nephew's fault,' he explained, grunting. 'He's a powerful big man. Great size entirely. Every time he came to see me, he was heart-scared of knocking things over. So I decided to make changes. Aye an' to your advantage too,' he added with a sharp nod. 'Did you ever hear tell of Sam McGinley or Rose Hamilton?'

'Rose Hamilton, yes. I *have* heard of her,' she said enthusiastically. 'She was Granda Hamilton's mother. He often talked about her. But I've never heard of Sam McGinley. Who's he?'

'Well, I don't rightly know either, but I found some letters your Granda gave me, ach, years an' years ago, and they're addressed to Mrs John Hamilton at Salters Grange and they start *Dear Rose* . . . Now Rose Hamilton would indeed be *your* great-grandmother on your father's side but, by coincidence, she used to live in that old house opposite the forge, just a bit away from the forge house where your great-grandfather and great-grandmother on your *mother's* side lived. That must've been where he found the letters. So Sam McGinley has to be some relative or friend of hers. Anyway, here they are. I hope they lead you to the family fortune. How are the family fortunes, by the way?'

Clare had already told him about their plans to make a move, but she had yet to tell him they now had a date.

Charlie had been all in favour of their move. He'd said that, with all due consideration, things were not looking good under this new Government. The so-called *new initiatives* were not going anywhere near far enough. They were encouraging hopes on the one side that weren't being met and upsetting the certainties of the other, so the old animosities were being stirred up again. He reckoned there'd be bad trouble, for no one was paying any attention to what was already happening. They'd do well to go before the whole thing blew up.

She'd just told him about Andrew's job in Fermanagh and was about to add that they had now got a date for the move when he stood up suddenly and asked her if she'd mind putting on the kettle.

'I've just remembered, Clare, I've a phone call to make about an appointment and every time I go to do it, something distracts me. I'll do it now before I forget again,' he explained, as he stepped out into the hall.

Later, as she walked home, she thought of the bundle of letters in her basket. She wondered what stories they might tell of people she didn't even know, who yet had this fragile link with her. Back in Headquarters, she gazed at the flowing handwriting, studied the stamps and the return address in New York State and decided that, like Charlie, she must not let herself be distracted. She parked them in one of the small drawers in her desk and promised herself there'd be time to read them in the wilds of January when there would probably be very little work to occupy her.

'Are you sure you don't mind being on your own, love?' Andrew asked, yet again, as he took clean shirts from the drawer. 'The house can feel so big and empty all on your own. Won't you be nervous?'

'Well I might be if it were *really* empty,' she admitted honestly, 'but dear old Sam Rogers is here for the first two nights and Jessie's talking about staying over the third one so she can make colour sketches in early morning light. If I do get twitchy, I can always ask June if Caroline could come over and stay. But it is *only* three nights and you can phone me as much as you like. You won't be paying the hotel bill, will you?'

'No, I won't. And *Yes* I will phone. But I may have to work with your man in the evenings, so don't be anxious if it's getting on towards bedtime before I manage it.'

'Aren't you afraid of leaving me alone with Sam Rogers?' she demanded, teasing him about the elderly bachelor who was one of her favourite regulars.

He raised his eyebrows. 'Sam may be the world's greatest expert on gripper treads and carpet laying supplies, but I can honestly say I don't think you need lock your bedroom door,' he replied calmly, as he zipped up his suitcase, a huge grin on his face.

By the Tuesday of Andrew's departure, the weather had settled into that soft, fine and dry warmth that the end of August often provided. He would have a lovely day for the drive. As she waved him goodbye, she felt so sad she couldn't go with him. She had such happy memories of the time they'd gone together, even if they would now always be tinged with the sadness of Hector's loss.

The previous day she'd picked roses for Hector, made them into a posy, wrapped it in wet moss in a polythene bag and placed it carefully in the boot. Andrew had promised to put them in water when he arrived in his hotel and take them to the grassy mound by the lakeside when he began work on the estate.

She turned away as the car disappeared from sight, a list of jobs already printing out in her mind. Routine things like the end of the month on Wednesday, preparations for a birthday party on Friday, bills to pay, and letters to write, both business and family. With her usual visit to Charlie on Wednesday afternoon and Jessie coming on Friday, she'd not have much time to feel lonely, not during the day at any rate.

The fine weather tempted her outside and she spent more time than she could really afford in the rose garden and the new herbaceous border, but she comforted herself as she worked by thinking how easily she could make up for it by doing chores in the evenings.

That first evening, she sat in Headquarters and got stuck into the paperwork until Andrew rang, in the best of spirits, full of interesting observations about the hotel where he and the Land Agent were staying. He even suggested they might just manage a brief visit themselves before June Thirty, as they called it, their private name for Departure Day.

Wednesday evening brought another phone call just as she was finishing her solitary supper. A short one this time. The work was going well, but there were complications. Lord Rothwell had gone back to Australia to visit his wife and had either mislaid the key for the safe, or inadvertently taken it with him. They were actually having to employ someone to come and break it open because they *had* to consult the original manuscript drawings of the estate.

'To visit his wife, Andrew?' she repeated, puzzled. 'Didn't she come with him?'

'Don't know, can't say,' he replied laughing. 'All sorts of funny things emerging about my distant cousin. Must go. I'll ring tomorrow. Be a good girl.'

'Can't say I've much opportunity to be otherwise,' she responded gaily.

Standing over the ironing board later that evening, a huge pile of their own ironing stacked on two kitchen chairs, Clare turned over what he had said. She wondered how any woman could bear to be so far away from her husband. But then, not all husbands were friends as well as lovers, and some husbands saw a wife merely as a provider of heirs, goods and services. Like ironing shirts, she thought suddenly, and laughed.

It was almost half past ten when she decided to leave the neat piles to put away in the morning. She could tell from the grumble of the television that Sam had come back from whichever pub he patronized and was settled for the late night movie. As there was no one else in residence, she could lock up right away and get to bed earlier than usual.

She put out the lights in the kitchen and looked up through the tall, barred windows at the pale, fading sky. The nights were dropping down visibly, but it was still not quite dark. She pulled the door behind her, stepped out into the corridor and felt a cool draught on her face.

She paused, puzzled. The enclosed corridor, often warm and stuffy in summer, only had a cool draught when they propped open front and back doors for precisely that purpose. She checked the back door just to make sure she'd locked it earlier and wondered if Sam, not the most collected of individuals, hadn't shut the front door properly behind him.

Afterwards, she realized the unfamiliar smell she'd caught on the air as she went upstairs should have warned her. But it didn't. She arrived in the entrance hall to a tinkle of the chandelier and the shock of finding three masked figures standing by the double glass doors. They were watching a fourth member of the gang going through the pigeonholes of her desk in Headquarters.

'Stop right where y'are, missus,' said the tallest of the guards on the front door, as she was about to turn, slip silently back downstairs and phone the police.

'Where's the key to the cash box?' he demanded, as he strode towards her, pulled out a gun and pointed it at her.

He was giving such a bad performance of a gangster that she wondered if the gun could possibly be real, but she couldn't risk assuming it was a fake.

'There isn't a key, because it isn't locked,' she said calmly.

'You'd better be tellin' the truth,' he growled. 'Over there and hurry up,' he went on, waving the gun around and directing her towards Headquarters where a slighter man, wearing a grey Balaclava and a black anorak was struggling to open the cash box.

'C'mon on, c'mon, hurry up,' said the Boss Man as Grey Balaclava fumbled and finally dropped the box, which fell open on the floor. It was empty.

'Right you, where's the safe?' Boss Man said harshly, turning towards her. 'We've not come here to go away empty-handed.'

'We don't have a safe,' Clare replied, keeping her voice as steady as she could manage and wondering if there was the slightest possible chance that Sam might appear.

'Ah, don't give me that,' he sneered, signalling to the two doorkeepers to come round behind her, in case she tried to get away.

'Why don't you look round my office and see for yourself?'

'Go on then. Have a look round,' he shouted to the one in Headquarters. 'Billy, give yer man there a hand for God's sake,' he added crossly, dispensing one of her guards to assist. 'Start goin' through the drawers of that desk,' he shouted. 'C'mon. Get started. Quick. We haven't got all night.'

It was at that point Clare recognized the smell she had picked up on the stairs. It was paraffin. The two doorkeepers had each been carrying a bottle which she had assumed was beer. Now the one behind her had both bottles and she had no idea what he might be going to do with them.

There was a crash from Headquarters as they knocked over her chair in their haste to obey orders. They pulled out the drawers, turned them upside down on the floor and started kicking the piles of paper apart. They weren't going to find any money, except the plastic box with the Petty Cash. What would happen then, she wondered. Quite without realizing it, she took a step forward to see better what was going on.

'Stop where you are, or you're dead,' the Boss shouted, startling her with the vehemence in his tone. One of the two figures dumping paper on her floor jerked his head up to see what was happening and in that split second she saw his eyes. Given they were the same eyes she saw every time she applied make-up, there was no doubt as to who it was.

'I told you we had no money, William,' she said crossly. 'Why don't you and your friends go home before the police arrive? Some of the guests will have phoned by now,' she said, looking directly at the Boss.

'Nah,' he sneered. 'Ye don't get us with that one, honey. We're more experienced than that. The new UVF, that's us, in case you don't know. We've been trainin' for a year an' now we're goin' to get the funds we need for proper equipment.'

Clare sensed a movement behind her and heard the sound of liquid being poured from a bottle. Before she had even thought what she could do about this new threat, the entrance hall was lit up and the chandelier tinkled again as a car swung round the turning circle and braked sharply at the foot of the steps.

'I expect that's them now,' she said, totally amazed at her own presence of mind.

William and Billy made a mad dash for the hall doors, almost falling over each other as they tried to get through them at the same time. Clare's guard wasn't far behind. The Boss paused only to ignite his 'gun' and throw it on the carpet behind her.

There was a sudden whoosh of flame as the doors swung closed behind them. Clare caught up the roses from the centre of the table, grabbed the vase in which she'd arranged them the previous day and splashed the water into the midst of them. Then she gathered up a pile of glossy magazines sitting beside the abandoned roses and dumped them on the small flames that survived.

Coughing and gasping for breath, she turned to find a large man she'd never seen in her life before, coming quickly towards her.

'Clare, are you all right?' he demanded. 'I'm sorry I couldn't catch them. They took me unawares for my mind was on other things. I'm Eddie Running and I was hurrying to catch you before you went to bed. I have a message for you from your friend Charlie.'

Seventeen

'Clare, are ye all right?'

Clare turned away from Eddie Running to see Sam Rogers moving towards them at a totally unexpected speed.

'I smelt burnin',' he said quickly, as he cast his eye over the scatter of magazines on the wet floor. 'ARP in London during the Blitz. You never forget the smell,' he added, as he inspected the charred carpet.

'Sam, this is Eddie Running. He appeared just at the right moment,' Clare explained, suddenly feeling she would like to sit down.

'Away and settle yourselves, the pair of you,' said Sam, looking them up and down. 'I'll bring a cup o' tea. I know where everythin' is for I go in an' pass the time a' day with the girls.'

Clare glanced towards Headquarters, the floor deep in paper, then led the way to the sitting room. Empty and dim, only the pale gleam of the newly-risen moon made the heavy furniture visible. She dropped down quickly on the big sofa in front of the fire.

'Eddie, could you switch on some of the lamps, please. I feel a bit shaky. It's probably those fumes from the paraffin.'

To her great surprise, Eddie laughed. He turned on the nearby lamps, looked her straight in the face and said, 'You're as white as a sheet. D'ye not think maybe you've had a wee bit of a shock?'

'I might have had a worse one if you hadn't turned up,' she replied, smiling weakly.

'Would you mind if I asked you a few questions while it's still fresh in your mind.'

'You sound just like a policeman.'

'That might be because I *am* a policeman,' he said, with a laugh. 'CID since last year,' he explained, a hint of satisfaction in his voice.

Clare wondered why Charlie had never told her his nephew was a policeman. Perhaps he thought she'd guessed. He was certainly the right height and build for the job.

'I saw *four* of them,' Eddie began helpfully. 'Couldn't miss them, they nearly ran me down. One was taller than the rest. Did *you* get a look at any of their faces or had they all covered up?'

'No, I didn't get a look at any faces, but I saw the eyes of one of them. I'm afraid it was my brother. He thinks we're rolling in money because there's a chandelier in the hall. He'd gone for the cash box in my desk, but it was empty. The taller one was acting Boss. He called one of the others Billy. My brother is William Hamilton. Eddie, I really don't want this reported, at least not till I talk to my husband.'

'Right. Don't worry about that for now. Let's just see what we can put together. Did they have any badges or distinctive markings?'

'No, I don't think so. Two of them had black masks and William and the Boss had grey balaclavas. Oh yes,' she added quickly. 'Boss Man said they were the UVF. That they were getting the funds they needed.'

'Clare, that is *very* helpful. We already know there are paramilitary groups forming. The Ulster Volunteer Force is one of them. There are others too and I'm afraid that sooner or later they'll have money for guns unless we can stop them.'

'Here ye's are now,' said Sam, bringing in a loaded tray. 'I brought mugs, they hold more. And I found the scones. Clare, you need something sweet an' I know you don't take sugar. Eddie, will you see she eats one of those while I go an' have another look at that bit of carpet an' lock the door till you go,' he ended, putting the tray on the sofa between them.

Eddie poured tea and handed her a plate with a scone well-covered in strawberry jam. 'Doctor's orders. They look very nice. I think I've had the same ones at Charlie's,' he said quietly, as she drank her tea gratefully.

'June is a great baker. I always take Charlie whatever's going when I go on Wednesday afternoons. It was wee buns today, because there's a children's party on Friday,' she explained, as she took a bite of Sam's jammy scone.

'I hear all about Drumsollen,' Eddie replied. 'I'm afraid all the disturbances have been bad for business,' he continued, making light work of his own scone. 'I'm surprised so many big firms are willing to come and set up new factories here, but then there are good incentives and they have their own security. As for yours, I'm afraid you'll need to keep that door locked in future and ask your guests to ring, unless you want to give them a key.'

He paused and watched her closely as she licked her sticky fingers. She glanced up at him and remembered he'd said he had a message from Charlie.

'I'm so sorry, I've kept you back,' she began. 'Will your wife be waiting up for you?'

'No, don't worry. I rang her from the hospital and told her I was coming to see you,' he said reassuringly.

'Hospital?'

'Charlie had a wee turn early this evening,' he began steadily. 'He was sitting on the sofa when I arrived, a kind of grey colour, so I took him straight to the Infirmary. They decided to keep him in for tests, so I waited till they had him settled and sat with him for a bit. He said you'd been to see him in the afternoon and I was to tell you if they kept him in for a day or two, he'd give you a ring. He said there was a call box patients could use. He'd seen it when he came to visit Billy Robinson after he fell off the tractor.'

Clare smiled and told Eddie how pleased Charlie was with his new phone and how he rang her now and again, saying he was just ringing to see if it still worked.

Eddie smiled and then looked down at his hands.

'Clare dear, there's no easy way to tell you this,' he began again. 'Just as I was saying *Cheerio*, Charlie had another heart-attack. It was very quick. I called the nurses, but he was gone before they got to him.'

'Oh no,' she said, her heart leaping to her mouth. 'Oh no, not Charlie too.'

'Clare, did you know Charlie had cancer?' Eddie went on. 'They thought it was one lung, but they did a second X-ray to make sure. He had an appointment a couple of weeks ago and the results are not long back. It was in them both.'

Clare shook her head silently. He hadn't told her he had cancer. She hadn't told him they had their date for leaving. No bad thing, either way, when you came to think of it.

'No, I didn't know,' she said slowly. 'He mentioned an appointment, but he didn't tell me what it was. Now I think of it, that wasn't like him.'

'Did you know what age Charlie was?' Eddie asked, his voice steady and strangely comforting.

'Yes, I do. Or rather, I can work it out,' she said counting on her fingers. 'He was ten years younger than Granda Scott, my grandfather, who died in September 1954. Granda was seventy-nine then and this is '65. Charlie must be eighty. Goodness, he didn't look eighty, did he?'

'He didn't do so bad then, did he,' Eddie continued gently. 'I didn't think he was that old either. He wouldn't even tell me when his birthday was, never mind how old he might be.'

'A bit of vanity perhaps,' Clare said smiling. 'I can't believe he's gone, Eddie, but I'll not wish him back to suffer.'

Eddie nodded and looked relieved.

'I have one request, Eddie,' she began, without a tremor in her voice. 'After the funeral you'll want a party. We're rather good at parties at Drumsollen. Ask as many as you want, there's plenty of room. No charge. You can bring what you want to drink, or give me a list and I'll see if I can get it cheaper from the Cash and Carry. What do you think?'

'I think that's a great idea,' Eddie declared, as he was forced to brush tears from his own eyes.

'How long did you say you were planning to stay?' asked Clare, as she walked down the steps on Friday evening.

'Here, you carry the small ones,' said Jessie, not bothering to reply. She dumped a bulging grip and a rucksack full of painting materials at Clare's feet and then manhandled two suitcases from the back of her new estate wagon. 'Harry wanted to know if I was leavin' him when he saw me loadin' up,' she went on, dropping the cases unceremoniously to the ground.

'And what did *you* say to that?' Clare asked, smiling to herself.

'Told him not to be so daft. Where else would I get my painting stuff cost price?'

To Clare's great surprise, Jessie came over and put her arms round her. 'Are ye badly cut up over Charlie?' she asked abruptly.

'Not as bad as I might be,' Clare replied, honestly. 'I keep remembering the cancer and that it had got into *both* lungs,' she said, wincing. 'I think if I'd had the choice I'd rather leave like he did.'

'When's the funeral?'

'Not till next week. There's another nephew in Canada couldn't get a flight any sooner. Come on in. You must be tired after the drive and humping all that stuff.'

'Clare, what in the name of goodness is that smell?' Jessie demanded, as she followed her into the entrance hall. 'Horrible. It's like raw onions,' she complained, turning up her nose and making a face, as she dropped her suitcases.

'It *is* raw onions,' Clare said. 'Not my idea and a long story. I'll tell you the story, if you tell me what's in those suitcases.'

'Bronagh,' Jessie replied shortly. 'Yer always talkin' about her an' I think she's a good sort m'self. D'ye know what size she is?'

'Fourteen, but she's on the cuddly side rather than the other. Why?'

'These are all my sixteens and fourteens. Some of them's never been worn. I only bought them to please my mother-in-law when she was tryin' to help me,' she explained. 'I hadn't the heart to wear them when I was bad and now I'm back to a twelve. She wouldn't be offended, would she?' she ended, suddenly anxious.

'No. Bronagh's too sensible for that,' Clare replied, shaking her head. 'Besides, she has two sisters she has to provide for. If anything's the wrong size she's a great hand with a needle. She's taken in trousers for me before now.'

'Great. Well that's settled. Now, what about your onions?'

'Did you not notice the new carpet?' Clare asked, looking down.

'Doesn't look new to me,' Jessie retorted. 'More like something Harry used to sell before he decided on pictures and antiques.'

Clare laughed aloud, convinced now that Jessie was completely restored to her old self. Sharp as a pin, as June would say, and a great eye for colour and design, as Harry had observed years ago.

'You're quite right, Jessie dear,' she said laughing happily. 'This *is* one of Harry's. He found it for us right back when we first opened and we had it in the best bedroom. Perfect match for those lovely old curtains.'

'So why did you bring it down?' Jessie asked suspiciously. 'What *happened* to the one that was here?'

'It had a brief encounter with some paraffin oil and a cigarette lighter and four boyos from the Portadown UVF,' she replied, grinning. 'I *will* tell you the whole story, but you mustn't say a word to anyone except Harry till I've told Andrew. I couldn't tell him on the phone for one of the boyos was William and I don't want him ending up in jail.'

'Huh. It'd be the best place for him,' said Jessie unsympathetically. 'Sure, don't you think he was behind the paint as well?'

'Yes I do. But what would you do if it was your brother?'

'Well John'd hardly be at that kinda thing and him a policeman himself, would he?'

Having agreed that June's onion recipe for getting rid of the residue of burnt paraffin and charred carpet was worse than the original smell had been, they shut the door of Headquarters firmly behind them and talked all evening as if nothing had ever come between them. As the fire burnt low, they began to speak again about Charlie.

'D'ye know what I mind best about yer man?' Jessie asked. 'Those dahlias of his. The ones he gave us the night my father shot himself and Aunt Sarah sent us out looking for flowers to spread around the stable floor after they washed the blood away. D'ye remember that? We got honeysuckle out of Robinson's hedges and then we went to Charlie an' he cut dahlias an' gave us wee roses with hardly any stem, but a lovely perfume. You poured water on the cobbles and put the wee stems where the water lay an' they kept fresh till after his funeral.' She paused and looked straight at her friend before she continued. 'Ye know, I told that psychiatrist fellow about that night an' he asked me the funniest question. He asked me did I ever think I would shoot myself. I told him not to be daft. Sure, where would I get a gun? But I told him I often thought of walking in front of a car. An' d'ye know what he said?' she continued, barely pausing for breath. 'He said, *That's good.* Now we know what the problem is. You'll be all right now.'

She laughed again and went on. 'To tell you the truth, I thought *he* was off his head, not me, but then he kinda explained that if we have a shock, a really bad one, it can get stuck somewhere in your mind and it can send out messages and we can't stop it. And if we don't understand about this we think it's real. Once we know the messages aren't real we can just say, *Piss off*, and it goes.'

Jessie burst out laughing again. 'Clare, if you'd seen yer man in his Savile Row suit and the old school tie, an' the accent you could cut with a knife, an' a straight face saying, *Piss off*, ye'd have split yerself. I thought I was goin' to disgrace m'self laughin'.'

'So, have you walked in front of any good motor cars recently? Mentally speaking, of course?' Clare asked.

'No, not one. It's gone away. It's gone clean away. Mind you, so it ought to have, given what he charged, but Harry says it was cheap at the price. He's always been very good like that,' she confessed, with unexpected gentleness.

At the end of the evening, they agreed that the smell of onions in the hall was fading, but they'd be really glad when it had gone. Clare climbed into bed feeling that, yes, she had indeed lost one old friend, but, to her great joy, another old friend had been returned to her.

Jessie went off after a late breakfast, her sketch book full of studies for the watercolours now to be her parting gift. This being June's monthly Saturday morning off, she had the whole house to herself and a long list of chores that needed doing. Andrew wasn't due back till late afternoon, so she tried to think which ones it would be most useful to have done before then. At the same time, she felt an equal and opposite desire not to do any of them.

She compromised by vacuuming as much of the dining room as she could get at, the tables still displaced after the children's party, and then tackled the large cardboard boxes into which she and Bronagh had piled the disordered papers in Headquarters.

It was a wearisome task sorting them out, for Billy and William had not only emptied all the drawers, they had kicked the piles apart looking for hidden cash. As she worked away steadily, Clare thought of the archaeologists who patiently reconstruct the history of a site, assigning each item to the correct level, even after various upheavals.

Totally surrounded by paper, thirsty and dispirited, she suddenly felt more than just alone. She felt lonely and a prey to sad thoughts. Could it be their Grand Plan and their high hopes of September

1960 had been merely an extension of the joy of being together, rather than a real possibility? She looked at the piles of paper she had managed to reorder. Bank Statements. Invoices for major items. Income Tax Returns. What had it all added up to? An empty house where the faint odour of onions reminded her of a young man, so obsessed by his own fantasy of stacks of cash just waiting to be picked up, that he could put her at risk in the way he had by telling the Boss Man how easy it would all be.

What if Eddie Running hadn't turned up when he did? She could have tackled two of them and William was a coward, but three of them was a real risk and she couldn't be sure the 'gun' was a fake. How would Andrew have felt had she been shot, or beaten, or burnt?

When she heard the vibration of a vehicle in the drive, she got to her feet before she'd even thought about it, rushed out and saw the familiar Royal Mail van sweeping to a halt at the foot of the steps. Hastily, she collected herself and went down to greet the driver.

'Good morning, Ernie, isn't it a lovely morning.'

'Mornin', Clare. Indeed it is, great for the time of year. Large fat one for your good man. Can you sign here, please? He's had great weather for Fermanagh, hasn't he? Will he be back for the funeral?' he said, dropping his voice by several tones.

'Yes, he'll be back late this afternoon. He had a bit more to do than he expected. And I wouldn't be surprised if this might be a bit more still,' she added, looking at the London postmark, the franking and the thick embossed envelope.

'No rest for the wicked,' he said, cheerfully, as he hopped into the driving seat and roared off.

She laughed, decided the morning was far too lovely to spend surrounded by papers and negative speculations. She carried the envelope indoors, parked it on her desk and fetched secateurs and a bucket. Just half an hour's dead-heading she told herself, then she'd make a pot of coffee and get back to the piles of paper.

Andrew looked tired when he finally arrived, but that was hardly surprising, she told herself, when he went to have a quick wash and change before supper. It was a long drive from Killydrennan and as Charlie had pointed out only a few weeks ago, the last place you could ever hope for a motorway was one running west to Fermanagh or up the far side of Lough Neagh through Omagh and Strabane to Derry.

It was hardly surprising either that Andrew hadn't noticed the changed carpet in the hall. Apart from the smell having gone and the carpet looking as if it had always been there, he'd been far too pleased to see her to notice anything else.

'That looks better,' she said, as he came back into the kitchen, his hair looking damp round the edges. 'Did you have to wear your suit all the time?' she asked sympathetically.

'No, it wasn't too bad,' he admitted. 'Henry Macaulay is a decent sort. Very public school, but then, I suppose you'd have to say, so am I. We wore outdoor stuff during the day, but the hotel was posh. Suits and ties for dinner obligatory, but the food partly made up for it, though I got so tired by the evening I could just about do it justice. I did miss you terribly,' he confessed, putting his arms around her the moment she'd finished putting hot dishes on a tray.

The table was laid in Headquarters, the fire lit, a bottle of wine ready to celebrate his return. The remaining cardboard box she'd pushed into a dim corner where the fall of the curtain almost completely concealed it.

'It is *so* lovely to be home,' he said, looking at the waiting table. He smiled as he touched her small posy of roses, then lit the candles for them. 'I'd rather dine chez Clare than any five star place.'

'At least I was able to cook your supper tonight,' she said easily. 'But I did let June do the dessert. No prize for guessing what it is,' she added laughing, as she served up *boeuf bourguignon*.

He ate so devotedly, Clare did wonder if he'd bothered to stop en route to have lunch. She poured more wine and saw him relax a little as the meal went on. How she was going to tell him about her late night visitors she had still not worked out.

'Did you manage to leave my roses for Hector?' she asked gently when they'd got as far as June's apricot tart.

'Yes, I did. In fact, I spent some time down there most days. They gave me sandwiches at the hotel and I took them to the lake at lunchtime. Not a lot about yet, but the regulars were there.'

'Is the house completely shut up then while Lord Rothwell is away?' she asked curiously.

'More or less. Mrs Watkins was there. She asked after you. She told me Russell has been given one of the gate lodges. They're too small for a family and one's been empty for a long while. Henry says Rothwell wasn't bothered about it, so they've set up a life tenancy to comply with Hector's wishes. It will revert to the estate when Russell dies.'

'How *is* Russell?'

'I don't know,' he said honestly. 'I can't read people like you can, but I can tell you there were other flowers as well as yours on Hector's mound. And it wasn't Mrs Watkins. I asked her if she'd put them there,' he said flatly.

As they finished their meal and moved across to the fire, Clare made up her mind. She was *not* going to tell Andrew about Wednesday night's invasion. It could wait until tomorrow. There was something about Andrew this evening she really couldn't make sense of. There was unease in almost everything he said, and yet, at the same time, there was a warm enthusiasm for everything they had here in this room, from the roses, to the food, to the fire. She watched his eyes moving restlessly round the room that had been the centre for the project that failed. Here, they'd been on duty for guests, had collapsed after the work of day or the week. Here they'd celebrated with friends and with each other.

'Andrew, is there something on your mind? Something you're not telling me?' she asked quietly.

'Maybe. I'm not sure,' he replied, looking at her uneasily. 'It may not be worth worrying over. As they say, it may never happen,' he replied, managing a smile.

'Well, whether it does or not, we could share it anyway, couldn't we? If it does, we'll face it, and if it doesn't we'll give thanks. How about some coffee?'

'Great,' he said, looking yet more abstracted as she poured for them both. 'Don't know where to begin,' he confessed with a sigh.

'Just begin anywhere,' she said encouragingly. 'It doesn't matter if it's not in logical order, just so I get the picture.'

'Well, Henry Macaulay was not quite what he seemed. Yes, there was a job to do, given all that work I did years ago had gone missing, but he was more than a Land Agent. He admitted that the second night when we'd been in the bar for a while. He's been working for the executors on a problem regarding the estate. It's Lord Rothwell's wife.'

'Good heavens, what can possibly be the matter be with Lord Rothwell's wife?'

'Well, she is *very* good-looking, I can say that. Henry had a photo of her in his file, but it seems she is of *mixed race*. No, no, not what you're thinking, my love,' he interrupted, as he saw the look on her face. 'It seems her aboriginal ancestors are no problem at all to the executors. No, their problem is that she was sent away from her family as a little girl. Apparently there were a lot of high-minded individuals who *wanted to save* children from their *native* families, so she was brought up in a Catholic mission school in Queensland,' he explained, taking up his coffee cup and emptying it.

'Oh, not again,' said Clare wearily. 'Is it any wonder I gave up the whole religion business as soon as Granda Scott died,' she demanded crossly. 'Sorry, love. I didn't mean to interrupt. Do go on.'

'Well, it looked as if the only way for Rothwell to have the estate was for him to divorce her. I think it was hinted in oblique lawyer's language that should he do so, the letter of the title could thus be adhered to and they could live together in Fermanagh with no one any the wiser. Being English, however, they'd forgotten the local gentry. They've been asking questions about his wife and they also invited him to become a member of the Lodge.'

'And how did he feel about that?'

'Apparently his comment was not considered the reply of a gentleman,' said Andrew grinning. 'I confess I liked him better after that, even if I've never met him.'

'So what's happening now? Hasn't he gone back to Australia to *see his wife?* That's what you said, wasn't it?'

'That's what he told Henry, but it seems now that he's not coming back. They were waiting in London for his *instructions in writing*. Henry said yesterday they'd had *a definite response* from him and it might only be a matter of a day or two until I heard from them.'

'Heard from whom?' Clare asked, totally confused.

'The executors, of course,' he said patiently. 'They'll send me the relevant documents and if I were to sign them, then, by due process of law, I would become the next Lord Rothwell.'

Eighteen

The little grey church on the hill where Clare and Andrew had been married five years previously, to the month, was packed to capacity. Clare almost smiled as she and Andrew made their way to the front pews where Eddie Running had insisted they sit with Charlie's immediate family. Charlie would be pleased. It looked as if the turnout for him was even bigger than for her grandfather.

She had been thinking of Robert's funeral as they drove up Church Hill when they found, to their surprise, a man, black-suited and wearing a hard hat, directing cars to park in a field opposite the churchyard gates. As they bumped over rough stubble, she remembered the field from long ago. Every Easter, her mother and father had visited Granny and Granda. Together, they'd all walked up the lane alongside the orchard from the forge house to the top of the hill, so she could trundle her egg with all the other children from Church Hill.

A changed world, she thought, remembering the ponies and traps tethered by the churchyard wall in October 1954. She'd come home from her first term at Queens, on a lovely autumn morning, to find her grandfather in his coffin. Charlie was with him in the sitting-room reading aloud from the local paper.

Now Charlie had gone too, her last link with this small piece of land where she'd once known every flower and tree so that at any season she could find something to put in the old, green glass bottle that sat on their table in the long, low house with roses over the door.

Andrew had given up Drumsollen, accepting that one cannot take back what was not given, freely and willingly, at an earlier time. Now, she too would have to give up what *had* been good, the goodness that *had* sustained her after the loss of her parents.

She had tried to give back to Andrew what he had lost and to keep for herself what had been so good, but it was something that could not be done. They had tried and tried again and finally failed, but in the process had learnt a great deal, especially about themselves.

Charlie had been part of that old world. Like Andrew's dream of Drumsollen restored, she too would have to let go her last link with that world of her childhood and young womanhood.

There were friendly faces all around her, known people who nodded kindly as she walked down the aisle to the seats marked out for them with carefully placed hymn sheets. This place would remain forever in her heart. It might well always be called 'home', but she no longer had any tie to the land itself.

On June Thirty, they would leave Drumsollen. Where or how they would find a life and a future, she did not know. That it would not be here among the little hills of her childhood was certain. Nor indeed would it be amid the isles and lakes of Fermanagh, a county unknown to her until a year ago, a place whose beauty had touched her deeply.

They sat close together in the whispering hush of the church as the choir in their new red robes filed silently to their places. She felt Andrew make small, restless movements by her side and immediately her mind moved back to Friday evening.

'Oh love, I *am* sorry,' she'd said, getting up and opening her desk. One large, white envelope sat in front of the empty compartments. 'This came this morning. I'm afraid I forgot all about it,' she apologized, as she handed it to him.

'Yes, I expect this is it,' he said flatly, staring at his name, at the address, at the postmark. He made not the slightest attempt to open it.

'What's wrong, Andrew? What *is* going on?'

Instead of replying, he tore at the envelope, a tough, fabric lined one which only came apart after he'd applied considerable force. From the ragged opening, several sheets of heavy paper fell to the ground. He bent and scooped them up.

'Here, look for yourself,' he said, thrusting them at her. 'Sign on the dotted line for a country estate and a guaranteed income for life. As much pasture for as many cows as you fancy. Gardens and gardeners, too, for your lovely lady wife. Jobs all round for good Protestant lads and lassies like our new neighbours the Brookes. Money in the bank and servants to do the work. All for one little signature.' He paused. 'Clare, I can't do it, I simply can't do it,' he said, his face crumpling, anger and distress tearing him in opposite directions.

'So what is your problem, Andrew? Who is asking you to do it?'

'Oh do be reasonable, Clare,' he almost shouted. 'We're broke. If you weren't working your socks off, we wouldn't have tuppence. I've made no money since I set up on my own, until this business in Fermanagh came up. My only clients are poor Catholics who couldn't pay my bills even if I did send them. And, on a plate, I'm handed everything I say I've ever wanted. Some of the best land in Ulster. And lots of it. A place for children to grow up. Exactly what I'd have loved to have had myself. And I can't do it. Not even for you,' he ended, choking on his words as he dropped his head in his hands.

'Good for you,' she said quietly.

'What did you say?'

'I said, *Good for you.*'

'And what exactly is good about it?' he demanded angrily, jumping to his feet and glaring down at her.

'You've always said you had difficulty making up your mind,' she began steadily. 'You said when you asked me to marry you, in bed in Drumsollen in April 1960, if I remember correctly, that you'd do your best, if I would help you with making up your mind. Those were the terms,' she continued, managing to keep her voice a lot steadier than she was feeling. 'Well, it seems you've made up your mind about something. That has to be good news.'

'You mean you don't mind?' he demanded. 'You'd give up *all* you're being offered?'

'I'm not giving up anything,' she said firmly. 'I have what I need. We do have one or two little local problems just at present, I'll willingly admit. Doesn't everyone? But we've managed well enough up until the present. So why should that suddenly change?'

She realized now that the minister had appeared, a young man new to the parish. He had not known Charlie very well, he admitted honestly, when he began his address, but he'd had the great good sense to talk to people who had known him all their lives. He proceeded to deliver a short synopsis of Charlie's life, interspersed with stories which exactly caught the essence of the man. There was laughter and a nodding of heads and Clare heard the odd whispered, '*That was yer man all right.*'

To Clare's great delight, the minister followed his tribute, not with the customary reminder of the shortness of life, the need for repentance and a proper attention to one's own salvation, but instead with a request for celebration and thanksgiving. The congregation lifted up their voices in full and hearty response. Clare did shed tears, more of relief, than sadness. Charlie would have approved entirely of the whole proceedings.

To Clare's amazement the party given for Charlie at Drumsollen after the funeral generated more business and bookings than many of the events she'd organized over the years with that aim in view. To begin with, the Canadian cousin for whom the funeral had been delayed decided to work through Charlie's vast archive to make it easier for sending back to Canada. One look at Charlie's bungalow, where he'd expected to live while doing the job, and he returned for two weeks at Drumsollen.

Clare's main preoccupation now became the selling of Drumsollen. She talked to her Bank Manager and found it was possible to register a property *quietly* with an estate agent. No board on the roadside, nor advertising in local papers, and therefore, no need to share news of their going with anyone but June and Bronagh and close friends.

What it was supposed to do was open the possibility of the agent being able to put a client in touch with her should the description of Drumsollen appear to meet their needs. That was exactly what happened.

'Good morning, Mrs Richardson,' said an unfamiliar voice, when she answered the phone one sodden November morning. 'My name is John Crawford and I represent Eventide Homes. I wonder if it would be possible for me to come and see you sometime next week.'

'Eventide Homes,' she repeated to Andrew that evening. 'What do you think of that?'

'Well I suppose it *is* a possibility,' he said dubiously. 'I've heard of several big houses being converted into nursing homes but I can't see Drumsollen fitting the bill. Surely you'd need lifts with two floors.'

'All things are possible if they have the capital,' she pointed out. 'That *was* our problem, wasn't it? We *might* have made it work if we could have refurbished, with phones and TVs and en suites for every room.'

'Are you sorry?' he asked abruptly.

'No, I'm not. I'm glad we tried, but there's no turning back now, is there? I think, though, we need to make use of all we've learnt. And we've got to do our homework properly. Have you got any further with *your* researches?'

For weeks now, Andrew had been poring over editions of *Farming News*, sent by Aunt Joan, and the *North Norfolk Property Guide* sent by Mary and John. What he was trying to do was see what it would cost to buy enough land to make a start, assuming land was available which Phillida seemed to think was the case. His problem was that their capital was tied up in Drumsollen. He had no idea what its sale might raise or how much he'd have available for either land or stock.

'Try not to worry, love,' Clare said, when he'd explained his difficulty. 'We might know better when this John Crawford comes next week. Which reminds me,' she went on quickly. 'We really need to lay the old entrance hall carpet down in Number One. We'll have to shunt it around to see if we can get the damaged bit under the wardrobe.'

'Why bother?' he asked. 'There are four other double rooms. We hardly ever have one double room in use, never mind four.'

'Can't give you an answer,' she confessed. 'Something about *rightness*. Not letting that business over the paraffin spoil a room. Especially when someone is coming to see the place. My magic, if you like,' she confessed, laughing. 'I'd like to put the room straight again.'

'What about your-not-so-dear brother?' he asked cautiously. 'Does Granny Hamilton know where he's living?'

'She says he's with one of my aunts who has no children. Apparently, he offered to do jobs in return for a bed. She doesn't see much of him, but he takes her to the shops in that car of his a couple of times a week. He's on the dole and not trying very hard to get off it.'

'Did she say anything about his choice of companions?'

'No, I don't think Granny knows anything about that, but then she never did pay much attention to William. It was Granda Hamilton who did his best with him. Granny just says he's no good and never was. Which is probably true, I'm afraid. Eddie Running says he's had a word with him and put the fear of God in him. Told him he'd be locked up for a long time if he was ever caught again with the UVF. It *might* keep him out of trouble. It might not.

Eddie says there's nothing I can do, he's unlikely to bother us again but there were his companions, so we need to be sharp on security just to be on the safe side.'

'I remember a world where no one needed to lock their door,' said Andrew sadly.

'And before that, there was a world in which many people were so poor they'd no need to shut doors because there was nothing for anyone to steal,' she came back at him.

'Point taken, my beloved,' he said, laughing. 'You may not have been trained to jump through the hoops of legal logic, but you certainly don't let anyone get away with a version of the past that leaves out the nasty bits. You do go for the *real* thing.'

'Thank you, my love. Now that I take as a *real* compliment.'

John Crawford turned out to be a graduate from Queens in his early twenties who owned up to the fact that he was fairly new to the job. He was, however, very sharp and Clare watched him scan every corner of every room as she took him round, as if he were making an inventory without benefit of pencil and paper. He was very pleasant when they came into the kitchen and he met June and Bronagh preparing for the sandwich round. He complimented them on the wonderful smells which had permeated the lower floor during the hour of his visit. Once back in Headquarters, he sat talking over coffee as if he had the whole day at his disposal.

'We do have three other properties already in the province, Clare, if I may call you Clare,' he said smiling, as she nodded and passed him a sample of June's morning's work. 'I still find it surprising that the relatives of elderly people who need care appear to be more concerned with the décor of our premises than they are by the provision of bathrooms or of lifting equipment,' he said steadily. 'You might not think that your beautiful chandelier or the polished wood staircase was a factor in the equation, but I can assure you it is. In fact, I can tell you now, I shall be recommending a visit by one of our Directors.'

'My goodness,' said Clare, surprised. 'But surely stairs like ours are the last thing you need with elderly people?'

'Practically, I have to agree with you, but we've discovered many relatives are *pleased* to see stairs. They don't want to be reminded of *disability*. What we have to do is to provide lifts in inconspicuous places. We have a standard building design which would work perfectly well here at Drumsollen. A two storey extension, roughly at right angles to the kitchen, where the garage and stable are at present. It would run out into that meadow area with the long grass as far as the edge of the property. All the essential medical and care services would be available there, keeping the public rooms free of equipment, apart from wheelchairs,' he said matter-of-factly, before pausing to help himself to another piece of cake.

'I have two questions I need to put to you,' he went on, pausing to munch enthusiastically. 'Firstly, there is the question of furniture and fittings, and the special nature of the pictures. I presume these *are* of a family nature. Does that mean that you would wish to remove them? I ask, because in the case of two of our other premises, we were able to offer a price to include *everything* in the property, including pictures and furniture. In fact, everything right down to kitchen equipment and bed linen, which would be immediately redeployable, as you can imagine.'

'You do surprise me,' said Clare, honestly, thinking of Archbishop Ussher and wondering what Andrew would have to say about selling off his remaining ancestors. 'I'll certainly be able to give you an answer quite quickly. Would tomorrow do?'

'Excellent,' he responded, nodding vigorously. 'Now the other matter is timing. We are in a position to make an offer right away, but we could not complete the sale, *were it to take place*, till the middle of next year. Purely a question of cash flow,' he said airily. 'We would prefer our new premises to be in next year's budget. What is your own time scale for departure?'

'Well, that looks as if it would suit us *both* very well,' he replied, when she mentioned June the thirtieth. 'I really do feel most positive about Drumsollen, but naturally I have to go up the line on this one. Can I phone you tomorrow when you've spoken with your husband?'

'You will be pleased to hear that Drumsollen *may* become the fourth lot of premises for Eventide homes,' Clare reported, as they drew up to the fire on a wild, December night with the wind gusting down the chimney, making the logs crackle and spark in the grate.

'So, I *was* wrong. There *is* a possibility.'

'Rather better than that,' she said encouragingly. 'Your man was quite enthusiastic. His timescale is a perfect match with our own plans. We just have a problem concerning your ancestors,' she continued lightly. 'Apparently, at the expensive end of the care market ancestors are welcome. He wants to know how you'd feel about yours staying where they are and their value being reflected in the purchase price.'

'Good Lord,' said Andrew, looking amazed. 'The answer is *Yes.* We'd only have been asking Harry to get rid of them anyway. What else did he say?'

Clare gave a full account of John Crawford's visit and expressed her cautious optimism that they might actually have an offer once they'd agreed on what he'd called *lock, stock and barrel*, a curious phrase, she thought, but familiar enough from her childhood.

'Then I'd really be able to go shopping,' he said with a grin. 'There *are* farms coming on the market in Norfolk. Not often, and not where we'd most like to be, but now at least I would know how much money we have to go shopping. That's a start.'

The offer came with the first Christmas cards and was the subject of much excitement. Even after deducting the remaining mortgage on Drumsollen and allowing for moving expenses, it looked like *a very nice, round figure*, as Andrew called it. There were enthusiastic phone calls to Aunt Joan, who was delighted things were now working out for them after all their hard work, and to Mary and John who promptly invited them to spend *next* Christmas with them.

'Of course we'll miss you,' Harry said, after Clare had spoken to both on the phone, 'but you won't be so totally tied down that you can't get home for a holiday now and then. You know you'll be welcome and the apartment's there up on the coast if you fancy a bit of sea air as well.'

The run up to Christmas was busy, much busier than the previous year, but as Clare said, 'Things never come when you need them most.' Happily, the extra income paid some extra bills and provided a larger Christmas bonus for June and Bronagh.

'Nobody deserves it more,' Clare said, when she passed over the small envelopes. 'The only thing I'll really miss when we go is having you both to talk to. The phone and letters isn't the same thing at

all,' she added, thinking longingly of Louise, and Marie-Claude, and
Robert, far away in France and of Helen and Ginny and other
friends, nearer at hand, but not visited for such a long time.

January blew in with unexpected gales and some very unwelcome
bills for the replacing of slates on the most exposed part of the roof.
Andrew continued his search for land in North Norfolk, but gradu-
ally accepted that there wasn't much point. Nobody would chose
to sell up at this time of year, barring emergencies.

Clare was concerned that he seemed so dispirited, with very little
work coming in to his office, not even the unpaid work he was
willing to do for applicants for Legal Aid. He was sadly disappointed
over the failure of the efforts he and Charles had made through the
Society of Labour Lawyers to get some focus on the question of
Civil Liberties in Northern Ireland.

When the Campaign for Democracy in Ulster had been started
he had been in such good spirits. He'd made her laugh by telling
her about the launch of the movement. A public house in Streatham
did not seem exactly the most appropriate place to go into the
history books, but that, he said, was where the Irish Trade Unionists
and the Labour Party members got together.

They had some good people too, he went on, an MP for one of
the Manchester constituencies, a lawyer called Paul Rose who'd been
called to the bar. They were trying to secure a Royal Commission
to look into the running of the Stormont Government and inves-
tigate allegations of discrimination.

It was clear by February 1966 that despite the bright hope of June
1965, when the CDU was launched publicly at a meeting in the
House of Commons, the campaign was confined to London and
Manchester. More disappointing still was that the Prime Minister,
Harold Wilson, had made clear he intended to take the same line on
Ulster as his predecessors and avoid doing anything that *might rock the
boat.*

'I just sit in my office and read about pedigree cattle. Anything
to avoid the local papers and the rantings and ravings of the Unionist
councillors should anyone have the temerity to suggest anything as
radical as equal rights,' Andrew said bitterly. 'I can't wait to get away.
Why don't we just look for a little house in Holt and I'll get a job,
any old job, just so long as I can do *something* useful. I could take

up maintaining gardens for old people, or drive them into Norwich to do their shopping. With all that money from Eventide we wouldn't starve for quite a while, would we?'

Just at the point when Clare was beginning to think it was, in fact, the only thing to do, something quite unexpected happened. Phillida's cowman, who had been with her for fifty years, suddenly decided to retire. Phillida was at her wits end to find someone to replace him. Then, on top of that, one morning early, she came out of the house, walked round the side of the water butt and fell on an invisible skim of ice, where it had overflowed after rain in the night that had frozen by dawn.

She had broken her hip, lain on the icy path till her daily help arrived and was now in hospital. Joan though she had a touch of pneumonia, but when she visited before the hip operation, Phillida insisted her horrible cough was only the result of bad temper as she lay on the path cursing, because she couldn't get up.

Nineteen

Clare thought the daffodils at Drumsollen were even lovelier than usual this year. As she stood gazing out of the window of Headquarters, there were not only more of them but they seemed brighter, their colour enhanced by the strong sunlight of a blowy March day. She remembered the year she had sent out the daffodil cards to all their former guests and discovered from their replies that the world had changed. For many of them, horizons had broadened and put air travel within reach. That had meant holidays beyond Ulster, one of the first changes that put their Grand Plan at risk.

She was still standing there thinking how hindsight could so easily point you to what you couldn't possibly have seen at the time when the phone rang.

'Joan, how lovely to hear you. Nothing wrong, I hope,' she said cautiously, well aware that Joan seldom rang and had never yet rung in the morning at peak rate.

'Well, yes and no, my dear. It's been a difficult couple of months for your two old crocks. Phillida's better. A lot better, thank goodness. That chest of hers nearly did for her. It's all right now, but the leg isn't. Oh, the consultant says it has healed, but Phillida says it's had it. She can't put her weight on it, or if she tries to, it aches horribly. We make a great pair, she and I, so long as we're sitting down. However . . .'

Clare took a deep breath. Joan's tone told her she'd not rung to report on their health.

'Now, dear, I hope this will be *good* news,' she said briskly. 'Philly's decided to sell up and go into sheltered accommodation. She's furious, of course, but she'll get over it. Besides, her cow man Jim is only holding on out of good nature. His wife wants him to retire and if you knew her you'd know he hasn't got much choice in the matter,' she added. 'She's no idea what the farm's worth, but she needs a lump sum for her new property and some capital for interest to give her pension a boost. She's totted it up and it comes to half what you're getting from Eventide, which sounds like good value to me. What do you think? Would Andrew be interested?'

'I think that's something of an understatement,' Clare said happily. 'I think he'll be ecstatic. He's been so downcast over not being able to find land in North Norfolk even now he has the money to buy it,' Clare continued. 'I've tried to tell him people don't make moves this early in the year and that something's sure to come up after Easter, but he's been getting terribly despondent.'

'Well then, tell him he'll be hearing from Philly's solicitor in a day or two. At least they can sort it out between them without a fortune in fees. Philly's man is a distant cousin and they've been friends all their lives,' she added by way of explanation. 'Must go now, my dear. Give me a ring when you've got it sorted. Looking forward to seeing you. Bye.'

Clare looked down at the phone in amazement. Joan had a habit of just disappearing, as if she'd felt her phone was running out, just as it used to when you put pennies into a slot in a public call box.

'My goodness,' she said. 'My goodness,' she repeated, as she put the receiver down. 'What an extraordinary surprise.'

She was just about to pick up the phone again and dial Andrew's number when there was a gentle tap on the door. She opened it and found Bronagh standing there empty-handed.

'I didn't think I'd earned my coffee yet,' she said easily. 'Come in and sit down.'

'Clare, I've got some news for you,' Bronagh began awkwardly. 'You've been so good to me, I wanted you to know before anyone else. Matt and I are going to get married. We don't know when, because I can't leave the two young ones, but we've made up our minds.'

'Oh Bronagh, what wonderful news. I am *so* delighted,' Clare said, getting up and hugging her. 'Andrew will be so pleased when I tell him. I can tell him, can't I?'

'Oh yes,' she replied, smiling happily. 'And I *am* going to tell June. But you first and *no one* else. We're not having a ring, because we're saving up,' she went on. 'Matt says there are houses to rent in Railway Street from time to time, which would be near his work. If we could get one of those, then we'd have room for my young brother and sister. He's been very good about that,' she confessed.

'I'm not surprised, Bronagh. He's a very nice man and he did fall for you in a big way. Whenever I think of him, I remember the stories my mother told about my father, when he had to wait around, because she'd got herself more or less engaged to someone else. He had to be so good until the boyfriend, who was supposed to be sending for her to come to Canada and marry him, turned round and married someone else.'

'Oh, how awful for her,' Bronagh said, her eyes wide with sympathy.

'Yes, she said it was a bad time for her, but it was all for the best,' Clare replied. 'She always used to tell me that some good always comes out of disappointments, if only you can see it. Not that I think there'll be any disappointment where you and Matt are concerned,' she added, smiling. 'We must cross our fingers and hope for a house coming up.'

They sat and talked for a little longer. Bronagh explained that Brendan had said he could manage the rent for Callan Street and could support his sister, Anne-Marie, until she went to university. She'd been told she'd almost certainly get a County Scholarship and he'd been earning quite a bit from odd jobs that still gave him time to study. He'd even been giving driving lessons to pupils who had a car of their own, after his success teaching his sister in Clare's car.

As Bronagh closed the door behind her and Clare dialled Andrew's number, she made up her mind about one thing. They were not driving from Liverpool to North Norfolk in convoy. If she could possibly afford to give Bronagh her car before she left, she would. One car would be quite enough for a farmer and his wife.

It was a week or more before their excitement died down enough to let them study the details of Phillida's offer more closely. Initially, Andrew had been concerned that the amount of land involved was simply not enough to support them and that the sum Phillida needed for her plans made it very expensive indeed. On the other hand, it *was* top quality land which he'd seen. It was in the right place, near to both Joan and Mary and John, which was a marvellous bonus. Documents arrived in stages so it took till the end of April for them to realize how generous Phillida had actually been.

For some time now she'd been working only a quarter of her land. The rest was leased by the year to adjoining farmers, the rents making up part of her income.

'But it is *leased*, Clare. Leased,' said Andrew happily, the documents and maps spread out all over the kitchen table. 'Not like Drumsollen where the land was sold. Gone beyond retrieving. When I get things going I can simply *not* renew the leases. It will be *my* land, whenever I am ready to expand, and we'll have enough to live on till I'm up and running. It is everything I've ever wanted,' he said, throwing his arms round her. 'Clare dear, I'm sorry. I said it's *my* land. That's just a manner of speaking. You know I mean it's *our* land. You do understand, don't you?'

Clare laughed. 'What's that expression about *scratching an Ulsterman and finding a peasant underneath*? Land hunger,' she continued, shaking her head. 'I've no problem with that. I'll even talk about *my* house if it makes it easier for you.'

'It's a bit run down, Clare, and I think she wants to leave most of the furniture. Will you mind terribly?'

'Well, it won't be the first time, will it?' she came back at him. 'So long as you don't forget how to paint when you start talking to your cows,' she added crisply. 'We have rather a lot of experience in the refurbishing department.'

'So shall I sign on the dotted line?'

'And become Farmer Richardson as opposed to Lord Rothwell?'

'Point taken,' he replied soberly. 'I'd very much like to sign. I have *made up my mind* but I'm asking if it's all right with you, because I won't if you don't think I should, however much I might want to.'

She picked up his pen and handed it to him.

As Clare and Bronagh drove back through the gates of Drumsollen after the daily sandwich run some two weeks later, a fresh, April day with the trees just beginning to leaf, Bronagh noticed some men in the large field that ran alongside the driveway.

'What d'you think those men are doing?' she asked, puzzled. 'They do look so funny digging with spades in such a big field.'

Clare stopped the car abruptly, got out and looked over the low hedge. Her heart stood still. 'If they are doing what I think they're doing, it is really bad news. In fact, quite dreadful news.'

'Tell me, Clare. Tell me what you mean,' Bronagh demanded anxiously, as she came to stand beside her.

'Do you see those little bits of wood they're sticking in the ground?' she asked. 'They're marking out a building site. The land was sold some time back to a builder, but the Planning Application was turned down. I'll have to find out what's going on,' she said getting back into the car. 'I'll drop you at the front and walk back. There must be a hole in the hedge on the main road that we didn't see.'

'Yes, there was, but it was only small. I thought maybe a cow had broken out. There were cows in there last week.'

'No cows now,' said Clare, distractedly, seeing all the implications printing out in front of her. 'I'll go and talk to them and see what I can find out.'

'No,' said Bronagh, putting a hand on her arm. 'Let me go. I'll get more out of them. In fact, I'm sure I recognize some of the men digging.'

It was quite a long walk down the drive, back along the Loughgall Road and into the field where the men were now running out tape measures, but it felt to Clare as if Bronagh had been gone for hours. Finally, she left Headquarters and went upstairs to the top floor, peered out through the bedroom windows with the best view of the field and the drive. She stood for what seemed a long time but there was no sign of her at all. Going downstairs again, she heard the hall door close. Bronagh was standing outside Headquarters looking pale and anxious.

'You *are* quite right,' she said, shaking her head as Clare came towards her. 'They were due to begin last month but we had such a lot of rain it was put off. Apparently the forecast is now very good so the bulldozers will be here tomorrow. They've taken on men for six months. Those are only a handful for this week. The foreman told me the show house will be ready by June and the rest by September.' She paused and looked closely at Clare. 'You're as white as a sheet. Is there anything I can do? Can I bring you tea, or coffee?'

'Thanks, Bronagh,' she said, shaking her head sadly. 'I think this is almost the worst thing that has ever happened me. Can you see Eventide wanting their "premises" behind a new estate? I'll have to ring Andrew, but a big mug of tea would help. And thanks for going to talk to the men.'

'We just mustn't give up hope,' Clare said, only hours later, when Andrew, who had come home immediately, held up his hands in despair.

'I saw the Planning Application when I put in my protest,' he said, furiously. 'And I had an acknowledgement when it was turned down. Some one has had a backhander since, I can be sure of that. *Brown envelopes all round*, Charlie would have said. Clare, what on earth are we going to do?'

'Well, we'll have to get Drumsollen on the market quickly. Board, advertising, the whole lot. It won't sell as a gentleman's residence, but there may be some commercial use it can be put to, like that castle that makes potato crisps,' she said quickly, recollecting an article she'd read recently. 'And we must tell Eventide. They'll find out anyway, but let's do the decent thing and save them the trouble.'

John Crawford was very upset when he heard what had happened. He was sure Clare was right, their offer would have to be withdrawn, but he was personally very sorry. It had been a pleasure to work with her. He wanted to know what plans they had and offered his help if there was anything he could possibly do.

But there didn't seem to be anything anyone could do. The value of Drumsollen was completely compromised by the building site. It was possible they wouldn't even have an offer at all in the new situation.

Clare rang the Bank Manager, who'd been a good friend for a long time now, then Harry, and then their estate agent. Roy Harkness said he needed to think about it. He'd get back to her. Harry said he had some thoughts. She was to keep her chin up and not let Andrew dig himself into a hole. The estate agent said they'd had one enquiry and they were looking into it.

Every day seemed like a week as she waited for developments. Yet the days flicked off her calendar with alarming rapidity. The contract of sale for the farm had not yet been drawn up, but it soon would be. Unless there was a reliable offer for Drumsollen the purchase would have to be called off. Phillida could not possibly be expected to wait for a sale that might never happen.

'Clare, Roy here. I have news for you. Not great news, but better perhaps than nothing. I've been checking out someone, who must remain nameless, on behalf of your estate agent. He's proposing to make an offer for Drumsollen, based on the land value.'

'Land value? What exactly does *that* mean, Roy?'

'It means he wants your driveway and the piece of land Drumsollen is built upon. We're probably looking at demolition of the house itself. How do you feel about that?'

'Roy, I hate to say this, but at the moment I'm only concerned with an offer. Have you any idea what he has in mind?'

'If I name a sum I would be breaking confidence, but if I say half of what Eventide offered you, I would not be giving away anything classified, would I?'

'Bless you, Roy. It's the nearest thing to good news I've had since we saw those men digging holes. Do you think the person offering is reliable?'

'Now there I *can* help you. Financially speaking, I only need to say *Yes.*'

When she told Andrew, he was not encouraged.

'But, Clare, my darling, even if we do get half of what we expected, enough for the farm, I grant you, we still can't go ahead. We have the mortgage here to pay off. On top of that there's the expense of moving and paying someone to help me, at least for a few months. There won't be any money coming in and I expect there are other small matters like the fact we might need to eat, or put petrol in the car. Even if the mortgage dissolved overnight, we will have no money at all.

'There *is* a little money from the leased land,' she said, matter-of-factly. 'That would keep us fed. The mortgage is the problem, I agree. We can't carry debt with no income.'

'So near and yet so far, Clare. Within jumping distance of the *promised* land, to coin a phrase. I can't see any way forward, can you?'

'Well, yes. I do see just one possibility.'

'You're going to sell your tiara? Sorry,' he said quickly, as he caught sight of her expression. 'I'm always flippant when I feel defeated. I apologize and will not do it again.'

'Good. We need all the cool we can manage,' she said quietly. 'As I said, I do see one possibility. I've been talking to Harry and he thinks we don't realize how the antiques market has taken off since he sold pictures for you six or seven years ago. Even the modest end of the market, bits and pieces of silver, real linen sheets, things we take for granted, get surprising prices at auction. He's coming up tomorrow to look into every corner and see what we might really be worth. He says we must *not* let this chance go. We have to grab it, even if he has to bail us out himself.'

'He said that, did he?' Andrew asked, looking round the room awkwardly.

'Yes, he did,' she replied. 'And he *meant* it.'

'Well that's it then, my friends, I'll stake my reputation on these reserve prices. Will that do? Do you think that will be enough?'

'Harry dear, not only would that clear the mortgage we'd actually be left with some cash in the bank. But are you really that sure the stuff *will* sell?' Clare asked, caution returning the moment she'd calculated the effect of the encouraging figure Harry had just shown them.

'I intend to make sure that it will,' he replied, firmly. 'Firstly, we go for *auction*. I know the best people to set that up. They do usually charge a fee, but they owe me some favours, so they may waive it. I then intend to circulate all my best customers and tip them the wink that this is one auction *they must not miss*. That'll bring them out of the woodwork, if they think there's money to be made, or items and examples to add to their collections. You'd be amazed what some of these people collect,' he went on, cheeringly. '*Now* will you go ahead and sign the contract for the farm?'

'Yes,' they said, both at the same time. 'Yes, we will.'

Twenty

The twenty-ninth of June 1966 was a brilliant summer day. Sunshine poured through the open windows and doors of Drumsollen and dropped patches of light on stacks of objects, piled on tables, chairs and floors.

From the moment the army of young assistants arrived from the auction rooms, clipboards at the ready, to lay things out, labelled and numbered, ready to be recorded for printing in the extensive catalogue, June and Bronagh had been struggling to save even the tiniest space on the kitchen table so they could provide coffee for everyone.

Clare could hardly believe what had emerged from cupboards and sideboards and had been pronounced eminently saleable. Delft and everyday china was stacked up on the kitchen table in perilous piles, Sevré and Royal Worcester dinner services were laid out more carefully in the dining room, battalions of silver alongside. Only the ancestors in their accustomed places remained untouched and indifferent, their details recorded in the colour supplement to the main catalogue.

'Well, that's it,' she said to Andrew, as he locked their bedroom door. A smart young woman with a barely discernable Ulster accent had warned him that if he didn't, it wouldn't be the first time a vendor had been left without a bed to sleep in or clothes to wear the next day.

'What shall we do?' she asked, as they moved upstairs and across the entrance hall to Headquarters. 'Where can we hide till it's all over?'

'Actually, if you don't mind too much, I did leave rather a mess in my office yesterday,' Andrew admitted sheepishly. 'But I *could* do it tomorrow, if you'd like me to stay,' he hastened to add.

One look at his face told Clare that the further away he was from Drumsollen today the better it would be for him.

'No, I'm perfectly happy to stay,' she reassured him. 'Besides, Harry will be arriving at some point and one of us should be here. I've locked up our lunch in the bedroom,' she added, laughing, as he kissed her and went out to the car.

So many last things, she thought. The last bottle of wine at the table in Headquarters the evening before the auctioneer's staff arrived to begin work. The very last batch of sandwiches made and delivered before the kitchen went out of action. The last picking of roses for the cut glass vase in the hall. The vase was still there, both it and the table tagged with robust brown labels and large black numbers.

Clare decided the safest place for her was the summerhouse. She climbed the steps, turned and looked back down at the expensive cars lining up before the house, their occupants stepping out, well-dressed and well-heeled, catalogues in hand. After their attendance at the Private View, marks had been made on chosen items, prices considered, bids were now at the ready.

She sighed. Tomorrow it would all be over. They'd made plans for disposing of what didn't sell. Harry would take any good stuff, various charities had been earmarked for the homely and domestic. June and Bronagh would deal with that, do one last tidy and leave Drumsollen to its fate.

She wondered if they might have to have a bonfire for the last residues of labels and wrappings and the thought of the fire brought back memories of the day she and Uncle Jack had cleared out the forge house. Then, the small amount of good, old furniture had gone to a sale room. His wooden chair she'd kept for herself, a companion through her years at Queens, but the old wooden settle where Charlie had sat across the fire from her grandfather, night after night, that had to be burnt.

They'd carried it out with the remaining rubbish and made a funeral pyre, like a Viking's funeral, she had thought, as she watched the sparks rise up into the pear tree. Rather different from the clearing of Drumsollen. She wondered how Andrew felt at this moment, or even if he knew what he felt. She was sure he had just needed to get away and keep himself busy while the impedimenta of his life was dispersed, the last emblems of a life he had not chosen being taken up and carried away into the lives of others.

By five o'clock the auction was over and June and Bronagh had the whole of the kitchen table on which to lay out picnic mugs and paper cups, scones and cake, for the last time. The auctioneer's staff came down and drank thankfully, munched their cake, said their goodbyes and hurried off back to Belfast.

Within half an hour, silence had descended upon the rooms that had been so full of noise and activity. Clare and Andrew walked around with Harry, amazed at the sight of bare, dusty surfaces so recently weighed down with objects of all kinds. Most of the smaller items of furniture had gone, but the larger pieces remained. They stood, looking strangely out of place, every one of them bearing a large, red SOLD notice and a printed sheet, the details needed by the drivers of vehicles that would arrive in the morning to carry them away to their final destinations.

Harry was delighted. He'd made some shrewd guesses, but even he was amazed at some of the unexpected results. With fees and commissions still to be paid, it would be some days before he could give them a final account, but he had not the slightest doubt that the sale had restored at least two thirds of what had been lost when Eventide had to withdraw their offer for Drumsollen, lock, stock and barrel.

'Harry dear, we don't know how to thank you,' Clare said, after they'd exchanged the few necessary words about the results.

'That's what friends are for, Clare. Isn't that what you once said to me?' he asked, kissing her on both cheeks.

He turned away, stuck out his hand to Andrew, then hugged him instead. 'We'll miss having you in Ulster,' he went on, 'but I've a feeling we may see a lot more of each other. It'll just have to be in more concentrated bits. I intend to see to it,' he said firmly, as he put his arms round their shoulders. 'Take care of each other in the meantime,' he added quickly, as he turned away, strode across the entrance hall and went out into the sunlight where only his own car remained, waiting at the foot of the stone steps.

After the heat of the previous days, June Thirty dawned damp and overcast. It was still raining as they left Drumsollen in the late afternoon, their last goodbye said to June and Bronagh on the front steps an hour earlier before the two of them stepped into the little blue car, now Bronagh's, as she set out for Ballyards to give June a lift home.

It seemed a long time since they'd driven through Belfast together, that quiet Sunday morning when they'd arrived home to the unwelcome greeting from her brother. It was only a year ago, but that year had changed everything.

Clare noticed there were Police wagons on some street corners, though the damp streets themselves were deserted. It was hardly surprising they were there when Loyalists had shot three Catholic barmen in the city, some nights earlier. A young man called Peter Ward had died. Earlier, a Protestant woman had been killed by a petrol bomb intended for the Catholic pub next door to her home.

She tried to push such distressing thoughts from her mind, but she had to admit it. Charlie had been right. They had done their best, but like so many before them, the only answer in the end was to take the Liverpool boat.

The lough was grey and flat calm under a dull, grey sky when they arrived at the docks, but by the time they'd queued to drive the car on board, left it being secured in the vast, empty cavern of the ship's hold and climbed their way up narrow stairs to emerge on to the wet deck, a tiny shaft of sunlight was striking the green copper turret of a church spire somewhere in the city.

They were so grateful just to lean on the rail and watch the last preparations for departure. Weary from days of effort, their minds full of comings and goings, phone calls to be made, documents to be signed, at last there was nothing more to do. They were on their way.

'Wasn't it funny about the chandelier,' Andrew said unexpectedly.

'Yes, it was,' she said, smiling. 'Even Harry was amazed at the price it fetched, but as he said, they're not made any more and few ever come on the market in good condition. I've felt guilty for years about how much it cost to restore when we were just setting out and couldn't afford it,' she confessed. 'It just shows you how wrong you can be.'

'But we weren't wrong about trusting Harry, were we?'

'No, we're fairly good on reckoning the people we can trust.'

'Perhaps because we trust each other,' he said thoughtfully.

'Maybe that's all one can ever do. Do one's best and trust that help will come. And it did, didn't it?'

Her words were drowned by the long, mournful sound of the ship's siren, telling everyone it was about to depart. There were bangs and clanks as sea doors closed and the remaining hawsers were cast off.

'So here we go, my love,' she said softly. 'Shouldn't the dark clouds open and the sun pour down and The End rise up on the screen in large letters?'

He laughed. 'But it's not the end, is it? It's the beginning of whatever comes next. Us together, making another life. Like we used to say, *Come rain, come shine.*'